Running TO HIM

MEN OF MONUMENT BOOK ONE

P.D. SINGER

ROCKY RIDGE BOOKS

This is a work of fiction. Names, characters, places, and incidents either are the product of the author's imagination or are used fictitiously, and any resemblance to actual persons, living or dead, business establishments, events, or locales is entirely coincidental.

Running To Him (Men of Monument Book 1)

Copyright © P.D. Singer 2020

Print ISBN-13 978-1-62622-082-9

Published by Rocky Ridge Books, Broomfield, CO

Thank you, Eden Winters, TD O'Malley, Angela Benedetti, Carole Cummings, Jackie North, and everyone else who believed in me when I had trouble believing in myself.

CHAPTER ONE

ONE STOP and half a mile to freedom. Tim couldn't wait.

Sunlight glittered off the signs directing staff and visitors to the offices, laboratories, or manufacturing buildings of the Monument Pharmaceuticals campus.

Tim guided his mother's late-model Chevy Cruze sedan down the curved lane flanked on each side by grass, still bright green in the early summer, and crabapple trees, part of Denver's great sea of spring pink. The blooms were a month fallen, turned to sour green knots of fruit.

Trying to ignore endless chatter coming from the passenger seat, Tim wished himself inside the single-story red brick laboratories lining the road. This was where he wanted to be, the culmination of years of hard work. But the reason that he would be dropping his passenger off at the front door instead of going in was as obvious as the passenger herself.

He'd learned to tune most of his mother's babble out over the years, but when she went into command mode he'd better snap to. Twenty-two years old, and it was as if she hadn't admitted he'd grown up. No way would he would subject himself to a professional career where his mother lurked just one building over.

"… I'll just have your father pick me up at the end of the day. You keep the car and do park at the end of the row so that my doors don't get all banged up, you know people love to slam into the car next to them. Go ahead and pull into visitor parking now, so you can just run in and grab the paperwork. With your qualifications and a good word from me you're a shoo-in at the Quality Control lab. Or maybe you want to be in Product Development. There's so much of the same thing going on in both labs. But you want Product Development. They have the new HPLC equipment." His mother pointed at an entry to a parking lot in front of the administration building. "There. Go there."

Tim ignored the turnoff and pulled up at the front door. He left the car in gear. "It's okay. I'm not going in."

Lorraine Ratliff was nothing if not insistent. "Oh yes, you are. All you have to do is collect the forms. I'm not going to bring them home for you. There really should be a limit on how much I have to do for you. It should be enough that I have the ear of the lab director."

They'd had this argument a dozen times and apparently they were going to have a thirteenth. "I have applications out all over the country, Mother. I am very invested in my job search."

His mother snorted. "Of course you do. However, there's no reason to go gallivanting to another state when there's a perfectly good pharmaceutical company right in your backyard."

He tightened his grip on the steering wheel until his knuckles went white. Working here would be perfect, except for everything, no, *everyone*, else in that backyard.

"Now come inside. I suppose you can leave the car here if it's only for a moment. If security creates an issue, I'll straighten it out." His mother nipped out of the passenger door. "Come along. Now."

Much as Tim wanted to stand his ground, it would be easier to just give her what she wanted. He didn't have to do anything with the paperwork. Comply, and his mother would get off his back. For couple of days at least.

"All right."

He'd have to move fast—the red and black polyester shirt and trousers he wore announced that he had some-place to be. It wasn't much of a job, but it paid at least some of the bills while he searched for more permanent work.

His brother Paul might make jokes about needing a bachelor's degree for food chemistry, but Tim hadn't given up hope on hearing from International Flavors and Fragrances about the opening in their laboratory. In the meantime, he could sling the wings at Cluckets. His career would be off to bigger and better things any day now. The ink wasn't quite dry on his diploma, but he wasn't taking any chances with the cash flow.

He hustled up the steps, having to wait at the top with the door open while his mother climbed more sedately. Natural dignity, high heels, or perhaps the way she enjoyed his dancing attendance upon her made her a few seconds slower. She offered her thanks at his courtesy with an "of course you're going to treat me like a queen" smile. Of course he would. She wouldn't have it any other way. And not that he minded, much, but the royal processional was eating into the brief moments that he had to collect the paperwork and then jet to work.

He followed her through the reception area and into a

cube farm, the institutional gray carpeting muffling their footsteps. So *now* his mother decided to hurry? When the rather nice scenery of a man's butt in navy dress pants poked out from behind a copier?

Not that he dared stop and admire, or even glance and admire. Not in his mother's office. Not anywhere near his mother. Not in a park or a restaurant or a mall or anywhere else on planet Earth if his mother was close enough to notice. Since she was near enough to say, "Come on, dear," and pull his hand, that was much, much too close.

Jerking his hand back, he followed her faster. His polyester uniform made him the frog in the punchbowl in an office full of people in business casual who verified DEA registrations and purchased raw materials. He'd fit in here better in the jeans and lab jacket of a chemist. Then he'd look like he wandered in from one of the buildings across the parking lot.

Perhaps she was embarrassed that her newly graduated son was dressed for serving lunch, because she shut her office door behind them. Bet everyone out there in the cube farm was glad it was him and not them on the wrong side of the door marked "Human Resources." Tim felt unpleasantly vulnerable standing on the guest side of her desk.

She thrust two forms at him with the demand of "Fill these out now."

He took a deep breath and a big chance. "I'll get right on that, Lorraine."

If she wanted him to be an employee here, she'd best get a taste of what that entailed on her side. Using her first name was a calculated risk: at home there'd be a snapped reprimand. Here? He'd find out.

"That's 'Mrs. Ratliff' to you, young man." She had to tilt back to look severely down her nose at him, even with

4

the two-inch boost from her high heels. She swung the door open and waved him out. "But I'm 'Mom' until you have an employee badge. Now scoot, Tim."

Agh. Mothers! Tim hunched his shoulders and all but ran out the door, past the nice butt that had reconstituted into six-foot-plus of buffness holding a mystery module. The kind of guy he'd like to meet someday, when he was free to be himself. When he could take the risk of smiling and finding out if the guy swung his way.

But not today. Not when he had somewhere to be in twelve minutes, and especially not when his mother was anywhere in the vicinity. Her "I-want-to-speak-to-your-manager" haircut was truth in advertising. She'd probably have the man raked over the coals for daring to talk to him.

Just one more reason why the paperwork in his hand would hit the trash at first opportunity.

———

So much for the printer workstation being a high output business model. The damn thing needed a full-time babysitter, and somehow Carson Eddinger had found himself elected to the job. Maybe if his colleagues didn't feed the hapless machine a steady diet of rubber bands and staples along with the endless paperwork to be scanned, copied, and otherwise dumped into the bowels of the business, he wouldn't spend so much time on his knees at work.

Hell, there had to be rent boys who spent less time on their knees and got more joy from it.

What lunatic excuse of an engineer put the paper feed in so it needed two levers and a twisty knob to extract a jam? Perhaps he should be grateful it didn't require a blood sacrifice and an incantation.

This time. He dropped a mangled yellow sheet on the floor and hoped he'd gotten all the shreds.

Carson stayed on his knees a little longer than he needed to extract the toner cartridge, which was empty *again*. With his head stuck in the machine and his butt out to the world, he could avoid speaking to The Harridan From Hell™. Yay, she was moving with purpose, and double yay, a small sip of revenge was his—Carson was only sorry that he was in the right position and wrong venue to slap his ass and tell her to "Kiss this!"

Now, the cutie she was towing behind her… Cutie ought to get a proper introduction to Carson's backside, with any slapping to be done for much better reasons. And knees time without any copier involved.

Dream on. So much time had passed since Carson's last enjoyable knee time that he couldn't rightly recall. Or didn't want to recall. He'd thought no strings attached was the way to go, until the emptiness of getting called someone else's name, or no one's name, became too much. Maybe if he was willing to take someone home, even let him spend the night, he'd have a better chance of something lasting.

He needed a name for Cutie. The spank bank needed a deposit. Or maybe not.

The guy was young, had to be at least ten years younger than his own thirty-three, and might not have a thought in his head.

Which wouldn't matter one single bit: fantasy fodder only said things that Carson wanted to hear. He could imagine erudite lines from Cutie's mouth, along with more dangerous imaginings, like "Fuck me, I love you!" That ought to satisfy all the needs Carson's right hand wasn't meeting.

His hang-dog demeanor could be fixed in Carson's

head too. He might look a lot more confident in different company. Wouldn't anyone getting dragged into Lorraine Ratliff's office look like they wholly regretted the events leading up to imprisonment? Carson certainly hadn't enjoyed his last session in the Chair of Tears. Not that he'd ever give that bitch the satisfaction of knowing.

She couldn't possibly not know how much he enjoyed being able to produce two emails from higher up, plus an invoice that she'd insisted didn't exist. Write him up for nonsense, would she? Not that he hadn't sweated bullets hunting for that invoice, which his nemesis the copier had scanned into the wrong folder. She'd been *so* confident she had him good that time.

He'd get another glimpse of Cutie if he stood here long enough, but Angie cleared her throat behind him. He jumped guiltily—how long had he been wool-gathering?

"Do we need to call the service center?" she asked, rattling the sheaf of papers at him. "I have to get these sent out on the afternoon mail, and if I have to run over to shipping to use theirs…"

"Honestly, government. You'd think they'd come into the twenty-first century and use electronic documentation already." Carson inspected the toner cartridge's change date, information he'd added a month ago with a silver Sharpie on the black plastic. "No, this will only take a minute."

Movement at an office door attracted their attention—he and Angie both swiveled to look. Jerking his eyes back to the cartridge almost as fast as he'd looked, Carson felt his fantasies evaporating like the mist they were.

"…Mom until you have an employee badge, Tim," had to be the biggest boner-killer ever uttered.

So Cutie had a name. Tim Ratliff.

And The Harridan from Hell™ was his mother.

Why hadn't she just named him "My Mommy Has My Balls In Her Purse"? Because that would explain his hunched over gait. His friends could call him Percy. If she let him have friends. Who in their right mind would risk dating anyone who came with a controller like her? Look how she was planning his life. And he was taking it.

If the poor guy ever managed to lose his V-card, Carson would bet either Mommy was leaning over the bed giving instructions, *blurggggggg*, or he was a lot more accomplished at sneaking around than the CIA. Or he wasn't, and the unfortunate partner was composting six feet down in the petunia bed in the back garden.

Nope, not a risk to take.

Not even a risk to imagine taking.

Back to dealing with the copier, which at least the bitch appreciated. Or at least she appreciated not being inconvenienced as frequently as the machine attempted. Not that she appreciated Carson dealing with the balky thing. Hadn't she ridden his back about "taking time away from your assigned work" for touching its innards? Like he could get anything done without a functioning copier/scanner.

First thing, seal the cartridge, or it would puke greasy black toner all over the packaging on the way to recycling. Carson turned it over gently, hunting the tabs.

Damn it all, here Lorraine came, with blood in her eye, and her mouth all pursed up like a cat's butt. "Don't you even think about it!"

He'd apologize for delaying Angie later. "Okay. I won't. You deal with it, Lorraine."

Carson thrust the cartridge into hand in a puff of black dust.

CHAPTER TWO

WES the overexuberant chemist swung around the side of Carson's cubicle like he was trying to pole dance on it.

"Lunch time!" the dervish in the Hawaiian print shirt yodeled. "Where are you taking me?"

"Who let you in?" Carson grumbled. He'd planned to go to lunch with Wes, but he had a stack of work yet to do. His spreadsheet lacked two thirds of the required data yet, a casualty of his time spent in the guts of the copier. Could all woes be laid at that misbegotten machine's wheels?

"Oh phoo, you're glad to see me and you know it." The chemist and sometime rock-climber executed a move meant for the walls of El Dorado Canyon more than a cube farm, manteling onto the cubicle wall, balancing on his hands with his feet a good three feet away from the carpet, sticking his tongue out at the fisheye camera on the ceiling. He leaned down into the adjacent cube to make smoochy noises. "You too, Angie. You guys love me."

"We'd love you better if you weren't knocking everything off my walls." Carson grabbed Wes's belt and hauled him off balance. Wes landed lightly, but his sneaker was going to leave a waffle print on that phone list. "Pick it up. Put it back."

"Somebody's hangry," Wes observed sagely. He leaned over to collect the fallen papers and pushpins without bending his knees.

Carson swiveled back to his desk to get his face out of Wes's ass. Little bitch did that on purpose. Trust him to make another snide comment without a word. If they didn't have an audience, he'd pinch that ass hard enough to make Wes flip to upright, yelling.

"Let's go." Carson locked his computer screen and pushed his chair back. "Come on, Angie, let's get the Energizer Bunny out of here."

Last thing he needed was someone complaining about horseplay in the office on a day that already contained the Toner Incident.

"That reminds me of a joke." Wes tap-danced after them. "What do you get when you put batteries in your rabbit?"

"No, Wes. Not now." Angie grimaced and sped up.

Carson lengthened his already long stride. Could they get outside before Wes uncorked his punchline?

"Orgasms!"

If he was waiting for laughter, he might be waiting a long time. Idiot just had to deliver his punchline outside The Harridan's open door. Maybe Carson had gotten all the way out of her line of sight before dodo egg attracted her attention.

"Ahem!" exploded from her office.

Carson kept going. Wes probably turned to blow her a kiss or twiddle his fingers in a cheery toodle-oo.

At last, on the other side of a door.

Plausible deniability—keep walking and hope the Harridan™ had enough else to do that she didn't feel the need to follow them. Carson unlocked his pride and joy, a black 2010 BMW 328i coupe, now making its third owner happy. Wes tumbled into the back seat, leaving Angie to tuck her skirt around her knees in the black leather bucket seat in front.

"Where are we going?" Carson aimed the BMW down the shady lane toward the gate. "And did you have to poke the bear?"

"Oh pfft. You're not hairy enough to be a bear. And I hardly poked you." Wes made up for the oversight with an index finger.

Carson twitched away, trying not to flinch hard enough to affect his sensitive steering. The car drove like an extension of his thoughts. "You're going to be eating stale sandwiches out of the cafeteria vending machine if you don't behave yourself for thirty seconds. Remind me why I like you?"

"Because there's never a dull moment around me, darling." Wes giggled.

Truer words were never spoken. Angie at least knew where the problem lay. "Were you trying to goad Lorraine?"

"My joke was probably the closest she's gotten to an orgasm in years. Unless you have another explanation for her cranky ways?" Wes leaned away from Angie's swat. "I'm hungry. Feed me. Now."

"You've been sniffing the solvents again, haven't you?" Carson gritted his teeth as they passed over the one-way exit's road spikes. "If it was ether, you'd probably be quietly passed out at your bench, so…"

"I say again, hangry." Wes tutted. "Dr. Wesley prescribes food and a stick removal."

For that, Wes forfeited any say in where they went for lunch. "We're going to Cluckets."

"Fine with me," Angie agreed.

"I had chicken for dinner last night," Wes complained, flicking the window switch and letting the road noise in at four second intervals.

Why had Carson reactivated the rear window switch since last time? He deactivated on an "up" cycle, just in time to take the car out of gear in the parking lot. "And you'll have chicken for lunch today, or a fish sandwich, or you can hoof it across the way to the taco joint and eat without us."

He almost hoped Wes would head the other direction when they got out of the car.

"Hangry *and* needs to get laid." Wes slipped his hand around Carson's elbow. "We're friends. I suppose I could offer a benefit, if it sweetens your mood."

"Just. Shut. Up. For five seconds!" Carson jerked his arm away. He'd never invited Wes into his home, even after knowing him for six years. And certainly not into his bedroom.

Angie swatted the back of Wes's head in solidarity, and for that, she earned an open door and an "After you, my lady."

Of course Wes sashayed in after her. Watching him from the back, Carson had not one scintilla of desire to take him up on what he knew was a semiserious offer. They'd spent enough time together to know Carson's sanity and Wes's lifespan would both fare better in friendship. Nope, watching Wes from the back was more for judging distance and degree of bend at knee and ankle to get maximum lift when the toe of Carson's shoe connected with Wes's buttock.

Carson put the fantasy of kicking Wes into orbit aside only because he studied the menu board quietly while they waited in line. In a few moments they were at the register. Carson hung back while his friends ordered and paid, wondering.

Yep, he'd seen a Cluckets uniform once this morning. This guy couldn't be… There were Cluckets franchises all over the city. And lots of staff at each one… There were probably a dozen young men at each location, maybe a quarter with dark brown hair, one or two of them with waves that peeked out from under their caps. Yeah.

Carson quit doing mental statistics the second he checked the name tag. Tim.

No reason to let on he'd seen the man's round trip to Mommy's office today. No call at all to show recognition. They didn't know each other. This was all "two piece dark meat, extra crisp, spicy, with slaw."

On-the-job Tim looked like an entirely different person with his shoulders back and his head high, working with pride, instead of hunched over, doing the scurry of shame. Looked pretty good, really, moving with economy and grace, distributing receipts, sauces, and forks with not one wasted action.

Angie found them a table. Wes, for all his grumbling, dove into his chicken with gusto, and finished off a drumstick before Carson had taken a third bite. Or maybe Carson chewed more slowly, thinking of what lay under that black rugby shirt with the red collar, and what those blue eyes would look like up close. Were his lashes stupid long or absurdly long?

Carson stabbed himself in the lip with the spork, dropping coleslaw down his shirt, where it dampened the printed galaxies and interstellar space.

Nope, no good reason to start fantasizing, not when he knew what kind of baggage the guy had attached to his umbilical cord.

"Smooth move, Carson." Wes giggled. "You can't even feed yourself. What did you do to your hands, anyway? Looks like you washed up in sulfuric acid."

Dropping the napkin on his tray, Carson surveyed his darkened hands. "Toner. Soap didn't even touch it. Have to try some Goo-gone."

"Rubbing alcohol," the feral chemist murmured absently. Carson mentally rescinded one PITA point.

"Lorraine and Carson played 'not-it' with a toner cartridge." Angie snorked instead of biting into a crisp thigh. "He was fixing the copier when she came barreling up out of nowhere. So he stopped. And she didn't like that either."

"There is no pleasing that woman." Carson had lost the game, too—she'd changed her mind once she got black puffed all over her manicured hands.

"Wonder how her family deals with her." Wes looked thoughtful. Probably best he was unlikely to find out. That expression could presage anything from a whoopee cushion to a call to the IRS.

"Probably by saying 'Yes, dear. No, dear. Anything you say, dear." Carson's next bite was more of a gnashing of teeth. Good. More boner killer. If he imagined that pouty mouth saying such things, he could rest easy about his dick never getting near.

Angie glanced back at the counter, where Tim dealt out more chicken and fries. "You know, I think the guy who served us was in this morning with her. He's her son."

"Cute, too." Wes craned completely around to stare. "His father must have muscular genes. He hardly has that sourpuss look."

"Shut up, Wes!" Jayzuz, the dolt wasn't keeping his voice down at all! "Don't talk about him behind his back."

"Okay, I'll go ask him directly." He scooted his chair away from the table. "Besides, he seems to be staring at you."

"He's staring at you, because his ears are burning from being talked about." Carson grabbed Wes's arm. Hell, his own ears were burning from listening to Wes. "Sit down, shut up, and eat your meal. Leave the man alone, he obviously has enough problems without you barging in."

"He does seem to be glancing over this way a lot." Angie, the little traitor, would have to agree with Wes.

"Maybe he likes green-eyed blondes. Girl blondes." At least Wes was sitting and eating, even if he did spew a crumb. No telling what stupid shit would come out of his mouth if he did go talk to the guy. "Too bad for you, Carson."

"Look, I do not even want to know which way he swings." Carson could tell a lie with the best of them. All's fair in self-defense, right? "Anyone he dates would have to pass the Mom test, and we all know his mommy hates me."

"He looks early twenties. Bet he can date who he wants." Wes swiveled around again, like staring would provide such answers. Carson cleared his throat, and Wes snapped back to eyes forward.

"You think Lorraine Ratliff's son gets to make his own decisions? Dream on, Wes. You didn't see him this morning." Carson dropped the last chicken bone onto his plate. "And I'm way past the point where I'm willing to sneak around, dodging someone's parents. High school ended fifteen years ago."

"So if mommy wasn't a problem, you'd ask him out?" Wes lifted an eyebrow.

"If his mom wasn't…" Carson knew a pipe dream when he heard it. Or a solvent-fumes dream. Or wishful thinking. Time to change the subject. "How about them Broncos?"

"Big men in tight pants, always in season." Wes smirked right through his companions' groans. "Time to get back to the lab, duckies. My digestion reaction's due to stop in fifteen minutes."

Carson was halfway in the car when he realized Wes wasn't behind them. No, the little fucker was at the counter, talking to Tim.

Did Carson have to drag him away by the scruff of his neck? Carson resigned himself to retrieving his soon-not-to-be-friend when Wes appeared, sucking on a straw hard enough to cave his cheeks in.

Wes tilted the driver's seat forward to slither into the back. "Relax. I just wanted a milkshake to take back with me."

They got all the way back to the admin building before Carson realized Wes hadn't cracked a "sucks like a Hoover" joke even once.

Why did that feel ominous?

CHAPTER THREE

THE MAN who'd seen Tim running away from Mom would have to be the one who'd shown up for lunch. There couldn't possibly be two men in deep blue dress shirts patterned with galaxies and nebulas, with hair full and nearly gravity-defying on top, but tapered close at the sides, almost as close as his beard was trimmed.

The one had already rocked his world, and not in a good way.

Nope, having Hottie McHotness see how Tim had run out the door hadn't done a thing for his self-esteem.

Suavely serving chicken and fries wasn't enough to erase his earlier humiliation. Best he could do was stand tall and speak clearly and get the order right. Big whoop. Wasn't as if Tim didn't know Hottie and his pals were talking about him. All that turning around and side eye. Probably having a good laugh at Tim's expense.

He'd replayed that morning fifty times in his head, trying for a result that left him some dignity. Yeah, he'd have to march, head high, shoulders back, away from an encounter where he'd said no and made it stick.

It was so much easier to do in his head. Where a lifetime of conditioning to say, "Yes, ma'am" could be thrown off without disastrous consequences.

Coming away the victor of a boundary-establishing encounter with his mother would take some practice. He'd started, even if he'd fizzled out, with not pulling in to the parking lot at her direction. He'd said no tonight to her doing his laundry. He'd managed on his own the last couple of years, not bringing full baskets home on the weekends like he had as a freshman and sophomore, and he'd fought to not come home more than two weekends a month this last year.

He could kick himself for not starting his job search earlier, though. Because now he had advice and commentary, and what could have been a final edit of his résumé had turned into a full-fledged rewrite.

"Because I'm HR, dear, I know what we're looking for," Mom said, and left massive blocks of red text using Track Changes.

Maybe so, but he was a chemist, and should have some idea of what a lab director would want to know.

He'd had to swap file names to send out his own version under her watchful eye.

And he hadn't gotten a single bite from any of the labs.

Maybe she was right.

Sorting and resorting his inbox didn't make any requests for interviews appear on his laptop. Even after he hit send/receive a fifth time. Tim closed his email. Maybe he should check the job boards again. Cast his net more widely.

Damn it. It was early days yet. Surely someone from a

drug company, or environmental lab, or plastics research, would need a guy with his skills. A BS in chemistry from a good technical university ought to fit in somewhere that wasn't… here.

He'd gone to a good school, he had connections, damnit. Maybe it wasn't the best school he'd been accepted by, but "it's close enough to drive." The hand that wrote the tuition checks had been very insistent on that part.

Tim opened his browser with a sigh. Maybe his résumé would be more impressive coming from a dot-edu address, but with graduation came a return to his old personal email. He would have liked something fun like labrat155@gmush.com, or makeitgoboom@whoohoo.com, but no, back when he was in fifth grade, Mom set him up as TRatliff@comment.net, "because that might not be available when you're older."

At least it was more businesslike when he needed it, and he could see the reasoning behind not using one of their ISP addresses on an eleven-year-old's choice, but what was wrong with makeitgoboom?

Fuck it. He'd gone along to get along, and what had that gotten him? Tim punched up Gmush, and hot damn, makeitgoboom was available!

Part of his new standing up for himself. Tempting as it was to fire off an email to his mother announcing the small rebellion, he stayed his finger on the send button. What she didn't know, she couldn't moan about. He could hear it now: "What if you get mixed up and send business emails from the wrong account?"

He wasn't five, for Pete's sake.

Who the fuck was Pete, anyway, and why was he still talking like a kid, even inside his own head? *Try it again.*

He wasn't five, for fuck's sake.

Not that he'd say it aloud, because his family didn't do casual crudity, but he would damn well flex some mental muscle.

He really wouldn't start spattering "damn" into family conversation because church, and God, and "decent behavior" and all that. Mom would have a fit, and then Dad would roar, and it just wasn't worth it.

Outside the house? Might just have to say something pungent when the situation required.

Because *for fuck's sake*, he really wasn't five, or fifteen, or even twenty any more.

He needed to get out on his own so bad he could taste it. Better see if Glassdoor had any new offerings. Maybe he should carpet bomb all the biotech places in Boulder, whether or not there was a listed job.

Hmm, a giant manufacturer of mozzarella needed a chemist? Tim adjusted his cover letter to suit and attached his résumé. Hope the work wouldn't put him off pizza forever. He never wanted another piece of fried chicken.

If he wanted clean clothing for work tomorrow, he'd better throw his uniform in the wash now. He could come back and locate another couple of prospects once the laundry machine was going. Which—sounded like the water was running.

He'd left something in his pocket, too. The guy in the bird-of-paradise Hawaiian shirt slipped him a napkin. Probably hitting on him. Or his idea of a joke. Oh yuck, had Tim slipped a neatly wrapped piece of gristle into his pocket because the guy acted like a spy? That absolutely could not contaminate his trousers one more second.

He dove at the laundry basket.

That wasn't there.

Oh, great. With any luck, Mom hadn't gotten any

farther than rounding up the dirty clothes. Tim flung himself down two flights of stairs.

He found his mother hurling dark clothing into the top loader like grenades. Dang, she was gonna put her hand right through the fabric, clearing pockets like that.

"Mom, thanks, but I said I'd do my own laundry now." You'd think she'd be glad to hand over the task, but no, here she was, *again.* "It's not a problem."

"Of course it's not a problem. All the better to hide, isn't it?" she hissed.

He hadn't been stupid enough to jack off into a sock since middle school. "What are you talking about? I'm not hiding anything. I'm just trying to be a responsible adult and do my own stuff."

"Oh?" could etch glass. "Then why are you running to the laundry room? Is it to keep me from finding this?" She snatched a white napkin with a red logo off the top of the dryer and thrust it into Tim's face. "Because I most certainly have found it."

Okay, not gristle. That would bring a scolding and a rehash of the Brussels sprout story from second grade.

"Since I don't even know what 'it' is, I have no idea what you're so upset about." Tim refused to back away, even though she waved the napkin unpleasantly near his nose. "Aside from it being paper that will make a mess if it goes through the wash."

She stopped shaking the napkin enough for him to take it and read the inked disaster. One sentence and ten numbers. Oh shit. The napkin didn't need to get wet to make a mess.

Carson thinks you're cute. 720-555-0154

An automatic apology leapt to his lips, but he stumbled so badly over the words that rational thought had a moment to squidge in behind the panic. He hadn't done anything wrong. Even if his mother expected apologies for anything from leaving a cup on the counter to the neighbor's dog barking.

He hadn't done anything wrong.

Tim closed his mouth firmly, and if he bit a chunk out of his tongue to keep the words in, Mom didn't have to know that. "I'm sorry" quietly turned into a "So?" loud enough to hear. Controlling his face gave him something to concentrate on. "Puzzled" was probably an expert move, so he went for "blank."

"So?" she hissed. "Why does Carson think you're cute?"

He spared a hate for this unknown Carson dude, because Tim could so have done without a confrontation after a long day on his feet.

Carson hadn't done anything wrong either. In fact, Carson probably hadn't done anything at all. The dude decked out in birds of paradise probably wasn't even Carson. Not the way he'd leaned in to whisper, "The big guy" like he was Austin Powers' weirder sidekick.

Tim shrugged. "Because I am? You mention my adorableness two or three times a week."

Oh, dangerous territory. Perilously close to backchat. But since he'd had to listen to her saying such embarrassing things to practically everyone they encountered together, he ought to get some mileage of his own out of it.

"Why does *Carson* have any opinion at all about you?" she snarled.

"Mother, I have no idea. I don't know Carson, I don't know if the man who handed me this was Carson or someone else." Absolutely true, pretend the bird of paradise guy's terrible spycraft was legit, spread the blame, then maybe no one would feel her wrath too deeply. "I didn't know he had an opinion one way or the other until just now. If he does. His friend might be pranking him. Or me. Wouldn't be the worst thing anyone's ever done at a fast-food place, though they usually destroy the bathrooms."

Instead of the staff.

Mom still had her rage-face on. He wasn't out of the woods. But he hadn't apologized, and he hadn't backed down.

Yet.

Discretion was the better part of valor—a tactical retreat while he was ahead might be in order. But he was standing his ground against an unjustified attack—another unjustified attack. The unfamiliar power made him light-headed enough to ask, "What's the matter with this guy Carson, anyway?"

His mother went back to hurling clothing. "He's one of *those.*"

Now that was damn judgey. "Those what?" snapped out of his mouth before he even registered that he was judging his mother. Finding her wanting. And sounding like it.

She muttered something and stuffed a pair of jeans into the washer without checking the pockets.

"I'm sorry, I didn't hear you." Dear God in Heaven, who was saying this stuff? Someone bound and determined to start a war, apparently, and who was using Tim's mouth.

She turned and snapped, "Homosexuals. If you couldn't figure it out from that note."

"I did. I fail to see why it's a problem." If he turned to leave with his back straight and didn't actually run, he might get the last word in.

"You fail to see—!" she shrieked. "You fail to see? He made a pass at you! He wants to recruit you into his horrible lifestyle!"

Nope, no escape yet. "Ma. I got a note with a compliment from someone who may or may not be him. That's hardly dastardly. I read it and go on about my life."

Actually, he'd like to be recruited a little more actively, but this suicidal mouth diarrhea had to stop somewhere.

"See to it that you do." The black and red shirt in her hands might survive her fingernails. It better: he had to wear it to work tomorrow.

Discretion was definitely the better part of valor here: he'd let her have the last word. Time to evaporate before she got to wondering just how Tim planned to go about his life. Fighting for the autonomy to do his own laundry, at least for tonight, was a lost cause, but an acceptable casualty of getting away with the napkin in his hand.

Win! Close, but a win.

More win—Carson thought he was cute? This opinion had been filtered through someone who dressed garishly enough to be seen from downtown Denver, so maybe Carson thought he was attractive. Or handsome. Much better. Had some dignity to it. But Carson thought… something good.

Once back in his room, Tim poked the number into his phone. Because he could dream. Not so much that he added the number as Carson. Nope, not leaving a blatant trail. Carson's new code name was… Tim thought a moment. Neil. His own middle name, easy to remember.

Because with Mom on the warpath, anything was possible. With a sigh of regret, he dropped the napkin into the trashcan beneath his desk. He could hug the words to himself.

Carson thought…

What Tim thought about what Carson thought would have to wait until the house was dark and his parents safely snoring. Not yet. Maybe a shower before bed… Nope, he'd already washed the chicken smell out of his hair tonight. He'd make sure there were lotion and tissues in the nightstand.

He did have an urgent issue to take his mind off Carson and his opinions. He needed desperately to figure out why his poor old Toyota wasn't holding a charge. Maybe it was something he could fix himself. Or get repaired at a reasonable cost. None of his buddies from high school were any more car-smart than he was, and the few from college who knew their nuts and bolts had gone on to the rest of their lives two time zones away. The internet might have some answers.

Dad wasn't much of a mechanic, but maybe he'd have some advice. He should be getting home from his church meeting any time now.

Footsteps sounded on the stairs. Angry thuds, damped by carpet worn down to the backing in spots, drew closer. Tim braced himself. Short of diving out the second-story window and hoping to do a pachinko bounce down the maple tree in the front yard, he was trapped.

"Why doesn't this bother you?" He should have known —once his mother got started it took an act of Congress to make her stop.

Having his back to her drew a prickling between his shoulder blades. She'd consider not turning around rude if not evasive and the beginning of a lie. Tim swiveled around to face her, refusing to bow his shoulders.

"A stranger having an opinion doesn't hurt me any." He met her eyes steadily. Little cringes got shunted to the side —he dared not give her any reason to suspect how not-hurt he was.

Mom blocked the doorway, her hands on the jambs. *You*

go nowhere until you've explained yourself rolled off her in waves. "What kind of man doesn't take offense to this?"

"The kind who doesn't think it's a big deal for a stranger to say something nice. It doesn't affect my life." Tim shrugged. *I don't know why you're making a commotion out of this* would be a logical follow-up statement, but he was pushing the boundaries awfully hard as it was. Mom would not take the deflection onto herself well. She never did.

"I'll tell you what kind of man doesn't mind another man calling him cute," Mom snarled. "A gay man."

Well, fuck. This wasn't just too close to home; this was smack in the living room. *Stay calm, stay neutral.* "I suppose."

Time to change the subject before she asked any more questions that didn't have answers he could give without lying. He could make the truth do sit-ups, pushups, and model like a lie, but he had to stick to facts, however strung together. "Mom, if you don't mind, I'm trying to find out about my car so I can fix it and give yours back."

He still wouldn't turn around to his computer without her agreement—she had such a touchy notion of respect.

She flung one hand up to the heavens. "I'm not done with you, young man. Of course gay men wouldn't mind, they want other men to think they're cute. Saying so's how they get together, isn't it?"

"I wouldn't know." Not from lack of wanting to know. Tim hadn't let anything hold him back except fear. The same fear that made tendrils of ice flow through his veins in the face of her questions. *Please let her stop now.*

"Are you sure? Are you absolutely sure?" She advanced two steps into his room, eyes blazing. "When was the last time you dated a girl?"

"High school, and you scared her off." Tim would run right now, if he wasn't pinned against his desk. "You called her a gold-digger and a slut and threw her out, remember?" Poor Emily, she hadn't deserved any of that for going to a movie once.

"And why not in college when I wasn't around?" Dear heavens, had her teeth really grown pointed? She was going to rend him limb from limb.

"No time. You wanted me to come home every weekend, and I did, until my workload got too heavy. Nobody was interested in that." Tim tried to scoot back again, but the desk ground into the back of his chair. "And the rest of the time I was studying or working. That 4.0 took a lot of time and effort."

"And now? You have time." Her fierce stare pinned him in place.

"I don't know anybody I want to date." *And if I did, I wouldn't bring them around for you to yell horrible accusations at them.* Tim's nails bent against the chair's arms. "And I *need to fix my car* so I can have a way to go out if I do meet someone."

"Don't you change the subject on me!" she bellowed. "Were you dating boys in college? When I couldn't keep an eye on you?"

"No!" Tim could say that in perfect truth. Twenty-two and never been kissed, except by poor Emily, who'd been called such names for one little peck. "You know that. You showed up for surprise cookie deliveries often enough to meet all my friends."

Horribly embarrassing, too. Chocolate chip check-ups, they'd called those visits, and the treats didn't nearly make up for the cringe factor of her hanging around late into the evening.

"Kept the gays from sniffing around you, didn't it?" She stood tall and triumphant. "Seems to be a little harder now. I told that fag Carson not to get near you, and what does he do not even three hours later? Slips you a note, telling you you're cute, and you like that! All 'it doesn't bother me' when you like it! I was right, wasn't I?"

She was always right. About everything. If you didn't believe she was right, just ask her. If you got the chance, because she'd already be telling you how right she was. Tim didn't dare argue. "It doesn't bother me, and what were you right about?"

"Honey's always right." Dad stuck his head in the door. How had he gotten all the into the house and up the stairs without Tim noticing? Oh, because his full attention was on Mom, and wondering if he should throw himself to the left or to the right if she did lunge.

"When I caught you with that stupid Tiger Beat magazine. And you lied to me, oh, no, no, you weren't gay." She shook an upraised finger in the air, punctuating every no.

"I was twelve years old. I had no idea what gay was, besides something you thought I shouldn't be. And that magazine had Selena Gomez and Miley Cyrus." No, Tim had no idea then, except that his friends called things "gay" when they meant "bad" and snickered like they knew what they were talking about. Once again, he was taking major heat for something someone else did, this time his then thirteen-year-old cousin, who'd left her magazine behind. "You know that was Jill's. She was mad you threw it away."

"I really don't think she left it under your bed. Did she?" Mom pounced. Dad hovered in the doorway, starting to speak and then stopping, like he had something to contribute. Maybe a little defense here? Oh wait, not against Mom.

Right then, what had been fear became anger. Why was he the target of such wrath? He hadn't done anything to deserve this grilling, and he was fucking tired of it. He'd done the good son thing, the obedient son thing, and what the hell had it ever gotten him besides a short time of peace and the loss of another part of his soul? He wanted those parts back, damn it!

"You even said Selena Gomez was cute. Does that make you gay?" Tim shot back. Not much of a comeback, but this was uncharted territory. His pulse thudded, driving ice through his brain. Getting any words at all past the boulder in his throat was a win.

"Don't smart off to your mother," Dad snapped. Of course.

"Great! After all the effort we spent on raising you to be a good God-fearing man, you turn out to be gay." If she spat at him, he'd come out of this chair and... Probably nothing. Just standing up—for himself—would be unfamiliar to them both.

What the hell? He hadn't given himself away, he knew he hadn't. Just not being mad about a note wasn't enough evidence for anyone. Except Mom, who had a steel-trap mind that caught fantasies as well as facts.

Well, this time she'd caught both.

And she could have it. She could fucking have it.

"Okay, Mom. You're right." Tim stood up, the ice in his veins turning to fire. She took a step back, her mouth open like a carp. He looked her in the eye, watching her unrighteous indignation battling over agreement and realization. Served her right. "You said I'm gay, I must be gay."

"Don't be ridiculous," Dad huffed.

"I'm not being ridiculous, I'm agreeing with my mother, who has declared me to be gay." Tim patted his hair in the most effeminate gesture he could come up with on short notice. "I'll work on being attracted to other men, starting right now."

Dad jerked back like he'd been bitten.

"Oh, don't worry, Daddy, I'm just gay, not creepy. You're safe. Let's see…" Tim went hipshot with one hand on his hip and laid a finger alongside his nose. "There's Ed Johnson down the street, and my coworkers, and Mrs. Hedstrom's grandson. Oh wait, he moved to California, he won't be around to ogle. Or, I know!" He flipped his hand palm up and added a shoulder shimmy. "How about Cars—"

"This is the most ludicrous conversation I've ever heard!" Dad interrupted before Mom found her voice. "What brought this on?"

Time to drop the posturing. "I got a second-hand compliment, and because I am not all butt-hurt about it being from another man, Mother declared me gay. Oops, I'm forgetting to be gay again!" He went with a limp-wristed wave this time.

She wanted to be right all the time, he'd give her right. This was war.

"Tho, Daddy, if thomeone pathed you a note thaying thomebody elthe thought you were cute, what would you thay?" Tim didn't straighten his wrist.

Mom turned to glare at Dad, taking the spotlight off Tim. He could breathe again.

"Uh, nothing? Shrug and go on doing what I was doing?" Dad looked perplexed.

"Okay, 'cause your gay thon needth to know how to properly path for thtraight." Tim flapped his hand limply again. Maybe the breeze would push his mother all the way out the door.

"This is beyond ridiculous. And as long as you live in this house, you'll keep a civil tongue in your head." Dad took Mom's arm and ushered her out. "Come on, honey."

Once his parents were safely downstairs, Tim collapsed on his bed. His heart rate might come down before midnight. What had he done?

Nothing. He'd agreed with his mother.

So what if his parents thought it was a tasteless joke? The truth was out.

CHAPTER FOUR

BEING LEFT UNINTERRUPTED by screaming harpies or balky machinery made for a pleasant morning. Neither Lorraine nor an incipient breakdown marred Carson's workday, twice running. This time the obnoxious one called in sick, instead of the required one. Good news, since his shirt was mostly white, with "paint drips" oozing down the shoulders and no toner marks. Made for a productive day to not deal with either of them—he had only three states left to go to complete this quarter's licensing requirements.

The Energizer Chemist bopped on in, shedding greetings like dandruff. He passed Carson's cubicle to Angie's, dropping into her lap for a quick spin. The screaming orange parrots on his shirt blurred into a ring of fire. He bounced up before she'd finished giggling around his name.

"Heya, Carson! Ready for lunch?" Wes dropped one eyelid. Maybe he was trying for conspiratorial, but he mostly looked palsied.

"Sure. Let's go."

They took Carson's BMW again, because they'd

learned not to let Wes drive. He'd highjack them to the best empanadas in Boulder or burritos big enough to beep all the way down in Arvada, consistently pushing the geographical boundaries for time vs eating, and Angie's car was a clutter of castoffs meant for a charity store.

"Cluckets, my good man," Wes intoned.

"Again?" They'd fought over having chicken twice in a row yesterday and ended up at a pho shop by dint of Carson driving right past the disputed restaurant. "What if I want Chinese? Or sushi?"

"Or a salad?" Angie stuck her oar in.

"Cluckets has salads. With chicken on top." Wes batted his lashes winsomely—Carson jerked his gaze away from the rear-view mirror before he gagged. "Please?"

"You'd think there was something else there besides food, you're so anxious." Carson was prepared to honor a nicely offered please. "Like you're getting your fix or something."

"Or something." Wes agreed. He practically skipped through the glass doors, executing a twirl while Carson and Angie followed more sedately.

"Gotta lay off the chloroform, dude." Carson got into line behind Wes.

"But it was a fine 2019 Chateau de Mallinckrodt, with a full body and a hint of sweetness." Wes inhaled deeply. "Ahh…"

Of course it was Tim's line. And Wes was right: the guy was cute. Well, good looking more than cute. Fine looking, and man, what a waste that he had the kind of baggage he did. If Carson didn't know what he knew, he'd take the chance to speak up about more than what he wanted for lunch. Instead of taking that wistful sadness out on Tim, Carson instead offered a wide smile. Retail and restaurant people got more than their share of shit from the customers: the least Carson could do was smile. At someone he wished he could smile at for other reasons.

Tim smiled back. Somehow a cookie ended up on Carson's tray without registering on the tab.

Carson dropped a napkin over it because the last thing he needed was Wes noticing out loud. He might draw conclusions.

Wonder if anyone in Tim's life was offering better conversation than "Two packets of ketchup, please."

They went in search of a table, and who should be there, staking out a four-seater table by herself in a crowded dining room, but Lorraine Ratliff. She had a medium soda cup and a tablet, and she faced the serving counter. They couldn't reach the dining area without passing right by her.

Please let there be another table available farther on.

She noticed them. Holy shit, did she notice them. If her scowl got any deeper, her forehead would end up on a map as Ratliff Ridge. Carson would still be polite. "Hello, Lorraine."

"Don't sit here." Man, right past the pleasantries of "May we, no," plus assuming that her company wouldn't give them all raging heartburn.

"Wouldn't dream of it." Angie marched right on by.

Lorraine wasn't done. She fixed Carson with a beady eye. "You shouldn't even be here."

Whoa. Time to sling some shit right back, and the bitch had given him the ammunition herself. "Me? You're the one who's contagious. I'm kind of surprised you're out in public. I'll let Dave know you're feeling better."

He turned to follow his friends to another table, seething. He had every right to be here, and what the hell was Mrs. "I'm not able to come in today" doing here?

35

Glaring at her son like every piece of chicken he served was coming out of her retirement fund?

Well, if some questions didn't just answer themselves.

Wonder how Tim had come to "deserve" the supervision. Bet that smile he'd offered Carson was getting marked down in some kind of detention book.

"Someone looked glad to see you," Wes remarked blithely.

"Sure wasn't Lorraine." The woman turned to glare at them, though the conversation probably didn't carry over the lunchtime hubbub. Wes wiggled his drumstick at her and blew a kiss. Carson restrained himself to a dirty look even though his middle finger yearned to salute.

"What's her problem?" Angie snarked. "'You shouldn't even be here!' like she has some say. For that matter, why is she here when she called in?"

"She's acting like she's standing guard. What the hell?" Poor Tim: had he been so very awful in his last life? Carson's food took the brunt of his wrath—he managed to strip most of a thigh with one bite and had to do some fancy grabbing to keep his paint-spatter shirt from becoming his chicken-spatter shirt.

"Huh," was Wes's contribution.

Alarm bells rang.

"Wes, what did you say to him when we were here the other day?" Was that milkshake a vector for a time bomb?

"Didn't say a thing." Wes put on his most virtuous air, nose high and butter unable to melt in his general vicinity.

"What did you do?" Carson demanded. He *had* to have done something—simple, specific answers from Wes always meant to listen for what he wasn't saying.

"Um, I may or may not have slipped him a note." He

tried hiding behind a crisp chicken tender, which might or might not get shoved up his nose.

With a breath deep enough to suck all the oxygen out of the room, Carson turned his scowl up to Lorraine-worthy. "What. Did. It. Say?"

"Help?" Wes beseeched Angie with hands slumped to begging-puppy paws.

Angie flipped her spork around to brandish it like a dagger. "Answer the man."

"Eep!" wasn't going to get him out of a damned thing. Wes cowered under their combined glowers. He should have been more afraid than he was—he suddenly reverted to his usually sunny self. "It said, ah, 'Carson thinks you're cute' and I think I got your phone number right. Be a shame if I didn't."

"What!" came out loud enough to make Lorraine turn around. Carson got his volume under control. That explained the cookie. He felt a headache coming on. "Damn it, Wes, don't you think I can manage my own social life?"

"No, not really." With that cheery pronouncement, the perp dove back into his meal. He came up long enough to ask, "Angie, do you need some help too?"

"Only to hide your body," she snapped. Thank God someone around here understood.

"Don't use quicklime, I won't decompose properly. The stuff doesn't do what you think it does." Wes unleashed another of his random factoids between bites. "Though I wouldn't leak *E. coli* and *Klebsiella* into the environment."

"You might be leaking long before you hit the ground," Carson grumbled. "Did you not consider that Timmy-boy is my worst possible choice?"

"You're resourceful." Wes waggled his finger in a way

likely to get it broken. "Besides, he needs some help too, and you might really like each other. Common enemies and all that. You'll have such fun thwarting her when she interferes in the wedding planning."

Weddi— Carson's brain shorted out with this extreme fantasy. There had to be some other explanation. "Have I offended you in some way that you'd wish the mother-in-law from hell on me?" Nothing was less likely to happen than Wes's fevered imaginings, but honestly, couldn't he say, "Hey, jerk, you shouldn't have done that" instead of taking this roundabout revenge?

"No, no, not at all. Are you making any progress with him?" Wes went politely interested, which was better than "tongue hanging out" prurience. But not by much.

"There is no progress to be made, you fucktard." Was Carson the only man at this table who knew better than to stick his hand into a running garbage disposal?

"Pish and tush, he's a sweet flower to be plucked and savored. I'm sure of it." Wes smiled sunnily and dunked a fry in the ketchup.

"I don't like you anymore." Carson dropped their friend code for "back off, shithead." Thing was, right now he kind of meant it. Wes knew the bad blood between Lorraine and Carson. Why was he pushing so damn hard?

"Oh, very well, I shall cease my efforts to bring you happiness." Everything about Wes drooped like a basset hound, the very picture of woe.

"Bring him grief, more like." Maybe Angie's full-body twitch signaled a kick under the table. "He's a big boy and knows what he's willing to take on."

Wes didn't recoil and howl in pain, so either Angie missed, or Wes passed up an opportunity for histrionics, a first.

Lorraine was still on vigil when Carson and his friends left without speaking to her. They were nearly to the car when the whirlwind struck from behind.

"Don't you come around here and bother my boy!" Lorraine shrieked. "You leave him alone and maybe I can undo your poisonous influence!"

What. The. Fuck?

He knew better than to take the bait, but Carson turned around anyway, his back against the Bimmer. This bitch was not going to run him off from one of his favorite lunch spots because she was hallucinating. "You're awfully upset about someone eating lunch. How high did the fever get?"

"I mean it!" she howled. "It's people like you who make good young men think it's fashionable to be gay! You've corrupted him, and I won't have it!"

"You've completely lost your mind, lady." He'd never meant the honorific less or the sentiment more. "If he's gay, he was born that way, and if he's not, nothing I can do about it. So—" *Fuck off, crawl back under your rock, eat shit and die* all came to mind, but this was someone he already had issues with. "—back off."

She looked ready to lunge, or spit nails, or both. Carson almost hoped she would attack—he could see the security camera over the restaurant's door. It would be lots of fun to be the aggrieved party in the legal free-for-all that would follow. If he could restrain himself while she got the first licks in, he might even get a couple of freebie punches as self-defense. God knew he had reason to understand the dance. He towered over her by close to a foot—he'd have to take some damage to prove he wasn't the aggressor, but it would be worth it. So worth it. Just, not the face, he liked that face.

Before Lorraine could make up her mind to strike, two

Cluckets employees came barreling out into the parking lot. One yelled, "Mom! Stop!" and the other just "Stop! Now!"

Tim and his accompanying Valkyrie swooped upon her. Tim shoved his way between Carson and Lorraine, pushing her back. "Mom, you can't do this!"

"Oh yes I can!" she snapped to him and then to Carson, "See! Corrupted! Now he's talking back!" She turned the venom back to Tim. "You're as bad as your brother!"

The other Cluckets staffer cut to the chase. "Ma'am, you need to stop this right now. You're harassing another customer. You've been loitering since yesterday and now you're causing a disturbance. You need to leave now, before I call the cops."

Damn, his rescuer got results, but she wrecked all Carson's fun. He was all set to sweep Lorraine's arms down and away from his face and take all her wrath on his torso. Then the voice of reason had to interfere. Lorraine would look so good in handcuffs.

Apparently "cops" got through to her. She still looked like she wanted to bite Carson's face off, but she backed away a couple of steps. "You're defending him?! Against your mother?"

"My mother is behaving badly. Please go." There was a quaver in Tim's voice, but Carson's big bad defender stayed planted, close enough that a half step would put them body to body.

Totally unexpected, and damn sexy, that Tim would come to his rescue.

"This isn't over, young man!" she snarled, and turned on her heel.

"Don't come back! You're banned!" the Valkyrie shouted after her.

Tim flinched, but watched his mother stomp to her car. Once the motor started, he turned around, jumping backward when he realized he and Carson were close enough to touch.

"I'm really sorry about that." Tim dropped his eyes. "She had a bad jolt the other day and she hasn't quite been herself. You're okay?"

"I'm fine. She and I work in the same building, so I've encountered Lorraine before. And, no offense intended, but she seems perfectly herself, only more so." Carson hadn't seen her dial turned up to eleven, but he'd been on the receiving end of sixes and sevens. "Thanks for standing up for me."

That wasn't the only thing beginning to stand up, not that Carson wanted to draw attention to it. Being cast as the protectee rather than the protector did a little something to his libido.

"You did good, Tim," the woman in the Cluckets shirt agreed. "But she really can't hang around here anymore."

"I know, Gail, but…. Throwing my mom out just wasn't…." Tim shrugged.

"It is now. Sorry, but it is." Gail turned to Carson. "Sorry that happened to you. How about your next lunch is on us?" She pulled a business card out of her hip pocket.

"Thanks. It's not your fault, but I'm not going to turn down good chicken." It would taste all the better for Lorraine being *persona non grata* where it was served. Carson pocketed the card.

A silver Chevy sedan roared out of the parking lot, its driver's face stuck on "cat butt."

Tim sighed, watching her. "There goes my ride home."

Gail patted his shoulder. "We'll work something out, don't worry."

It probably wasn't the ride so much as what waited at home. Carson could only be glad he'd lucked into a good job just before the meltdown of 2008 and kept it—his days as a boomerang kid could be counted on no hands at all. If he had to live with his mother and stepfather again.... They did say orange was the new black.

"Hey, Carson! We need to go." Angie summoned him back to reality from the far side of the car. Lucky her and Wes, they had 3000 pounds of steel between them and the fury.

Carson bitched all the way back to Monument Pharma, not letting his pals get a word in edgewise. They didn't deserve to speak: Wes had engineered the situation, and Angie... Well, she hadn't killed Wes for him so....

Until she redeemed herself in the parking lot with a *ding!* that chimed from Carson's pocket.

"Shut up already and listen," she said. "I just sent you a video."

"What? Oh wait." Carson shushed her until Wes had to admit defeat and go back to his lab. Let him be eaten with curiosity. Carson and Angie headed back to the cool cave of the admin building, the summer-hot tarmac cooking their feet right through their shoes. The parking lot didn't contain Lorraine's silver Chevy broom.

"Video?" Carson prompted her.

"Yes, indeed, Lorraine's little fit has mostly been recorded for posterity. Once she started screaming, I thought— I missed the first part, but you should have some nice ammo if you need it. Or if you haven't uploaded anything to your YouTube channel in a while." Her words were light but came in fits and starts. "I really thought she was going to hit you, and.... Well. Big man, small woman...."

What a wonderful, wonderful human being. If he swung even the slightest in Angie's direction, he'd marry her for this alone. At least he could hold the office door for her. "I wasn't too sure myself. Thanks. I, ah, have a use for it already."

Carson didn't follow her to his desk. Making a small detour down a corridor, he was glad to see the third door down open. He stuck his head past the sign reading "Human Resources Director." Dave Pfeiffer looked up from his computer screen at the intrusion. "Hi, Carson. What's up?"

"Got a problem." Carson closed the door behind him and sat down in the managerial version of the Chair of Tears. Shouldn't be him sobbing after this talk.

"Do tell." Dave closed his screen and aimed his full attention on Carson.

He wouldn't start with the pettiness of an illicit call-off, though Dave could figure that out for himself. No, straight to the heart of the matter. "I've been having some issues with Lorraine. You remember how she tried writing me up, and you may have heard how she lit into me for fixing the printer and then not fixing the printer."

Dave nodded, his face impassive.

"In light of further developments, I don't think it was about the printer. I think it might have been more about this." Carson activated Angie's treasure. "See what you think."

He hadn't seen the video yet, so whatever angles Angie shot might not show Lorraine frothing at the mouth, but the audio was clear enough. Starting at "...poisonous influence" and going all the way past the Cluckets manager's golden phrase of "You're banned!" Carson had to listen to her hate all over again.

So did Dave, and his scowl deepened. "This is connected how?"

Carson forced himself to relax. "The copier incident was right on the heels of her son coming into her office for some paperwork. I saw him run in and out, didn't speak to him. He might not even have seen me. She told me "Don't even think about it," which, what? I always fix the copier, but maybe that wasn't what she meant. Then I've had lunch where he works a couple of times, didn't say anything that wasn't related to ordering food. So I don't know where she gets her notions, but I don't appreciate her attacks."

Dave handed the phone back. "Do me a favor. Forward me a copy of that. I can't do anything about incidents that happen off-site, ugly as that was, but interesting how the Cluckets woman mentioned her loitering."

Good, he'd caught that tidbit. "No problem." Carson tapped his screen, and Dave's email program chimed a soft acknowledgement. "Can you get her to back off of me? I just do my job around here, you know? I don't have any involvement with her precious son."

"Wouldn't matter if you did. He doesn't work here, and even if he did, it wouldn't be a problem if you were in different departments." Dave drummed long, elegant fingers against his desk. "She shouldn't be taking her private frustrations out on you no matter what. Particularly not about you being gay. That's not just law, that's corporate policy."

Good, Dave had his back. "Thanks. I gotta get back to work."

He strode back to his desk, thinking hard. Shouldn't matter, even if, huh. Keep her private frustrations to private time, huh. Was apoplexy still a thing? Well fuck her, she didn't get to tell Carson how to live his life, and if he could get her to stroke out? Win. Besides, the guy was cute.

He waited until Angie stepped away from her desk to search for "Cluckets near me" and dial the restaurant. Two rings and then: "May I speak to Tim?"

"Speaking."

"Hey, this is Carson Eddinger, with the black BMW, from this afternoon's excitement with your mom. Seems like it's my fault you're on foot. How about I give you a ride home?"

CHAPTER FIVE

A SHITSTORM DAY just turned to sunlight and rainbows.

"Um, wow. I, uh…" *Oh jeez, he called! What do I do? I can't — I shouldn't— Mom'll be so pissed. But he's— Oh! He offered!* Tim choked out, "Sure. G-great."

"What time do you get off?" came in a sultry purr over the company phone. Or maybe it was a manly growl and Tim was so twiddipated by the sound he couldn't tell the difference. Or maybe he wanted to hear growls and purrs so bad his imaginings covered up the sound of a rusty chainsaw. Because if Carson kept talking, Tim would be getting off before he hung up the phone.

"Seven, if you don't mind waiting." *Please don't mind, please don't mind….* Tim could probably convince Gail to let him off early, but—

"Not at all. See you at seven." That had to be a smile in his voice. Like he was really looking forward to letting a guy who smelled of chicken grease contaminate his fancy ride's upholstery. Maybe the seats were leather. That wouldn't hold the scent too badly.

Tim held the handset to his chest a moment, the golden, unexpected offer fading into a dial tone. Carson called. Carson called *him*. Carson cared enough to make the offer.

Carson made the first move. If it was a move, and not just pity for the adult whose mommy couldn't admit he'd grown up and out of the sandbox.

He and Mom were going to have to come to a better understanding, because she'd been way out of line today. Yesterday too, but she hadn't run screaming after anybody. Carson said he knew Mom from work: maybe bad history was why she lit off after him.

But hey! The guy knew about Mom and still picked up the phone. Tim went back to slinging the chow with a lighter heart and a deep desire for the clock to march at quadruple time and to slow to a crawl.

Because Carson offered to take him home.

Where hell awaited.

———

Seven o'clock did finally arrive. Tim punched out, his heart thumping. *It's just a ride ho*me, he told himself, but they had to start somewhere. Even if it never went one minute beyond getting out of the car.

Aside from smelling like work and wearing a uniform, this was almost like a date. Yeah, a microscopic date. All the anticipation and "do I have something stuck in my teeth?" without any of the expectations of having a good time and maybe getting... Kissed was about the extent of Tim's experience, with an unwitting beard who had neither given nor gotten a good time out of it.

Hope he could get into the front seat without his boner

announcing itself to the world. Or to Carson. Maybe he was just being nice and his friend was having some fun with him. Tim wanted a little more assurance before bringing boners into play. Which—too late. A black BMW polished to a blinding gloss rested in the one parking place with shade from a spindly tree. Carson leaned against the trunk like he was exactly where he wanted to be, one hand partially in his trouser pocket. Not like he was flashing his groin, but so fine. With a smile. For Tim.

Tim gulped. "Hope you weren't waiting long." He stealth-admired Carson uncoiling and swinging around to the driver's door. The lock clicked to let Tim into the lap of luxury.

"I took care of some errands while I was out." Carson looked so at home in that black, yep, leather bucket seat, his arm outstretched along the back of the passenger seat so he could crane over his shoulder to back up. Even though the car had a back-up camera. His hand brushed Tim's shoulder on its way to the gear shift, which he cupped with a grip that did funny things to Tim's groin.

Smoothing into the forward gears, Carson asked, "Where are we going? Home, or…?"

"Home." Tim gave the address. "As much as I'd like to go anywhere else in the world, the parents are expecting me." Man, did he sound like a dork. "All things considered, today may not be the best day for pushing the boundaries of their expectations. All that post-college freedom hasn't materialized yet."

"Not sure it materializes as much as you summon it into existence." Carson spared a sideways glance from the road, just in time to catch the deep flush burning Tim's cheeks for the admission. "Depending on the parents, the spells can be simple or complex."

"Wish we had time for a side trip to Flourish & Blotts then." Tim sighed. "Or that the magic was real."

"GPS, find Diagon Alley," Carson commanded. "I didn't remember the name of the bookshop until you said it."

Tim's memory was getting a little fuzzy on everything but the way Carson upshifted and downshifted the six-speed manual. "I binge-read Harry Potter last year."

"A nice refresher since the books have been out so long." Carson swung the BMW south on Wadsworth Parkway.

"First time reading them for me." Tim bit the bullet— Carson knew something about his mother, and much as he didn't want to look like the world's biggest baby-man, this could be a signal that he needed some help in getting to what he hoped Carson could want too. "I read a lot of things in college that my parents didn't want me to read. They were kind of iffy on the Narnia books, so you can imagine…"

"Got your horizons broadened at school, did you?" Oh good, Carson didn't sound judgey. More like—you go, buddy! "That's what a well-rounded education will do for you. Not all of it comes in a classroom."

Maybe Carson could get into a little practical biology. Maybe Tim should quit such dangerous fantasies and definitely he should keep the object of his mother's wrath out of her sight. He didn't really know where she was, but home sulking seemed like a good bet. They were almost to the house. "This is going to sound dumb, but… Let me off a couple doors down. Don't put yourself in the direct line of fire twice in one day. She'll probably yell at me a while, but no need to let her have at you too."

"Okay." Carson swung around the second to last corner. "Any chance of getting your own wheels?"

Agh. That. "I do have an old Corolla, but the battery isn't holding a charge and it's been stranding me. I haven't figured out if it's the battery or something else." Tim had spent most of his Google-fu chasing more job leads instead of car problems. Getting a better job would let him hire a mechanic and get out of Dodge.

"I know a little something about cars. I could take a look." With a glance at the navigation screen, Carson slowed and pulled over in front of a two-story frame house with small columns of brick at the front door. It looked like every other house on the street, all cookie-cutter sameness. The paint might vary but the roofs were a uniform brown. Were there three floor plans to choose from, or four, and did flipping the blueprints over do anything to add variety? "Is that your car?" He pointed to the red subcompact parked on the street three houses ahead of them.

"Yes. And yes, I wish you could, but…" Tim lifted his hands in helplessness.

"Are you going to do any summoning or not?" Carson snorted. "The worst that happens is I can't fix it either."

No, the worst that could happen was… Was… Mom would yell, and Dad would back her up, and…

They couldn't cut off his allowance, they hadn't given him one in years. If they tried changing the password to the router, he could piggyback on a neighbor's unsecured network. Someone real close had the gold icon and five bars. His phone? Might be a risk.

Not so bad, really.

Or they could make him get his own car insurance and health insurance, or they could make him move out. Or they could…. Tim didn't want to find out how high his mom would escalate, right after she'd all but attacked Carson in public.

He didn't want to believe she did that, or that she might cut him off. And the only way to not find out was to not provoke her. Because that's just the way she was.

"I...guess not. But thanks. And I appreciate the ride." No, he'd provoked Mom pretty hard, taking a side that wasn't hers. Pushing it harder? Scary dangerous. Even if the prize was a couple of minutes with his wet dream walking. Tim opened the car door.

"It's okay, kid. I owed you one for today."

Was that disappointment on Carson's face? And "kid?"

Tim snapped around. "I did do some summoning today, dude. I had to tell my mom off and make her leave, for you. Do you blame me for not wanting to make things worse?"

"You did." Carson tapped his lips and then glanced sideways at Tim, his head cocked like a challenge. "Seems to me you ought to push the advantage while you have it, but she's your mom and not mine. And thanks for doing that, by the way. For a minute there I thought it was going to get a little ugly."

"It will." Tim could see the coming storm. "But not for you."

———

Damn. So close. So fucking close. The kid had almost taken Carson up on his offer. Would have been such a great poke in the snoot for her too, to see the hated gay guy elbow deep in the guts of her son's car that she and dad couldn't, or maybe wouldn't, help him fix.

Carson watched Tim amble down the street. No hurry

to get to his front door and confront his mom again. Tim did have a point—there would be some fallout from today's display of spine. Bet every chair in that house was a Chair of Tears.

Why was the guy still living at home? Had he majored in political science or English literature? Working at Cluckets couldn't be putting that much in his pocket, but surely he had some plans.

Tim disappeared into the house before Carson set the car in gear again. What was he waiting for? A shriek of terror so he could ride to the rescue? Hah—if he went pelting into Lorraine's house for any reason, he'd be testing out her willingness to use Colorado's Make My Day laws. Best to go, and hope Tim retained or could relocate his earlier resolve.

He pulled away from the curb and into a stately second gear. An old woman came down the walk from the front door of the house on the far side of the Ratliffs', small but militantly upright, and—familiar? Could it be?

Carson pulled to the curb. She watched him from the mailbox.

"Mrs. Hedstrom?" Carson stood in the open car door, not coming closer. "Is that really you? I'm Carson—"

"Carson Eddinger, if you haven't just grown up!" Her initial suspicion dawned into recognition. Her face blossomed into a smile, her teeth white among the wrinkles. "How nice to see you!"

She did remember him! He might have been lost among the tides of high-school kids that flowed through her classroom, trying with varying degrees of success to learn trigonometry and navigate adolescence. Then again, maybe he was memorable for all the wrong reasons.

He came around the car to give her a hug. "How are you doing?"

"Oh, you know, life is life." She patted his back and let go to look him up and down. "Are you on the way somewhere? Do you have time to come in and catch an old teacher up on things?"

"Sure!" Even if he didn't really, he'd make the time for Mrs. Hedstrom. "That would be great."

He escorted her back up the walk, with overlong grass swishing against his ankles. The grass had invaded the space between the pavers. Mrs. Hedstrom stumbled. Carson caught her arm before she hit the flagstones. "I really do need to get after that," she apologized.

"Once you find your round to-it?" Carson had long since lost the paper disk she'd handed out to the class, but the thought stayed with him.

"Now you have your round to-its, and no excuse for not getting your studying done," she'd said, and held squadrons of hormonal teenagers to her high standards. She'd taught a lot more than math.

"That and a good cushion to sit on, and maybe a hydraulic jack to get back off the ground." Her voice was wry. "I'm not as young as I used to be."

Not just time had changed, but space. Carson always associated the smell of chalk and textbooks with Mrs. Hedstrom, and a feeling of safety. Math could confuse you, but not hurt you. Instead of a line of textbooks under the window, a row of brushed aluminum canisters lined the beige Formica counter, next to a fluted glass blender that had to be older than he was. A sheet of chocolate chip cookies cooled on the stovetop, and the digital timer clicked down the seconds until the next pan would emerge from the oven below. Their glorious scent filled the kitchen. A metal mixing bowl full of water and utensils rested in the sink.

She waved him to a seat at the gate-legged table covered in red-checked gingham.

Laying out a plate of cookies and pouring out coffee, Mrs. Hedstrom bustled around her kitchen in a domestic way Carson had never seen. Disciplinarian, yes, and teacher, and once as avenging fury, but nothing so homey as hostess laying out refreshments for a guest. He bit into one of the cookies. "These are really good."

She sat down at the kitchen table and picked one to nibble on. "Thank you. I used to send batches up to Fort Collins for the neighbor boy, but he's graduated now, and back home. I suspect he'll be over tomorrow."

Before explaining why, she turned the subject. "Tell me, Carson, what has life brought to you?"

More than he would have had if she never walked into his life, and he couldn't exactly thank her for it. "I went to college on a scholarship, majored in business, and I'm working at Monument Pharma in licensing. It's not real glamorous to talk about, but it's stable. So it's good." Really good, aside from the harpy who had it in for him, and he'd settle her one way or another.

"That's wonderful, dear." His old teacher pushed the plate of cookies at him.

For her he'd eat the whole plate and spend his weekend working out. Not only that, but home-made cookies had never been part of his landscape. He wasn't about to turn down chewy morsels of numminess.

She cocked her head and nodded in that old, familiar way, mostly seen when a student successfully found a cosine or cubic volume. "I always thought you'd be a success."

She had? He wasn't just *That poor dear, he's been through so much* to her? "I don't know about success, but I'm comfortable and stable."

Mrs. Hedstrom laughed. "When you get to be my age, you realize that's a highly underrated version of success. And you are driving a lovely car."

Everyone made assumptions about the BMW. He didn't have the heart to disagree with this angel from his past. "Thank you. I did get a good deal on it. And it's fun. Maybe I should take you for a ride down Highway 93, just to feel the wind in your hair. We could have lunch in Golden. Or Evergreen."

It would be fun. Some times of day the less than arrow-straight highway running along the foothills west of Denver was nearly deserted. Perfect place to open the throttle. Whip around the hogback. Sail past the reservoir. Pussyfoot through the sprawl of Golden until he got to C-470, where speed limits were suggestions, until it was time to make a right at Morrison and blaze through the canyons up to Kittridge. He shivered, imagining putting the pedal down through the curves, owning that mountain road next to Bear Creek.

"You sound just like my husband did, back when we were dating, although his bribery involved a '67 Mustang and a night at the Broadmoor." She smiled with her gaze far away.

"Erm, how is Mr. Hedstrom?" Guiltily aware of eating a third cookie with next to no inquiries about her life, Carson noticed how quiet the house was—their voices competed with the whir of a fan and little else: the calico cat had sniffed his trouser legs in silence and went on about her way.

"Passed on two years ago, dear." Her eyes lost their focus, looking into the past.

"I'm sorry." He'd never met the man, but this angel of a woman shouldn't endure such a loss. Not when she'd…

"Don't be sorry. He was eighty-one, and led a fine, busy life. The man went skydiving for his seventy-second birthday, can you imagine? Cackled like a loon all the way down too, and managed not to break anything on landing, either. And took me hot-air ballooning for our fortieth anniversary. We made a lot of memories, Stan and I." She jerked back into the here and now. "Isn't there some sweet young man you'd like to make such memories with on your way to lunch in the mountains?"

She'd known, she'd always known, though how, Carson couldn't have said. She'd had a few wise words to help him with—who was it back then? Tony Bianchi? She'd known back in those hellish days when he'd arrived in her classroom winded and aching, and she'd never thrown a word of shade at him. Her damn neighbor could afford to take some lessons.

"Not really. Not exactly. Maybe." Carson twiddled the last bit of cookie into crumbs and glanced up at her. "We just met."

Tim might enjoy the trip. Lorraine would hate it. Carson would enjoy Tim's pleasure twice as much for Lorraine hating it.

"You do that," she said brightly, covering his hand with her own. "You deserve the happiness."

"Thank you." Tears stung behind his eyelids and threatened to roll down. By sheer force of mind over surface tension he kept them from escaping. If aliens ever needed to know why humanity should be spared, he'd show them Mrs. Hedstrom and her quiet goodness.

"Are you doing okay?" he managed to ask.

"Yes, I am, although some things around the house are

a little harder to keep up with." She patted his hand one last time and took up her coffee cup. "I've been thinking about hiring a handy man. I'm really not ready to give up the house."

"You shouldn't have to." Carson snapped to attention. His own pristine townhouse wouldn't suffer for waiting a week or two or three for its next little upgrade, but Mrs. Hedstrom's house probably hadn't had a firm hand doing maintenance in a long time. This was her *home!* "I'd like to help. Make a honey-do list for me, okay? I'll bring tools, if you don't have any."

"There's a shed full in the back yard. And a few in the kitchen drawer." She looked taken aback.

"Good!" Carson could hear a drip from the kitchen faucet even with his back to the sink. If a roll of white plumber's tape didn't lurk on his workbench, he'd find one at the hardware store. And the yard needed some love for sure. "How about a lawn mower?"

"In the shed." She looked confused now, as if this shouldn't be happening. "Carson, dear, you don't have to…"

"Yes. Yes, I do." He'd never been more certain of anything. "Mrs. Hedstrom, I *owe* you. Even if you'd tell me it was just the right thing to do. So what time can I start the lawn? Can I disturb the peace around nine o'clock? Before the day heats up too much?"

"You don't have to give up your Saturday morning for that. The neighbors usually help me, either the father or the son." Her voice shook, as if she wasn't expecting the kindness.

Well, she deserved all the kindness ever. And if Tim or his dad had appointed themselves lawn care, they needed to see how it was done, because this sweet old lady shouldn't have to risk a broken hip bringing in the mail because they decided to skip a week.

And Carson had a plan. So, so easy. He'd learned "This is a done deal" speak from the best, sitting right next to him. "Nine o'clock it is."

"Okay." She wasn't arguing, good. She changed the subject: bad. "Speaking of fathers and sons…."

She wasn't referring to his father, who'd taken off without a backward glance when Carson was barely old enough to remember him. No, she meant—

"That scum who married my mother is out of prison." *Prick, waste of oxygen, fucking piece of shit* were more accurate, but not words he'd say to her. Stepfather was more than Carson would acknowledge: it implied some kind of bond. "And my mother took him back. We don't speak much."

No, not one word had he given her. She'd made her choice and her choice wasn't her son. Never had been.

"I can't say as I blame you."

Bless her. She knew the story. She'd been part of the story. The rest of the world might bleat, "But faaaaaaaaaaaamily," but not Mrs. Hedstrom. Her calm acceptance of his reality made Carson plan to caulk every seam, stop every leak, and snip every sprig of plant life into submission.

He should have been here long ago.

He had extra reasons to be here now.

CHAPTER SIX

Tᵢᴍ ᴡᴏᴋᴇ to full light and the oily grumble of a nearby lawn mower. The dull roar teased at his mind—hadn't he promised someone? Yes, he had, and he'd better get over next door before his mom stuck her head through the bedroom door with a grouchy reminder.

Everything out of her mouth was likely to be grumpy for a while. She'd started to light into him last night for his "disloyalty", but that hadn't worked so well for her, had it? Because Dad wanted the whole story. "My boss almost called the cops on Mom" and why was enough for Dad to give her a stern admonishment to "watch herself."

All the same, Tim planned on avoiding the direct firing line as much as possible. Since he had a Saturday off, for a wonder, that meant a full day of dodging.

Sleep was well and truly murdered by that overexuberant gardener. Tim could add to the racket. He found a pair of basketball shorts and a ripe T-shirt. The day was warm and would only get hotter, no sense in stinking up another.

Breakfast would be nice, except the potential for meeting Mom in the kitchen was awfully high. Best to do that while wearing the virtuous stains of labor.

He really needed to get out of here, if a bowl of cereal had to be weighed against a confrontation. Maybe he'd take his laptop for an afternoon in the library.

The racket from the mower grew louder. What cruel neighbor was up and laboring so early? Tim stuck his head out the window to find the source. Which was next door. Oh, my.

A man, tall, buff, and showing it off in nothing but sneakers and shorts, a hat, and maybe sunscreen, pushed the mower in straight lines. He wasn't wearing a shirt, showing off rippled abs and pumped arms. And when he reached the end of the row, he'd turn around to show off his ass, which promised to be just as nice as the rest of him. He gleamed with sweat. The bill of the ball cap obscured his face, but the sleek black coupe in Mrs. Hedstrom's driveway might as well have been a neon sign.

Tim couldn't get out of that smelly T-shirt fast enough. A fresh shirt for a sweaty job was a small sacrifice. He dove into something clean, a little frayed, and tight enough to announce that it had been in his drawer since before his growth spurts kicked in. As long as it didn't say Wayne Carle Middle School on it, the shirt was perfect. He checked. Nope. Some band whose music he couldn't recall. Which was fine. With any luck, he wouldn't be wearing it long.

Why was Carson here, mowing? Not once, ever, had Tim seen Carson in the neighborhood, and he sure would have noticed. Have to find out.

Out the front door fast and undetected, and then saunter next door.

He had to shout his greeting to be heard over the mower. "Hey, Carson!"

He got a smile and a wave, and more grass fell to the blade. Tim moseyed to the shed. Gloves, weed whacker, and cord, good start. He started at the edges of Carson's completed passes, and if he whacked the grass a little short when he got an eyeful of his fellow groundskeeper, it would grow back. He hoped.

Because damn, did Carson look good. Striding up and down the lawn, his muscles playing under his skin, dancing beneath the sheen of sweat and sunscreen. Coconut and gasoline fumes made a strange perfume, mixing with the watermelon scent of the cut grass.

He had to mind his edging around the flower beds a little better or he'd behead the blooms in his besottedness. Maybe he should weed instead, and then he could admire more of the gorgeous sight. Lightly tanned man under the cloudless blue of a Colorado sky, doing work he looked to be enjoying. As seen from the vantage point of Tim's knees. He'd like to kneel at Carson's feet and… He'd have to figure out what and how. Right after he managed when and where.

Maybe crouching over would disguise the wood he'd popped and had no chance to adjust. Like he could stick his hands in his shorts and fix the hard, throbbing problem that dueled with his skivvies.

All he needed was his mother popping her head out to see what was going on. She'd probably have a fit about him working outside in public with Carson. Hey, he could snap back with, "You think I should leave him to do my task alone?" *Please let her stay inside.*

The fear helped with the woodie problem. A little.

On the other hand, grabbing the dandelion digger out

of the shed gave him a moment's privacy. Maybe he should stay in here and rub out a quick one. If he had anywhere to land the splats. Poised to cross that bridge when he came, the sound of his elderly neighbor's voice made Tim rethink that plan scant seconds before the point of no return. *Damn it!*

Adjusted and frustrated, Tim emerged from the shed to attack the thistles trying to hide among the lavender and daylilies.

"There you are, Tim!" Mrs. Hedstrom brandished a blue spray can. "Did you remember your sunscreen?"

"Erm, no, ma'am." Forgetting was a good thing this time. "Would you get my back?" He tugged off his shirt, which he *thought* Carson appreciated silently, and held his arms out so she could spray him. She misted him front and back, and he took his chances on his face, stepping away from the choking cloud once a layer deposited on his nose. He tucked his shirt into his waistband, letting the sun heat his bare skin. "Thank you."

Thank you, thank you, thank you, he meant, because here came Carson with a big grin, leaving a close-cropped path in his wake. The smell of new-mown grass was gonna give Tim woodies for the rest of his life. Did Carson like what he was seeing as much as Tim did? Staring would have to wait until Mrs. Hedstrom bustled back inside. If he could last that long. *Hnnngh.*

He took his frustration out on the thistles and bindweed.

"Lookin' good" in Carson's voice could have meant his work or himself: Tim wanted to believe one but knew it might be the other. He'd filled out enough to make his ribs disappear and his shoulders not be bony, but he wasn't in Carson's league. Wonder how much gym time that took, especially for a guy who ate fried chicken a couple times a week?

"Thanks." Tim dumped his victims into the black trash bag Carson held out. "I think we did a pretty good job."

Carson surveyed their efforts. "I think we did too."

"We".... Tim liked the sound of that, but had to confess. "I was going to do this today, but you beat me to it."

"Twice the hands, half the work. I'm glad your family helps Mrs. Hedstrom. She's good people." Carson gazed at the house. "She's done so much for others."

"I grew up as much in her house as in mine." Tim had run in and out as freely as if he lived there, and only been gently admonished to put away the Legos when he was finished playing. "The Hedstroms were... are... like auxiliary grandparents."

"Lucky you." Carson dropped the last bag of clippings into the green receptacle in the alley.

Yeah, he was. Mrs. Hedstrom's welcome, homework help, and dare he say it, love, had almost made up for the other winners in his familial jackpot.

The lady herself stepped out onto the back deck to summon them. "I have iced tea!"

The sun was heavy, not yet oppressive, but they'd been working hard. A cool drink wasn't exactly in the same league of wonderful as pulling Carson close and finding out if the sunscreen would let their bare chests slide or make them stick, but it was the best Tim could get right now. Since Carson was pulling his shirt on to follow their summons.

At least he'd gotten a good look before that traitor T covered up Carson's muscular, smooth torso. Tim followed suit and led the way up the deck's staircase.

The kitchen was dim compared to the brightness of the rising-noon sun. Tim blinked, adjusting to the indoors, which smelled of lemon furniture polish and pine. He knew more than saw the gate-legged kitchen table with its four spindle-backed chairs and settled down with his elbows on the red-checked cloth.

"Sit down, fellas. Have some tea." She doled out tall glasses tinkling with ice, to pour against a chorus of pops and snaps. "You did a lovely job. Thank you."

She brought a plate of cookies over, setting them down with a small hesitation. Tim really shouldn't grab like a brat, but... There were plenty for Carson too. "Mmm. Good as I remembered."

Mrs. Hedstrom tucked herself into a chair. "I wasn't sure you still liked them."

"Sure do." Tim had to pause long enough to swallow or he'd be a crumb fountain. "It was really nice of you to give the recipe to Mom, too. My friends thought they were the bomb. I had to fight them off to get any."

"How... very odd." Her lips settled into a thin line for a fraction of a second. "Well. Enjoy, dear."

"Sounds like there's more to that story, Mrs. Hedstrom," Carson lifted an eyebrow, which Tim could see now that his eyes had adjusted to the lesser indoor light.

A chill grew in Tim's belly, unrelated to the cold drink freezing its way down his esophagus. "Mom never asked for the recipe, did she?"

"No, she didn't." Mrs. Hedstrom played with her glass, swirling the ice cubes around with a straw.

"Then... I owe you four years of thank yous for the care packages, don't I?" The chilly drink and cookie went to iceberg inside him. He and his friends had eaten those cookies a couple of times a month. Every chocolate-chip check-up. "You must have thought I was an ungrateful monster. I am so sorry." He couldn't bear to look at her: he rubbed his eyes, buying time. "I don't know what to say to make this right."

"It isn't you who needs to say anything more." She patted his shoulder, more of a forgiveness than he thought he deserved. "You didn't know. And now you've said thanks, and you are welcome."

Still. "My mom owes you a big apology. I'm going to have to say that too. Because I don't think she will, she never does say sorry." Tim could already hear her defense for being called out. *"Do you feel better now that you've said that?"* was as close as she ever came to admitting she'd erred. "So, I'm sorry someone else took credit for your kindness."

"You're a good man, Tim." Mrs. Hedstrom smiled at him, but a flash of anger underlay her words. "You shouldn't have to apologize for your mother."

"I seem to be doing that a lot lately." He couldn't bear to look at Carson, who'd deserved amends only yesterday.

"I'm going to tell you a fact of growing up, Tim." The cricket-sized grandmother drew herself up into a thin, wizened sage. "That is, you separate from your parents. You are not extensions of them, even if they've trained you to be such. Right now you're trying to be the part of your mother that is good and kind. Those are good things to be, but only if you are being them because that is who you are. You can't be that for someone else. They are who they are, and the world will deal with them accordingly."

"I know, but… I'd prefer if most of the world didn't think my mom deserves a boot to the head." Tim mumbled. The man Tim wanted to impress sure had reason to feel that way.

"Then she needs to behave in ways that don't elicit nice warm thoughts of kicking her." The sage *tsked*. "You've heard that actions have consequences?"

"Of course." Most of his actions had some consequences he didn't like, if Mom didn't approve. He'd learned to either not do those things, or hide them better. Which...

"You're trying to ward off the natural consequences of her actions for her. If she doesn't get the feedback, does she learn to do differently?" Mrs. Hedstrom's white brows rose.

"No, but... She is my mom."

"Yes, she is, and you love her. Which is fine and good, but there comes a point where you have to love her as an autonomous adult, not a dependent child. Which means acknowledging that she is fallible, and it also means letting her take responsibility for her actions. Which is also what she should be doing for you, now that you're a young man." Mrs. Hedstrom refreshed everyone's glasses with more tea.

"The other side of this is that your mom, your parents, are not in control of you, except as much as you allow them to be. You can be guided by them as far as you think is correct, but there comes a time when you simply have to do things your way."

Might as well put up a neon sign for Carson—*Not in your league!* Tim wanted to slide under the table. Which wouldn't do a thing to reverse Carson's opinion of him. Even worse was the reason why.

"That's a tough one, since I'm still financially dependent on them." Yesterday was payday, and Tim's check had been painfully light. Cluckets didn't schedule anyone not management past thirty-two hours a week, even if you'd been with them since high school.

"That's something you must decide for yourself, dear. Along with what you consider necessities." Mrs. Hedstrom took a long pull at her tea. "I've had to reevaluate those from time to time. A schoolteacher's pension only goes so far. And still, I'm happy."

Carson might have been part of the woodwork for all the expression in his face. He was a good ten years older than Tim; he'd been down this road. All independent with a decent job and driving a great car, like he had his life together. He had to know from experience.

If Tim couldn't impress him, he could still get the benefit of Carson's experience. "Did you go through this with your mom?"

Carson's voice had the sound of a mining bore biting through solid granite. "My mother is feeling the consequences of her actions. She didn't like it then, and she doesn't like it now, and that's her problem, not mine."

Tim recoiled. "Wow." His mom frustrated him, babied him, and scared him, but Tim still couldn't muster that much venom over her. What the heck?

Mrs. Hedstrom didn't twitch.

Carson shook himself. "Sorry. I guess the short answer is yes. The long answer is 'we're not going there.'" He scrubbed at his face with one hand. "Um, you've had a lot laid on you here. How about we go take a look at your car? My tool kit's in my trunk."

———

Talk about a mixed bag of a morning. Carson could count half a dozen wins, and a big old punch to the kidneys.

Win the first: Mowing Mrs. Hedstrom's lawn without a shirt, and pretty much without a word got Tim up, moving, and pitching in. Nice to know he could be lured by partial nudity. Or by keeping a promise.

Maybe that was win the second, too, because her lawn looked good, the tripping hazard on the front walk was gone, and she wouldn't have thistles breeding thistles all over the property.

Win the third: Tim managed all that yard work with a boner. Looked like he might have nipped into the shed for a bit of relief and didn't get it—Carson didn't know how to describe that face, but frustrated was part of it, and embarrassed, and a little frantic, too. Guess Lorraine might just be right about how gay her son was. Eh, stopped clocks managed that same trick twice a day.

Win the fourth: Mrs. Hedstrom doing a number on Tim's head about growing up. That woman was a gift to humanity for sure.

Tim couldn't have known he was delivering a right hook to the nads when he'd asked about Carson's experiences. Few people knew what he'd been through, only one Carson would talk to, and Mrs. Hedstrom wouldn't say anything. He couldn't imagine telling the whole story—too humiliating, even now. Tim would have to find his role model somewhere else. A garden variety bitch should be easy in comparison.

Guess Tim got his own kidney punch with win the fifth. Lorraine Ratliff got exposed for a snake, but it couldn't feel good to find that out the hard way.

And win the sixth? Here Carson was, exactly as he'd imagined, bent over into the engine compartment, ass up, poking around. Let boyo have a good long look. And maybe even get his vehicle working again. He'd turned Carson down once, but not twice.

"What, exactly, has it been doing?" Carson thought he recalled something about the battery.

"Terrible squeak, the battery doesn't hold a charge, and

the steering isn't quite right." Tim's left leg jiggled nervously in the corner of Carson's vision, and while it was a nice leg, the motion was making Carson a little queasy.

"How long since you've driven it?" The purple nitrile of his gloves kept the oil and smudges off his hands, letting him poke and prod without a guaranteed Lava soap scrub.

"Monday. I stopped because the steering didn't feel safe."

Carson stood up, careful not to whack the back of his head on the hood. "Smart. Think we can get this puppy started?" He really didn't want to risk a jump start with the BMW. He could fix a lot of things, but a fried electronic dashboard wasn't one of them.

"We have a portable charger. Let me get that." Tim motored off in the direction of the house.

Carson stepped back about three feet. The mature elder bush just to Mrs. Hedstrom's side of the property line with the Ratliffs cast a glorious pool of shade, fifteen degrees cooler than the direct sun. The umbrellas of fine white flowers wafted with a sweet scent, drawing enough bees that Carson wouldn't risk swiping a palm over the pale fuzziness of the blooms.

And it shielded him from view if Sneaky Snake happened to look outside. Carson wouldn't mind getting caught, but only when he'd gotten enough done on the car to do Tim some good.

His partner in crime reappeared with the charger, its jumper cables wrapped red and black around the handle. Tim set the charger down and expertly connected the cables. "I'll give it a minute or two, and then start it."

When Tim did turn the key, a banshee shriek nearly deafened Carson. It settled to "newborn infant wails" levels of awfulness. Carson plugged his ears with his relatively

unsoiled pinkies and peered into the engine. This was…
fixable.

He turned an imaginary key at Tim, signaling to cut the
engine. The screaming died quickly, as all moving parts
whirred to a halt.

"That sounds even worse with the hood up." Tim shivered. "Any idea?"

"Oh yeah." Carson quickly unbolted the engine cover
and set to investigating. Prodding the pulleys and the
serpentine belt, he checked for looseness and waggle. No
waggle. "I need a little bit of water."

Tim dove into the passenger-side footwell and came up
with a nearly empty water bottle of a store brand. "Will this
do, or should I go into the house?"

"Perfect. Turn the engine on again." The horrible
screech came back full force and cut to nothing when
Carson splashed some water on a pulley and belt. Couldn't
get a better diagnostic and look like a hero at the same time.
The shriek died, letting Carson speak into the relative
silence. "Ever replaced the serpentine belt?"

"Is that what it's called?" Tim helped him peer at the
offending part. "I haven't. The previous owner,
who knows?"

"How many miles do you have on this beast?" Carson
guessed he was looking at a 2003 or 2004 model and
expected a high number. Not quite as high as what Tim
told him.

"A hair over two hundred and twenty thousand. It had
probably a hundred forty when I bought it." At a sharp
glance from Carson, Tim blushed. "And yes, it was
wrecked, too. You can't buy much for two grand."

"Hey, it's run this far. It can run farther." Carson

dropped the hood and stripped off the purple nitrile. "We need to make a trip to the parts store."

Tim stayed quiet on the drive over, just a quick trip down the main thoroughfare. He had to be doing sums and getting terrible totals, because he asked, "What do we need and how much should I expect? Maybe it would be cheaper to buy another car?"

"If I'm right, nothing that awful. Thirty bucks or so." Carson led him to a spinning rack of black rubber belts, coded for size. "What year is the Corolla?"

"Two thousand four."

He selected the loop coded for that year and model and let Tim pay with his debit card without comment.

"You think this will do it?" Tim turned the belt over and over, fingering the grooved inner surface.

"Should. It's not a pulley squeal. The serpentine belt drives the A/C, the power steering pump, the alternator. All the good stuff. The belt starts to fail, the systems go unpowered, and if the belt breaks, the car stops, but not before the fan blades shred. And you definitely don't want that happening at highway speeds."

Carson had the hood up again and twisted the bolts with a ratchet, his anxious watcher hovering over his shoulder. This wasn't working quite as well as he'd hoped: Tim had a distressing ability to focus on the problem.

He pulled the old belt out, and let Tim help him thread the new one over one pulley and around the other. "I'm tightening the belt with the tensioner, which is right here," Carson explained. "And we want to be sure the belt is running without a wobble. Might have to adjust a pulley or two."

But no, when Tim fired the car up again, the engine turned over for the jump, and stayed running at a normal purr. He came around to the front of the car to help Carson admire the internal workings. "Everything that should be spinning is spinning."

"It sounds right."

Good thing the car did, because the air split with a hideous shriek of the human variety. "Get off my property!"

"Sure thing, Lorraine." Carson didn't budge. He didn't have to. He turned to face his nemesis. "See? I'm not on your property."

She stopped out of arm's reach—his arms, not hers, he noted distantly—and kept shrieking. "You need to get away from my house!"

"This is a city street. It's public property. See how my feet are on the asphalt?" Pointing virtuously downward, he taunted her with logic.

Tim seemed to be hiding behind Carson. Guess he'd found logic a weak shield before.

"I say you need to go away! Quit touching my son!" Her face turned a dangerous shade of purple. Was this what imminent stroke looked like?

Carson spoke over his shoulder. "Tim, have I touched you?" He tried to smile encouragement.

"No." A weak but correct answer. One Carson intended to change as soon as possible.

"Okay, Lorraine, explain how I'm supposed to stop doing what I'm already not doing?" How far could he goad her?

She didn't take the bait. "You need to get your hands off my car!" She clenched her fists at her sides, quivering with rage.

Now that he hadn't anticipated. Could be a problem. "Tim, is this really your mom's car?"

"No." Tim stepped up to Carson's side. "It's mine. I bought it with my own money four years ago. The title's in my name only, and I gave you permission to work on it. Mom—" He took a deep breath, like the oxygen was courage. "You need to calm down."

Oh, dear God in heaven. Carson didn't know shit about women except to know that telling one to calm down was the Wrong Thing To Do. He wanted to throw his arms in front of his face lest she detonate complete with shrapnel.

"I'm calling the cops!" She shook her fist with the words, and then sprinted back to the house to make good on her threat.

"Good luck with that!" Carson chased her with laughter.

"Um, Carson, I think she meant it." Tim whipped the old serpentine belt nervously.

"Oh, I'm sure she meant it, and I'm equally sure that if they stop laughing at her long enough to send someone out, she'll get told not to waste resources. You live here. I'm working on your property, which is sitting on a public thoroughfare." Ratcheting the last bolt back on the engine cover, Carson figured the car should continue purring. "Now, if she threatened to call the homeowners' association, I'd be worried. There's probably rules about working on vehicles in this neighborhood."

"You really think this won't be a problem?"

"Nah. On the other hand, we don't have to be here if the cops do show up." Carson knew the perfect poke in the snoot for Lorraine "Stick up her ass" Ratliff. "Let's go for a test drive."

CHAPTER SEVEN

TIM PULLED FORWARD, past the elder bush, before Carson got in. Guess he wouldn't want to step on Mom's property in any way, just in case. After the initial shock of her threat wore off, he could see Carson's point. Once again, he—they—hadn't been doing anything wrong when Mom blew up.

He had to stop with the knee-jerk reactions.

Seeing her in the rear-view mirror, running into the street flailing, only inspired him to drive faster.

"Where to?" He was really taking Carson out! Somewhere. Kind of.

Hey, he was driving an amazingly handsome and confident man around on a Saturday afternoon. So close enough to taking him out.

"Let's get on the highway toward Boulder, head up Flagstaff Mountain," Carson suggested. "It'll be cooler up in the hills."

Coming down the slope of Davidson Mesa on Highway 36, the red tile roofs of the University of Colorado dominated the view of Boulder. "Did you go to CU?" was as good small talk as any. Anything that didn't include Mom was a great subject.

"No, I went to Metro. Got enough of a scholarship that I could work part time and still graduate in four years. I wanted to go to CU, but...," Carson trailed off. "Metro worked well enough."

Tim understood. Metropolitan State, in downtown Denver, had been his classmates' third choice of fallback schools, not first choice. "I wanted to go to the School of Mines, but my folks said if they were going to pay that much, I'd go to Colorado Christian University. Which, no way!"

"Big gap between Mines and CCU's curriculums. Did they want you to be a pastor or something?" That grimace had to be an opinion on pastors.

Tim agreed—he was so sick of getting advice on how to live his life that he couldn't imagine handing out advice for a living. He didn't want turnabout, he wanted out of that cycle. "Don't give anyone ideas!" How the hell did something as innocuous as "where did you go to school" turn into a horror story? "I argued for University of Rochester, they've got a great program, but nope, too far away. I thought that was a selling point, actually, but I got overruled."

As he had so many times before. That time the argument was "Your brother went far away to school and look how he ended up! You aren't going down that path."

Damn it, he was gonna launch completely and never get overruled again. Tim steered west on Baseline Road, which narrowed and grew clogged with cars around the wide expanse of Chautauqua Park. Hikers, couples pushing all-terrain strollers, and dogs in bandanas dotted the broad meadow at the base of the mountain. If there was a parking place to be found, it would fit a Matchbox car. Tim wasn't going to waste his time trying to find it.

He kept going up the mountain. The road hairpinned around a nearly full parking lot, and an elegant restaurant loomed over the curve. "Here, maybe?"

"This is a trailhead," Carson pointed out. "I don't mind a little hike, but we didn't bring water."

"Let's keep going." Tim hadn't thought about the water issue, and he did want enough privacy to talk without dehydrating on the way.

Another turnout appeared about a mile farther through the twists and turns, and nothing passed them from either direction when they left the car. A path led downhill from the road, more of a suggestion than a track, with grasses bent down instead of bare earth. They scraped by the serviceberry bushes and the mountain mahogany growing amongst the sparse pines. A chunk of pinkish-gray rock twinkled with facets where the sun struck between the dappled shadows. Wide enough for four to sit, and as close to flat as could be hoped for, the rock overlooked the steep drop to Boulder on the plains below, the northern 'burbs of Denver where the Monument Pharma campus lay, and a little farther south, the blue jewel of Standley Lake, partially ringed by houses.

Carson pulled up some rock, dangling his legs over the edge. "Pretty view."

How close dared Tim sit? Not touching, no, but... Close enough to mean *I wouldn't mind if you did.* He had to scoot around a bit to keep a ridge from gouging into his butt, which put him about an inch closer than he planned. Their feet hung over, a good four feet from touching the steeply sloping ground.

"Yeah. And quiet."

Sound carried this high up, but motorized noises were so far away. The wind creaked the pines, swaying the tops against the fierce, unmarked blue of the sky. Insects chirred in the grass—if any jumped, please let them jump the other way. Bees bumbled in and out of the yellow cups of the pasque flowers. A stand of aspen rustled downslope. A metropolis of three million people stretched out at their feet, and still they might have been the only men on the planet.

"You never did say what you studied." Carson leaned back on his hands, his gaze focused on the plains below.

"Chemistry. At CSU. Fort Collins was as far as I could get." Fifty miles needed to be five hundred, but he took what distance he was allowed.

"Seems like there ought to be plenty of opportunities with that." His statement was quiet and matter of fact, but he might as well have shouted, *"What the fuck are you doing at Cluckets?"*

Trying to get the fuck out of Cluckets and into a lab, that's what he was doing. "There are. I have a million résumés out."

Another topic he didn't want to continue until he looked like a complete loser. He wanted to shine in Carson's eyes, and every avenue seemed to bring him right back to "pathetic basement-dwelling goblin."

Time to pick a different path. "How do you know Mrs. Hedstrom? I've never seen you at the house." Tim would have noticed for sure.

That got Carson to look down at his knees. "She was my tenth-grade math teacher. The one I'd list for 'which teacher changed your life' if anyone ever asked."

A striped ground squirrel scurried through the grasses

at their feet. Tim crossed his legs up on the rock. The squirrel probably wouldn't run up his leg, but... And it put his knee an inch or so away from Carson's thigh.

"How'd she do that?"

Carson turned to meet Tim's eyes, one side of his mouth quirked up. "First day of school, she told us, 'If you need an A so badly you'd cheat to get it, don't. Come see me, and I'll *give* you that A. And I will make sure you understand the material well enough to deserve it.'" He had the old lady's phrasing down perfectly, just an octave deeper.

"Since math was my weakest subject—then—I was the kid who had to take her up on it. She helped me figure out why I was struggling so much, and caught me up on some basics I'd missed earlier. Made a lot of things easier. Made a lot of things possible. My whole life, really. I wouldn't be here without her." He turned back to the glorious vista.

"That sounds like a lot of credit to give trigonometry." Math had always come easily to Tim, He hadn't had reason to use differential equations since acing the class, and didn't know if he ever would.

"It wasn't all math." Carson found a loose pebble and flipped it into the grass. The ground squirrel skittered deeper into the undergrowth. "But it's all I'm going to tell you."

Twice he'd been warned away from parts of Carson's past. "Okay. I won't ask. But this is a yes or no question. Is it okay to ask about coming out? I promise it's not idle curiosity. And it doesn't have to be today."

"I... don't think my experience would be all that helpful to you," Carson said, speaking slowly and to the aspens below. "But we could talk about stuff. Are you thinking about telling your folks?"

"I already did. They thought it was a joke, an ugly,

tasteless joke. Because of the way I told them." The heat from Carson's thigh warmed Tim's knee in a way that was no joke. "Until she started believing it."

"That... sounds like a unique coming out. What did you say?"

"You may have noticed that Mom likes to be right?" Like the tide liked to come in, welcome or not.

Carson nearly choked trying to hold back a snort. "Yeah, I've noticed."

Tim took a deep breath. "She found that note your buddy passed me and jumped to some conclusions. Not that they were wrong conclusions, but based on insufficient data, and she came roaring to accuse me of being gay. So..." Looking back, Tim couldn't believe his audacity. "I leaned into it. Hard."

His confidante lost any semblance of trying not to laugh. "What did you do?"

The laughter was contagious, and in retrospect, it was pretty funny. Tim managed to speak somehow. "I kind of pranced around and lisped, and totally declared that my mother was always right and obviously that made me gay, starting right then." Tim demonstrated his hand gesture on the last line.

Carson lost it completely, falling backward. If he laughed any harder, he'd roll right off the rock. "You didn't!"

Damn, but he was beautiful, with his shirt riding up and his defined abs flexing with each guffaw.

"Oh yeah, I did. She did a dying trout imitation and my dad told me to keep a civil tongue in my head and dragged her away." Too bad the aftermath wasn't as funny. "Unfortunately, she's now trying to do damage control."

Carson sat up, his laughter spent. "I suppose that

explains her recent behavior. Except she lit into me once before Wes handed you that note. General prickliness?"

"I guess." Tim studied his knuckles. "Thing is, what do I do now? She's tried the "Now I'm telling you to be straight" trick, and I went 'Beep boop, contradiction, contradiction, does not compute' which went over like a lead balloon." He'd been lucky she'd said that after he'd pulled into the Cluckets lot and not before. Only escaping behind the counter into the kitchen had ended her tirade.

Carson sat up and pulled his shirt down over the lovely valleys in his belly. "Even if you wanted to retract what you said—"

"I don't. It's true and I don't want to fight the fight twice." Too honest for his own good, he'd been told. Probably true.

"You're going to be fighting some part of it with someone your whole life." Carson winced. "Hell, she's not even my mother and I'm fighting it with her. There's a lot of Lorraines in the world."

"Yeah." What a thought. A whole network of Lorraines, each with a Tim and a grouping of Carsons multiplying, until the misery engulfed the world, with overlaps so two or more Lorraines could torment each one... Brr.

"Anyway, where on the spectrum of 'mope for a while and then accept it' to 'ship you off to pray away the gay camp and burn all your baby pictures when it doesn't work' do you think she falls?" Geez but Carson had some cheery notions.

"Since we have screaming denial, I think moping would be an improvement. I don't *think* she'd try the prayer thing." Tim cast back through his memories. Their church wasn't exactly welcoming, but still a long way from blanket condemnation, and he'd never considered what kind of hate he'd get from that direction. Not that it mattered all that much to him: he went because the parents insisted, not because he felt all sorts of community, fellowship and love of Jesus. Nope, church was more of a way to spoil a good morning's sleep. Did their denomination even try "pray away"?

The parents, on the other hand...

Tim had never imagined anything but complete rejection from them if he accidentally slipped and revealed himself. Living on the streets and getting a GED at age fifteen. Burying himself in debt at twenty trying to finish school.

He wasn't fifteen, he wasn't twenty, he had a degree and a car and a job, even if it wasn't his intended career. His mother could turn her back and he wouldn't starve.

He'd hurt. But he wouldn't starve. And he had all the tools to make a good life for himself.

"Good news is, you're what, twenty-one?"

"Twenty-two." Somehow that extra year was important to claim, like it would help Carson take him more seriously.

"Okay, twenty-two. You're not a minor, and they can't control you to the point of forcing a pray-away. It would be unlawful imprisonment if you didn't consent. Which doesn't mean it's never been tried, and you'd go through hell getting to official attention. I sincerely hope that's not one of her probable reactions." The mistrust in Carson's voice didn't inspire any confidence. Would Mom go that far? Would Dad go along with it?

"I've always anticipated just... getting thrown out. Disowned." Tim spoke his worst fear. "Getting the rest of the family to reject me. I always figured on getting out and far away, and leading a life they don't share enough to question, and let them think what they like."

Carson placed a large, warm hand on Tim's shoulder. "We can safely assume that plan is shot. This is where I apologize for someone else's actions. I'm really sorry Wes's little prank blew up on you in such spectacular fashion."

Well fuck, all this turmoil and it was a prank? His life got turned upside down and fucked sideways and it was a *prank?* Tim jerked away and scooted two feet down the rock. If he hunched up any harder, he'd be a gargoyle. "Your buddy Wes is an asshole."

Dropping his hand slowly, Carson nodded. "He is. He shouldn't have been an asshole to you. And he *will* be apologizing directly to you, that's non-negotiable. Or he'll find my size ten shoe turning into a butt plug." A pause and a deep breath. "Thing is, Wes might be an asshole, but he wasn't wrong."

What? Tim glared sideways through slitted eyes.

"I do think you're cute. Well, good looking, not cute. But like he meant, I noticed you with both eyes." Carson *looked* perfectly sincere. And he was saying the words Tim longed for. Then he kept talking. "I just wasn't going to do anything about it."

"Because my mother is a bitch." He spat the words.

Carson flinched. "I wasn't going to phrase it like that, but yeah, you do have some problematic family, and I've already had issues with her at work. However..."

He dug the hole, let him dig himself out. Tim waited.

He held out an arm, curved as though to pull Tim against his side. "I'm gonna do the time, I ought to do the crime."

Tim didn't budge. "So you're only interested because

my mother hates the idea. Thanks a fucking lot." The obscenity came easily this time. Big jerk. Way to cut a guy.

Carson dropped his arm, and his face fell almost as far. "That's not what I said. I said I'm interested against my better judgement. I'm going to get the blame either way. So are you, because my idiot friend decided to broadcast something I said that I didn't expect to go beyond my lunch buddies. I didn't mean to offend. I should have considered A, that you're angry, and B, that you might not even be interested. Though you did give me a cookie."

"Yeah, well, it felt like flipping her the bird, to flirt right under her nose." Against his better judgment, huh. Like Tim was a questionable choice... That hurt, and he wanted to hurt back. "Maybe I gave away a lot of cookies those two days."

Carson turned back to the view of the cities below, with his knees up and his arms wrapped around them. "I can see the appeal. I hope if any of your other baits pay off, they don't get you into as much grief as I have."

"Maybe the repetition will wear her down." There wouldn't be any repetition. Tim hadn't sweetened anyone else's lunch. And hell, he was a questionable choice, as long as he had the millstone named Mom around his neck. She took cockblocking to new heights.

That thought made him uncoil and head up the hill. "I guess we better go, before she puts out an APB on you for kidnapping."

He'd meant it as a sour joke, but Carson seemed to be taking it seriously. He clipped his seatbelt on the passenger side with a frown. "With you clearly in control of the car, and able to state your case, they wouldn't have much cause..."

"Geez, Carson! I was joking!" Tim turned around to

begin the trip down the switchbacks into town, a trip he found more harrowing than the climb.

"Yeah, well, I have learned that 'half in jest, all in earnest,' and the one time you don't think two steps ahead is the one time you wish you had. She already threatened to call once." Carson was silent for most of the ride, but once Tim made the turn into the subdivision, he spoke again. "Tim, you didn't really finish the thought about what kind of fallout, but… If push comes to shove, call me. I caused the problem, I'll put a roof over your head."

"And that's the only reason I should call you?" Good to know he had an ally, but the rest stung hard.

"You call if you want to." Carson grinned, a ray of sun through the clouds. He got out of the car with a cheery wave. "You have my number, right?"

"Assuming your asshole buddy got it right, yes."

"All right then." Carson strode one door down to his BMW, looking just as fine from the back as a man could look. Tim watched him pull away, and sat in his elderly econobox, dreaming. Carson was the sexiest man he'd ever met. Even his car was sexy. And he'd held out his arms to Tim.

In a more perfect world, he'd have taken the opportunity up on the mountain and put his arms around his companion. He'd have learned all about the delights of getting kissed in the warm sunshine, and maybe getting naked in the grass. He could have found out what pulling a man's firm torso against his own was like. Instead, he'd thrown the invitation back in Carson's face.

Like a petulant child.

Maybe he did have some growing up to do.

He'd start right now.

He touched the empty icon next to "Neil's" number.

The phone rang and rang. With each trill, he died a little. Would Carson answer? Had that jerk Wes given him the wrong number? Or misremembered a digit? Had Tim transposed numbers entering it into his phone?

"Hello?" Thank God, that was Carson's voice. But so neutral. Oh. He wouldn't recognize the number.

"It's Tim," he finally remembered to say. "Wanna look at some eagles?"

CHAPTER EIGHT

IF DRIVING LORRAINE INTO A SCREAMING, frothing mess was Carson's only objective, today was a rousing success. Try to throw him off "her property," would she? Claiming a public street as her very own, no cootie-bearing gays allowed, really? Grandiose much? While he was doing a sorely needed favor, no less, she was threatening to call the cops, and for a reason that wouldn't hold up. Man, did she look like an idiot in front of her son!

The pop-eyed, fist-waving fury was a bonus. All her Stairmaster time paid off—she ran into the street faster than he'd expected. Suppose all that adrenaline had to go somewhere. He would have taken a video of her impotent raging, but Tim had shot away from the curb and around a corner in what was probably a good maneuver of self-defense.

Unfortunately, even with the wins of this morning, the fallout might not be worth it. Carson could deal with whatever shit Lorraine dreamed up for him, especially since her boss was in his corner, but Tim didn't have that kind of defense. He hadn't mentioned much about his other family that sounded supportive.

Some families were like that—one bigger than life and twice as demanding member could steamroll everyone into doing things their way.

Carson had poked the bear and left Tim in the cage.

That the cage was only as locked as Tim let it be might take a while to sink in. Bless Mrs. Hedstrom for pointing at least part of that out.

Didn't keep the bear from rearing up and slashing everything and everyone in reach while they ran to the exits. *If* they ran to the exits.

Tim didn't seem so bruised that he couldn't get out.

Carson hadn't put this whole mess in motion, but he'd sure stirred the pot. And he'd have been good and furious at anyone who'd done the same to him, back in the day. He rubbed his nose, feeling the knots of cartilage under the skin. He hadn't stirred up that kind of shit for Tim, had he?

Maybe leaving the poor guy alone and letting him keep his head down around Lorraine for a while would let things go back to whatever version of normal Tim could live with.

And if it was all too late for that, Carson would take him in, help him get on his feet. He'd just have to suck it up about having another person in his private space.

His townhouse was plenty big for a second person. Especially if that person wanted to share the bed. Tim was good company. Really good company.

Too bad Carson'd fucked up the chances of spending any more time with him. Tim wouldn't forgive him any time soon for the shitstorm that was no doubt breaking over his head even as Carson drove off counting the day's tally.

He was almost back to his townhouse when the phone rang. He didn't recognize the caller: the number had the local 720 prefix. Probably spoofed by another telemarketer: they'd grown pestiferous. He'd let it go to voicemail.

Except—the one person he wanted to hear from had a number that wouldn't register yet on his caller ID.

He accepted the call, ready to cut it off in three words or less.

"It's Tim" came after a pause long enough that Carson reached for the "end call" button.

"Yes, I'd love to look at some eagles. Where do we find eagles?" Of all the things Tim could have said, Carson would not have predicted that.

"Not too far out of my neighborhood, actually. There's a small parking lot on the north side of Standley Lake, on the south side of 100th. Meet me there—is nine okay? You were up that early today."

"Not a problem." Carson wouldn't be doing any carousing into the wee hours. "Are we hiking or running?"

"Good idea, we can run by the lake too." Tim seemed perplexed, like he didn't often plan outings, even though he was off to a good start.

"Sounds like fun. Um, did you get into the house without incident?" Carson didn't think the screaming would have died down so fast, but maybe cooler heads had prevailed.

"Haven't gone in yet." Tim's sigh gusted through the phone. "Um, if I don't show tomorrow, it's not because I'm blowing you off, okay?"

"Should I come looking for you?" If Tim got locked in the basement, Carson wouldn't mind taking an axe to Lorraine's door.

"Let's hope it won't become necessary."

With The Harridan from Hell™ on the warpath, it

couldn't be entirely ruled out. "If I don't see you by 9:20, I'm ringing your doorbell."

And probably getting screamed at, and trespassed, and all sorts of interesting fallout. Nothing he couldn't roll with, if it wasn't a blow to the face. Well, he knew how to deal with that. Now.

"Thanks, Carson. See you tomorrow."

———

Okay, he hadn't completely fucked up with Carson. Not only was he willing to come on a cheap date, he had Tim's back. Maybe. He was pretty good at standing his ground when Mom was telling him to leave. Make that damn good. He hadn't flinched or backed away, and he'd given Tim the courage to speak up.

Course, he hadn't said anything that wasn't the truth, but it was a truth Mom didn't like. She'd pitched a fit when he bought the Toyota without her input or her name on the title. Guess he'd been wiser than he knew back when he was eighteen—he could have had something much newer if he'd taken Mom up on her offer. A two-year-old Kia Soul in lime green to drive versus a car he owned—he'd wavered enough to send her to the bank for financing.

She was still likely to be pissed when he went inside. He'd have to wait until the next geological epoch to completely outwait her temper. But—best defense was a good offence, and he'd managed once. Just have to think up a few choice lines.

And get them out past the rock in his throat. *Okay, deep breaths. Think of Carson.* No, don't think of Carson—he didn't want to face his mother with a woodie. She wanted him to stand at attention when she spoke, just not that kind of standing at attention. Blech, that took care of the problem. *No, think about how Carson stayed calm in the face of ranting, stuck with logic, and didn't let himself get rattled.*

Tim could do it. Really, he could do it.

As convinced of his ability as he could be with only himself for a pep talk, he headed into the house.

Mom met him at the door. The purple tint was gone from her face, replaced with a scowl. "Where have you been and what have you been doing?" she snapped. "With that, that, man!"

"We took the car for a test drive, talked, and came back." Not exactly what Tim could have done, but the truth was a nice shield.

"I suppose you two talked about me?" She followed him into the kitchen.

There wasn't any denying that—when someone chases you away with shaking fists, they're bound to get talked about. Tim poured a glass of water from the tap. "Some." Drinking kept him from elaborating.

"I can imagine what terrible things he said. And the rest of the time you, what? Had sex?" She came too close into his personal bubble for comfort. Why? So she could intimidate him? Or sniff him? Joke was on her for that one—he whiffed of this morning's yard work.

Putting the glass down on the counter let him step back enough to take the full stage. Tim clasped his hands against his heart, head tilted melodramatically. "Oh, no, Mother dear. I am untouched. I am thtill a gay virg—I mean, gay virthin." Sweeping the back of his hand to his forehead, Tim lamented to the ceiling. "Alath, I am twenty-two and unkithed!" He held his pose of woe and waited for the storm.

"Damn it, will you knock it off with the dramatics!" she snarled. "I asked you a question."

She might deny he was an adult, but it was a lot harder to deny that he was nearly a head taller than she. He dropped the pose, setting his shoulders in righteous firmness to stare down. "I answered it. And it was an intrusive question and shouldn't have been asked."

Uh, oh, he may have gone too far. Her eyes widened at his rebuttal—*how dare he?* written all over her face. Tim wasn't quite sure how he dared either, except to back down now would get him torn apart for having shown spine.

"You just mind your manners!" She pointed a finger toward his nose.

"I did." Tim bared his teeth in a not-smile, knowing how the hawk felt when it stooped for the kill. "I thanked Mrs. Hedstrom for the cookies."

She dropped her hand, realization dawning in her eyes.

"*All* the cookies."

Tim left her standing in the kitchen with her mouth hanging open.

If he worked diligently, he could send off another dozen résumés today. He wouldn't hold out for his dream job, not when he only needed to get out. A prize awaited, one he could claim only when he was out on his own. A prize wearing Carson's face.

CHAPTER NINE

IF HE KEPT to a reasonable pace, Tim would be at the parking lot in fifteen minutes, and his minutes were ticking away. He tossed the third shirt back in the drawer. Ah, there it was, a gray ribbed tank with arm holes high enough to run without chafing. It looked right with the black running shorts with the side notches nearly at his hips. He surveyed himself in the mirror, hoping Carson would like what he saw. Shoes, check, stretches, check, water bottle, check, ready, go!

Tim had one hand on the doorknob when he remembered—wallet. He tiptoed upstairs.

His father stood at the top of the stairs, rubbing sleep from his eye. A familiar but unlovely sight, with wild, graying body hair covering a bare paunch lapping over striped pjs. "Good, you're back. We'll be headed to church, so get cleaned up. I want to get there a little early."

"Morning, Dad," wasn't an agreement. With any luck, he'd be too groggy to notice.

Oh, shit, no, Tim was not going to church this week. He

slipped past and into his room. Where— Yes! He stuffed his wallet into his pocket. Keys, check! He eeled out again and didn't answer his father until he was already on the staircase. "Not going to church today." He didn't take the steps two at a time, but he didn't slow down either.

"What! Yes, you are. How else are you going to meet a nice Christian girl?" Damn, Dad was more awake than he should be. And he'd been talking to Mom, no doubt.

"Tho thee can teatth me how to put on mathcawa?" got Tim to the front door. "Later, Dad!"

Whoot! Free! He headed up the street toward the main road.

Not so free. His phone vibrated against his hip. Nope, not Carson. And nope, not answering it. Tim punched it to silence and killed the buzz. He refused to respond to the pull on the leash. Not today: he had a date.

The poor phone was probably getting blown up sky-high, but he wouldn't check the carnage until he was ready. And that might be hours from now.

He took the shortest, but most exposed route, trading time against visibility.

A familiar coupe sailed past him with only fifty yards left to the rendezvous spot. It turned into the dirt parking area with Tim hot on its wheels. He rounded the wooden fence in time to see Carson emerge, a vision in microscopic red running shorts and a white singlet tighter than his own. Rawr!

Maybe he should have put on a jockstrap.

When Carson started stretching, bent sideways and spread wide, Tim grew certain he should have put on a jockstrap.

"Hi!" might have been a grunt, but it was also sweet music. Them getting together yesterday was probably a coincidence, but this morning, it was all on purpose. This gorgeous, confident man had turned up in an out of the way spot for no other reason than to be with Tim.

Against his better judgement. Carson was here. Because... the draw was just that powerful? Tim could hope. And hope to be enough to make Carson not regret getting involved.

"Okay, where are we going?" Carson asked after he'd stretched enough to turn Tim weak in the knees.

"Let's follow the path to the shore on our way to the ranger station. It forks and then goes to the observation blind." Tim pointed west. "How fast do you like to go?"

"How about you pick, and if it's too fast for the old man, I'll slow us down?" Like Carson was an old man, yeah right. Older than him, and—more worldly. And more buff and more together, more experienced, and more... whatever Tim was, Carson had to be more of it. Including faster. Dear Lord, this was a terrible idea, trying to impress an older, more sophisticated man.

Tim set a pace he could maintain for miles, heading downhill toward the water. Carson matched him easily, dropping behind when they passed other hikers or the occasional fisherman planning to drop a line in the reservoir. The prairie was broken by the random juniper looming over the grass and sage. They avoided the camping area, where tents and more than a few enormous RVs had parked in untidy rows.

"Really roughing it, aren't they?" Carson spoke easily, his words sounding conversational against the *slap slap slap* of their feet against the red dirt path.

"The cubmaster called camping a state of mind. If we hadn't camped here, I probably would never have gone." Tim's dad had gone along for a couple of weekend events, but never for the camping up in the mountains. Too far from creature comforts, or too far away from Mom, who had called him away from the lake more than once. "At night you can hear the coyotes."

"Coyotes?" Carson sounded unconvinced.

"Yeah, they wander into the neighborhoods in search of fresh poodle for dinner. There's foxes and raccoons and prairie dogs all over the place. The reservoir is a nature preserve. That's why there's no development on this end." Didn't everyone know this? How long had Carson lived in Denver? A question to ask later.

"You did promise me eagles."

A few high wisps of cloud marked the brilliant blue sky, but no raptors. Three huge white birds in perfect formation flew over their heads, their necks pulled back into S curves. Flabby yellow pouches wobbled beneath their bills. "We're getting there. We can start with pelicans."

Carson stopped running and stared after the birds, which banked the other way as if with one mind. "Those are pelicans. Those are fucking pelicans. Who the hell knew there were pelicans in Colorado?"

Tim pointed at an island not far from the shore, where masses of brown and white seethed and honked. "Lots of pelicans. The brown ones are cormorants. Yeah, in Colorado. And Wyoming and Nebraska. All the big bodies of water have them."

"Huh. Who would have thought?" Carson ran on, turning to examine Bird Island as they trotted past. "I believed you about the eagles, but pelicans?"

Well, well, Tim had a city boy on his hands. Maybe he could impress Carson better than he thought.

The morning sun beat on their shoulders, where a light breeze licked enough to keep the heat at bay. The dust puffed up behind them when Tim veered them uphill. The path became a two-track road, rustling with tall grass. The seed heads, already losing their spring green for summer brown, tickled Tim's ankles. A grasshopper clicked and chirred a long flight across the road, far enough ahead that they wouldn't intercept the nasty thing.

Their trail took them into a stand of shrubs and through a wooden fence, marked with warnings not to disturb the wildlife. "We must be getting close."

"Nearly there." They rounded a stand of juniper, pungent in the sun, revealing a wooden blind. The three-sided hut had a roof and a large glassless window in the long side. No one else was there to see the eagle's nest, so they'd have the shade and the permanently mounted binocular telescope to themselves, at least for a while.

"Here, eagle, eagle, eagle." Carson leaned one knee on the wooden bench beneath the window. The naked prairie rolled for a mile or so to the stand of ancient cottonwoods, gray and leafless.

"Let me get this focused." Tim leaned down to meet the eyepiece. He aimed the telescope at the ragged platform of sticks and branches. "Oh, hey, we got movement!"

"Really? What am I looking for?" Carson was a warm presence at Tim's back.

Acutely aware that he was bent over enough to stick his ass out at his companion, Tim rose to let Carson have the 'scope. Now Carson was the one with his butt poking out so provocatively. Round and firm, just right for two hands….

Tim shook himself and tried to find his voice. "That mess in the tree is the nest. There's a mating pair that's used it for years, and they hatched two eggs this season. You're looking for the babies."

Carson peered, and whooped. "Oh my God. That is a, well, it's something with a beak. And ugly."

"If it's anything besides the eaglet, it's in trouble. Here comes Mama. Or Dad, I can't tell which is which when there's only one." Hot damn, if there was anything worth looking at even a quarter as much as Carson's ass, it was a bald eagle bringing breakfast to the nest.

"What?" Carson lifted his head to track the incoming eagle, and then returned to the eyepiece. "Fuck, this is…"

Yeah, it was. It really was—he'd reduced Carson to amazed and incoherent mumblings, even with their pants still on.

The eagle touched down with its prey. Carson stayed glued to the telescope, oblivious to anything without feathers. He provided a running commentary of "It's tearing the prey apart, it's kind of dirt colored, might be a rabbit. One of the babies is begging…"

There might be some begging in Tim's future too, only for permission to run his hands over the delectable mounds of buttock only inches from his groin. Two pair of running shorts were in the way, and some words of welcome, or Tim would be interrupting the birdwatching. His cock couldn't get any harder, could it? His heart had to be thudding loud enough for his companion to hear.

He might have whimpered, just a little. Enough to penetrate his companion's concentration, because Carson looked up with a guilty start. "Oh hey, I'm hogging the telescope. Here, you look."

Tim *had* been looking at exactly the view he wanted most, but he did put his eyes to the 'scope in time to see the adult poke a bite of meat into its offspring's beak. Which, yeah, cool, but he'd seen the eagles before, and he'd never had Carson standing next to him in barely-there shorts, with his groin closer than anyone's groin had ever been before. Close enough to touch, if he reached.

"Here, you take another look." He'd offer the lion's share of the viewing to Carson just to bask in how much he was enjoying what Tim offered. Would Carson turn that kind of rapt attention to him? Or would he be just another pleasant diversion in the clothes-off department?

"This is so cool. Really getting to see the eagles." Carson shoved his face back into the telescope.

Fuck but the man was enticing. That red fabric stretched across his butt mocked Tim—*I get to cup his buns and you don't, nyah nyah, I'm all over his balls and you can't touch..."*

The temptation to reach out might kill him. Maybe Carson wouldn't mind, but here, where they could have company with no notice at all? Not a great idea when privacy was an illusion that could shatter in a heartbeat. Tim removed himself from the blind to read the informational posters about nesting and chick-rearing. He had to get himself under control.

Carson joined him, scanning the bar graphs about days spent nesting and days spent incubating. "Mama flew away."

If only. "She'll be back."

"Um, speaking of which, how did it go yesterday after I left?"

"Not as bad as it could have." Tim felt an evil grin grow. "In fact, I shut her down rather hard."

"Teach me your ways, master!" Carson implored, his eyes dancing.

"Remember I said I leaned into her announcement? I did some more leaning." A dramatic reenactment left

Carson howling while Tim lamented to the sky that he'd never been kithed.

When he'd recovered his breath, Carson said, "That's too bad."

Wait, what? Tim had accomplished the impossible. "I did have to throw in a dig about Mrs. Hedstrom's cookies, but I think I did damn well. She left me alone for the rest of the day."

"Oh you did, you did." Carson dashed a hand across his eyes, a last chuckle heaving his chest. "I meant about the kithing. You ought to be kithed." He lost the mirth—his smile went knowing, seductive. "I'd like to kith you now."

"I'd kiss you back." The time for joking was over. Tim met Carson's eyes with all the heat he could muster, enough to set the prairie around them on fire.

"Good." Carson pulled Tim into the shade of the blind and, oh god, closer yet. Not touching, not yet, those few inches might be two miles. Throwing himself at Carson wouldn't be… or would it? That thought got lost in the bend of Carson's neck, enough to touch his lips to Tim's.

Much too tentative. Didn't Carson hear how Tim would kiss him back? This first brushing contact was electricity through them, but not enough, not nearly enough. Tim closed the gap, daring to press himself against Carson's chest. Oh, damn, belly to belly. Groin to groin.

Carson was as hard as he was, fuck. Hard and pressed close from top to bottom, from lip to thigh. Tim moaned and opened his mouth.

Zero to sixty in no time flat. Tim didn't have the patience for hesitant groping—he might not have a speck of experience, but he knew what he wanted. Years of pent up demand, of adolescent fumbling that had never happened and now never would, because he was a man, holding a man, this man, Carson. All elegance and confidence and poise, and Tim would kiss him like he meant it.

Oh man, Carson was solid and real in his arms. Not like last night or the night before, when he was imaginary and fit in a twin bed with Tim only because he was insubstantial. Not now. So real, his chest a wall of warm granite, his back a firm platform for Tim's hands.

With Carson's arms wrapped around his back and their mouths mashed together, Tim was in heaven. Heaven had hip motion too. Frotting had been a word in a book. Now it was cock to cock. The hard column of Carson's cock rammed against Tim's belly, banging into his own over-heated erection. Clothing might as well not exist—they thrust against each other. Tim's hips moved without his willing it, but oh…

Carson broke the lip lock to do something different and just as wonderful. He trailed his tongue down Tim's neck, delving into the hollow behind the strap muscle that popped out when Tim turned. That spot… And his ear, getting treated with the gentle nibbles and puffs of breaths, and back to his neck…

"No marks," Tim mumbled, the only flawed thought in his head. The rest of his mind was *More! More! Yeah!*

"No marks," Carson agreed. Dear lord, what that man could do with his tongue, and one hand on Tim's ass.

So that's where the noses went. Tim found Carson's lips again, hungry for the press of his mouth. And he wanted Tim just as much. *Guh.*

"I'm gonna…" became *Oops, I did,* but the best oops ever. Spurting and throbbing within his clothing, Tim went up in a blaze to set the grasslands on fire. In Carson's arms. With his cock thrusting against Tim's. He moaned, and then Carson stuck close and gasped his own pleasure.

They held each other, panting, until time returned. Carson might not have been as wobbly as Tim, but if he was, they could hold each other up until the trembling stopped. Or longer. Lots longer.

Carson seemed as content as Tim to hold the embrace, his lips near Tim's ear. Tim leaned into Carson's neck, half-drunk with the scent of warm man in fresh sweat. They ought to hold each other close until they came up again, because what else could they find to do?

The crunching up the path barely penetrated Tim's awareness, but the piping of "Mama, why are the mans hugging?" certainly did.

He whipped around without releasing his grip on Carson—not letting go of his fig leaf. A woman pushing a baby in an all-terrain stroller and a small child in a dinosaur shirt stood on the open side of the blind. Nobody he knew, at least.

Welp, no semi-stiff to disguise now. Tim wanted to bury his face back in Carson's neck. He didn't.

"Because we like each other very, very much," Carson announced. "And we liked seeing the eagle babies. The telescope's pointed right at them. They're funny looking and gray, not brown with white like the mama bird. She flew away a little while ago but she or the daddy might be back."

Carson's impromptu lesson on eaglets bought them some distraction. They eased out past the woman, who wasn't concealing her smile all that well.

"Race you!" Carson shouted and took off. The man could move a whole lot faster than he had on the way out.

Tim had an extra gear too. Maybe two extra gears, when Carson threw a challenge over his shoulder. "Catch it, and you can—it." He filled in the blank with a pat on his own backside.

Challenge accepted—they were halfway back to the car when Tim caught up and delivered a light slap on that delectable cheek. Oh man, he'd just touched Carson's butt. He'd been invited, well, challenged, and he'd won the prize. Carson jolted with the surprise and kept running. Tim paced him, pulling huge lungfuls of air in to maintain his sprint.

Not much farther. The BMW grew closer. The moment of truth grew closer. Tim had patting rights now—how would he redeem them? Did Carson mean that? He must— he'd frotted and cuddled, and he was smiling now, while they walked the last fifty yards more sedately for a cool-down.

"You're fast," Carson noted. Tim basked in the acknowledgement. "Do you run any of the local races?"

"Nothing that requires an entry fee." Cluckets didn't pay well enough to generate an extra fifty or seventy-five dollars for the privilege of competing. But he wouldn't be at Cluckets much longer. He *couldn't* be. "Next year, the Bolder Boulder."

"I ran this year, in the E wave."

Well, if Carson hadn't just announced he could match a better pace than today's. Tim's last 5K race would qualify him for the D wave. Maybe Carson had an extra gear he hadn't used yet. Maybe Carson wanted to be caught. Since he was clearly faster than almost anyone else.

"We ought to train together." Carson wiped his forehead with a sweat-banded wrist. "And there's races this summer and fall."

Oh yeah. Carson just put the keys in Tim's hand for spending time together and getting sweaty. "That works. We can compare training methods."

"And motivation factors." The BMW flashed a

welcome. Carson swung Tim to him for a kiss. "I might need a lot of motivation."

"I could probably find something to get you going." Tim stole another kiss and broke away. He desperately wanted more smooching, but they were in full view of the street, and anyone might drive by. Had his cum soaked through his shorts?

"Get in then." The BMW clicked its door locks at Carson's touch on the key fob.

Tim would pop open just as obediently. "Where are we going?"

"My place." Carson headed the land-rocket to wherever home was.

Tim couldn't wait.

CHAPTER TEN

WHAT THE HELL was he doing? Carson tried to stop asking himself that and just do it. It was okay—Tim was harmless. He could bring someone into his personal domain if he wanted to. And he did—he wanted private time alone with this sweet, uncertain young man. Despite his drawbacks. Maybe because of them, but… Maybe Carson was feeling protective. Or horny, or …

They didn't have far to go—Carson's townhouse was a few blocks off the main drag, about a mile south of Tim's house. The development was three two story units with garages per building, angled for the illusion of privacy. The spiky clumps of Spanish bayonet growing beneath Carson's windows and around his patio provided a very real privacy, and anyone who got past them still had to deal with windows. The filigree twists of wrought iron were as functional as bars.

He pulled into his driveway and cut the motor. He needed a few deep breaths before getting out of the car.

Tim noticed. "Um, you don't have to…"

Shit, the kid thought Carson's hesitation was about him.

"I want to." Damn it, how was he going to explain this? "I, ah, don't have a lot of guests over."

"I don't care if the place is a mess."

"It's not that." *Find something half rational, Carson. You invited him over, you want privacy with him, the best place is behind your front door.* "I'm just, really, really protective of my space. So it's weird to bring someone in. You're my first guest in a long time."

He bought the townhouse eight years ago. He got rid of the roommates seven years ago. The rent didn't make up for the traffic.

Yes, it was weird, yes, it was reclusive, but Carson felt much safer keeping his haven to himself. Now he had a guest. Well, he'd made a huge, out of character offer before he knew how much he liked this guest, because he could conceivably have Tim around for the long term if his family situation really blew up.

For a moment, Carson regretted poking Lorraine. But just for a moment, because this sweet young man waited to be invited in.

"This is one of those 'we're not going there' things, isn't it?" Tim waited while Carson unlocked the wrought iron and glass safety storm door and tapped a code onto the keypad.

"One day I'll tell you the story." Maybe. One day might be very far away. Remembering the humiliation had no part in the joyous horniness of this first encounter with Tim. He wanted to be everything Tim could think he was: confident, collected. Desirable. Explaining would kick the shit right out of that. Carson ushered his guest in and slipped off his shoes. Tim left his at the door as well.

The mess that wouldn't bother Tim would most certainly bother Carson, therefore, it didn't exist. A single coaster sat on the coffee table, two of the other three roosted in a kitchen drawer, the fourth on the bedside table upstairs, next to a lone book. Carson checked—he had straightened the aqua and royal blue cushions against the turquoise throw on the pale gray couch this morning. The colors echoed the huge seascape painting on the wall behind. Bright ceramic fish swam in and out of the walls.

He liked the white walls and the gray ash laminate flooring; they seemed pristine and clean to him, so much so that he'd snapped up the gray ash dining table and chairs when the furniture store closed out the line. They went so nicely with the ombre area rugs in all the colors of the ocean.

"Wow, I like it. It's like living in an aquarium." Tim smiled when he found the school of angelfish darting behind the flat screen TV.

"Thanks. It's a work in progress." Not so very long ago, the main floor had been decorated in "Early Eclectic" aka "Salvation Army Chic," with aging beige "realtor's special" carpet. The upstairs only showed its thrift store origins if you looked closely. "Welcome to my humble abode."

"I'm honored to be here." Tim stayed in one place, as if he didn't quite know what to do next.

Carson could sympathize. Going straight to bed seemed a little crass. The mess at his hip squelched, aid from the strangest quarter. "We're sticky. Want to clean up?"

"Um, yeah."

Carson led Tim up the stairs and into the master bedroom. The master bath had the bigger shower, plenty for two.

He hadn't planned on company today, though he'd

hoped, enough to make the bed up fresh and shove the hamper into the closet. And set out fresh towels, which emptied the linen closet of everything but his enormous beach towel.

One man alone didn't need much. And he had all he needed, just barely, to make a guest welcome.

Might as well lead by example—Carson stripped off his singlet and hung it from the towel bar. His shorts had a spot at the hip, evidence of their enthusiasm. Couldn't remember the last time he'd creamed his jock, but for an intro to gay sex, no pressure for more, he didn't mind. Tim had to start somewhere.

Peeling down was a good start. Tim squished some liquid soap into his skivs, working up a lather. "I'm glad that woman and her kids didn't come along five minutes earlier."

"Me too. Us mans needed to finish the busy part of the hugging." Carson slipped out of his shorts and went to drop them in the hamper. Hope Tim was watching, because the view was nice, even if he did say so himself. Freshly shaven buns framed by the wide elastic of his jock strap flexing their way to the hamper—yup, good for a gasp.

And on the return trip, the view was even better. Tim, clad in nothing but socks and a blush, standing at the sink scrubbing furiously at his underwear. He had his groin to the vanity, but the rest was open to view. A lanky runner's build, with some width at the shoulder, lightly defined muscles in his legs, maybe two inches shy of Carson's own six feet. His chest was sprinkled with hair at the breastbone, looking natural and unclipped.

Calling him adorable out loud might set this sex project back a while. Carson came up from behind to slip his arms around Tim's chest and peer over his shoulder, trying to meet his eyes in the mirror. "Looking fine, my man."

"I am?" kind of squeaked. "I—thanks," sounded more nearly normal. "You too."

"Thanks." Dropping a kiss on the edge of Tim's ear, Carson kept his hips back from Tim's butt. Much though he wanted to plaster himself into the valley of that sweet virgin crack. Not touching might be impossible without letting go and backing off—his cock was filling again. Carson turned to start the shower. "Join me?"

Tim hung his wet underwear on the towel rack and stepped through the frosted glass slider. He turned his back to the spray and opened his arms. His smile was sweet and tentative, with the confidence dial turning up with every centimeter Carson came closer. Body to body again, with nothing in the way. Mouth to mouth again, more gently now that their first crazy rush peaked, but with the promise of wildness. Tim held on with an iron grip, and he sought Carson's tongue with his own. The water beat down on them—nothing outside their skins mattered.

The enclosed tub was their little world inside Carson's little world, with the perfect population of two.

———

Naked. With another man. At last. And it was Carson. Gorgeous, kind, with enough flaw to make him real Carson. In the shower. In his arms. If Tim thought too hard he'd wake up and this would all disappear.

Couldn't risk that—Tim opened his mouth to restart the dance they'd begun at the eagle blind. Carson seemed just as enthusiastic as before, if slower, more thorough. He'd follow, learn.

Would he learn everything at once today? He shivered in spite of the warm water beating on his shoulders. Would Carson find him lacking now that they were together and alone?

Not so far. Not with one arm pulling Tim close and the other hand cupping his cheek. One thumb scraped against Tim's light stubble, an unbearably erotic gesture when their wet skins suctioned together from belly on down.

Carson kept kissing him. Like he liked it, he really liked it. Tension ran out of Tim's shoulders with each caress, going south into his hips. Not that he could keep from grinding his groin against Carson any more than he could stop his heart from pumping every drop of blood he owned into his dick.

Kissing was wonderful, kissing was grand, why hadn't he ever kissed anyone before? Oh yeah... But he had Carson for his first kiss and his first frot and his first... whatever they chose to do. What would they choose? Would Carson be upset if they didn't do everything right away? Tim wanted to do everything, eventually. But... did Carson expect eventually right now?

"Whoa, Tim." Carson pulled back enough to run his thumb over the seam of Tim's lips. "You're thinking so hard I can smell burnt oil."

Busted. He closed his eyes. "I just... don't want to disappoint you."

That got a chuckle. "Tim. The only thing you could do that would disappoint me is to leave and swear you're not coming back. And even if you did, I'd have to accept that." He moved his thumb to make way for a brushing kiss. "I don't have a list with ticky boxes in my head, if that's what you're worried about."

"Um, how did you know?" At least part of his blood rerouted to his cheeks.

"It's not a big leap when twenty-two and never been kissed starts kissing, et cetera." Carson's smile was a crinkle at his eyes from this close. "But don't freak out about it. We do what we do, and we enjoy each other along the way. All that et cetera? It's fun. Let me show you."

Carson turned Tim around to face the spray. His hands traveled up and down Tim's front, pulling him tight. His erection bumped at Tim's cheeks. "I thought..."

"Shh. You're feeling, not thinking right now." Carson shifted so his cock rubbed against Tim's taint, poking into his balls from the back. "Just enjoy, okay?"

Oh, okay. That was Carson's cock rubbing, where no one had ever rubbed before. With anything. And that was Carson's mouth, where Tim's shoulder met his neck, nibbling and licking. Tim let his head fall back, barely letting him nuzzle into Carson's ear. "Feels nice."

"Good," came with the faint graze of teeth. Ohhhh... And brush of palm against nipple... Ohhh... If he knew what to do with his hands, he'd do it.

Tim reached back, finding those firm handfuls of ass he'd seen framed in white elastic. The muscles played under his hands—flexing for his benefit? But damn, when Carson reached for the body wash and made lush trails of bubbles up and down, and then down farther...

Tim trembled to feel another man touching his cock for the first time. Someone else's long, strong fingers taking matters in hand. Letting go only to cup balls that were drawing up close to Tim's body already.

"Mmm, you shaved?" Carson mumbled into Tim's neck.

"Um, yeah? I thought I should…" Thinking was hard right now, but he'd debated with himself in the shower last night, and thought either way he'd be wrong, but…

"It's sexy."

It was? He'd done it right?

"Also sexy if you didn't. Either way, rawr." Carson said *rawr* with his hands too, sliding his way back up Tim's shaft.

"So it's okay I didn't do my chest?" Where Carson was playing and had already figured that out.

"I know why you didn't. It's okay." He shifted his lips to Tim's jawline. "You feel great."

Carson was definitely feeling him great. So great. "It's not gonna take much…"

"I wanna feel you come."

Hearing the wish was enough to force Tim to grant it. Carson held him while his world went incandescent and the glory spurted through his cock. He pulsed against Carson's hand, painting the tile with white ribbons and splats.

The aftershocks sagged him against Carson, who made up for his shaky knees with strong arms. Twice now. With this wonderful man who murmured sweet encouragements in his ear, like "Yeah, want you to feel good."

He did, oh he did. And there was more to feel— Carson's erection still rubbed between Tim's legs. He turned to kiss Carson full on, as much as he could with not enough air in the room to fill his lungs.

"What should I do for you?" Tim had to do something to the stiffy now trapped against his belly. Right?

"Mmm, let's go to bed and decide there." Carson snaked an arm around the glass slider to snag a towel. He wrapped Tim in a terrycloth hug.

Dear God, he was really going to get into Carson's bed. This was so far beyond what he'd imagined when he'd made the invitation. What had he imagined them doing? Looking at bald eagles, and then...? Somehow this, but not this, because this was too much for now, getting into bed with anyone else was for someday, not today, but someday when he didn't have to look over his shoulder.

He couldn't freeze Carson for that someday, though... it would be so perfect if he could transport the wonderful sight of this naked and erect man pulling down the light blanket into a future where he wasn't afraid to reach out.

He had now, and Carson. Tim left the towel behind and crawled onto the king-sized bed, where Carson leaned against the pillows with his arms out.

"Erm, what do you like?" Tim scooched around until he had his arm behind Carson's neck, perfect for kissing him. And getting a view. All the way down to what was up. Whoa, Nelly.

"Everything." Carson rested his hand on Tim's forearm, which curved around Carson's chest almost naturally. "There's no timetable, there's no checklist, there's just what you'd like to do at the pace you want to do it." He added a lick of tongue to Tim's lower lip. "If you say stop, we stop, if you say let's change up, we change. This is supposed to be fun."

"But—if you aren't getting real sex, will it be fun for you?"

How did voicing his biggest fear turn into being flipped to his back with a stern, naked man on top of him? Carson pinned him down top to bottom and spoke from nose to nose.

"This is all real sex. I don't define sex as getting a dick shoved up my ass, or shoving mine in."

That was gay sex the terrifying way. Tim swallowed

down the boulder in his throat. "When you put it like that, it sounds pretty scary."

Carson backed off from noses-touching range and his voice softened. "Sorry, but… It's not anal or nothing at all, you know? I guess you don't, that's why we're talking. If we do that, it'll be because we both want it. It doesn't have to be every time, or any time. We've had three orgasms between us so far, so this is pretty damn real, don't you think?"

"So did I lose my V-card in the shower? Or back at the eagle blind?" Tim wasn't about to argue the realness of what they'd done, but… What was supposed to count for popping his cherry if it was all real sex?

Carson opened his mouth to speak and closed it again. Another attempt, and he still didn't explain. Finally, he shook his head. "I don't think I can answer that for you. Because yes, we had real sex, and I can still see that it might not be enough for you to count." He ran his fingers through Tim's hair, his mental gears turning so hard Tim could hear them grinding. "But that only matters if you think it's an event. I think getting some experience is a process. Because there's gay guys who've never tried anal, and virgin is the absolute last word I'd use to describe them." Carson chuckled. "Does it matter?"

Yes, it did, in some weird ways that Tim didn't want to examine too hard right now. Two people in the bed were enough; he didn't want parents and church and societal expectations in there with them. "It's always seemed like a rite of passage."

That got a grimace. "I suppose. Seems like this whole virginity thing comes with a lot of baggage, half of it not applying to guys." Carson swooped in for a kiss. "For being two horny dudes in a big bed, we sure are talking a lot.

How about you tell me when we've done something mile-stone-ish?"

"We have." Carson couldn't know how big a milestone Tim passed by asking him out this morning, or for every-thing they'd already done. A milestone in claiming the life he wanted to live. "Let's do some more."

CHAPTER ELEVEN

BEING the lower layer was nice. Not that he'd planned it, but Tim wasn't about to change it. Not when Carson lay on him like a hot, muscular blanket with added groin features. Which—oh man. They were touching, cock to cock. Good thing he was lying flat, or he'd have fallen at the thought.

Carson was giving him mouth to mouth even without a fall. Like this, and this... All lips and tongues, every hot breath thrusting their chests together. Was he really holding Carson? Tim risked sliding a hand down to cup one firm buttock. Oh yeah, he was. And Carson liked it—he could feel the smile twisting their kiss.

He could stay like this forever, thrusting up against the most amazing man he'd ever met. Coming twice already slowed him enough that he wouldn't blow his load between their bellies any time soon. He'd come in Carson's hand, where else could he...

Tim rolled them over, wanting the control of being on top just as much as he wanted to be held down. Carson flipped gracefully to his back. Tim didn't follow completely.

If he wanted to touch Carson's cock, he'd have to forego lying on top, but what a small price to pay for the first-time joy of wrapping his fingers around another man's erection.

Oh man, Carson was so... so...so... Hot and heavy in Tim's hand, throbbing with his heartbeat. For Tim. He wanted to explore, he wanted to hold on, he wanted to look, he wanted to keep kissing.... He wanted it all, and all at the same time.

Gggnnnnhh, the way the soft skin traveled over the firm column... Tim forced himself to slowness, savoring the feel. Carson's ragged breathing must mean he was doing it right, but he had to know for sure. "Is this good?"

"Oh yeah." Carson ran his fingers through Tim's hair. "Real nice."

Tim had to see what he was feeling. He came up on his elbow to run his gaze down the gorgeous length of Carson's body. All the way down to his cock, where droplets of clear fluid clung to the tip. He watched the skin bunch up ahead of his hand, covering the plum-purple head. He could lick those droplets away, Carson would let him....

The enormity of what he was doing hit like a ton of bricks. Pleasuring another man now, when he was days or weeks or a month away from safety and independence, what was he thinking? Three tries to find his voice let him rasp, "Is it okay if this is all...?"

"Told you, it feels good." Carson nibbled Tim's shoulder. "You're driving. Though if you want me to come, go a little faster."

No he didn't want, yes he did, he could run before they did anything more, anything he might have to admit to before the Spanish Inquisition, no he didn't, he wanted to slide his tongue down Carson's body until he bumped into that stiff cock...

Tim pumped faster.

Carson helped, lifting his hips, thrusting into the circle of Tim's fist. Oh fuck, he was gonna make Carson explode any second. Yes. No—something important would change, but yes. Yes.

Hell yes.

Carson helped with that hell yes, pulsing and spitting white globs against his belly. Tim had made him do that, brought him to the brink and over. Carson was coming, because of what Tim did, and it was beautiful.

He held on while Carson softened and caught his breath, hardly daring to move. Maybe a tissue would be nice—Tim groped at the side table to snag one. Should he lick instead? Carson was smiling, so getting mopped up couldn't be that bad. Another kiss, soft and brushing across Carson's forehead, would take his mind off other mouth activity.

His lover—was Carson his lover now? His boyfriend? Fuck buddy? Amused, or horrified, but willing bystander to the drama of Tim's life? Too much to think about now. Carson, yeah, Carson, was lifting his mouth for a kiss. Well, all right.

"That was wonderful," was a wisp against Tim's lips.

"Hand jobs might be the only thing I'm really good at." All that practice on himself had to pay off somehow.

"Yet. Don't discount native talent." Carson turned them to their sides on the cool edge of the bed, the crisp cotton wicking away their heat. The overhead fan twirled white blades too fast to see, wafting more coolness against their skins. Carson brushed his fingertips up and down Tim's flank. Tim shivered. "Besides, if you're paying attention and reacting to your partner, you're doing fine. I'm happy. You?"

"Yeah." The happiness squished all Tim's breath out in one big sigh. "I am."

"Good. You gonna stay happy if I get a little more active?" Wow was Carson gorgeous when he smiled from nose-booping range.

"Yeah." At least he thought he would be. Or maybe being the center of Carson's active attention might make him break into self-conscious pieces. Self-conscious *happy* pieces, hardly worthy of the man's notice but getting it anyway. He'd take it.

Sweet merciful... oh man... With Carson kneeling over him, brushing his lips from neck to nipple, trailing his tongue over the rise of a pec and down into the valley of sternum and farther. Was he dipping his tongue into Tim's navel? Did his chin just bump the tip of Tim's cock? That had to be the rasp of his close-clipped beard.

All that, and more, poised over Tim's body like a derrick of dick. Carson explored up and down, but not down-down. He left Tim's cock strictly alone except for that accidental touch, and he had Tim gripping the mattress hard enough to make divots.

The graze of Carson's teeth against his biceps made him shiver again, or was that from the barely-there caress of a sated cock against Tim's hip? Was he really one big erogenous zone? Quivering under every brush of Carson's mouth said yeah, he was. Carson could touch anything he wanted. Anything at all, and he was getting intimate with the inner bend of Tim's elbow.

Gah! The tension might kill him, if his dick didn't explode first. So hard he throbbed a double beat against his belly, and Carson wanted to suck on Tim's fingers? *Hnnngg.*

Oh yeah, he was coming back to horniness central, up Tim's arm, down his chest... Would he keep going? Was there about to be some mouth to cock action? At last? Tim hadn't just been waiting while Carson teased him mercilessly today, he'd been waiting his whole fucking life for this.

Oh jeez—Carson just licked down his hip and was coming back straight up the middle. With his tongue.

Right up Tim's shaft. To the tip. Oh fuck. He was gonna come down, with his mouth open. YES!!!!!!!!!

Or no. A big no. This was one of those milestone things. And he could never lie about it.

Tim jolted upright, catching Carson's face in his hands. "Wait."

Carson blinked. "Um, okay."

Jesus, there was no way to say this without sounding stupid and too young and mommy-whipped. Once the thought appeared it was there, and sucking out every bit of joy. "I can't do this yet."

"Okay." Carson swiveled and sat up, ending cross-legged, his hands in his lap. "Wanna talk about it?"

Talk about it? That was worse than stopping! No, Tim did not want to talk about how he couldn't lie back and let the most amazing man in the universe suck his cock! Not that there was much left to be worth sucking on—as soon as he'd imagined that fateful conversation of not honestly claiming to be inexperienced, he'd started wilting. Gawd but he was pathetic.

"I can't—I mean—I'm sorry, but … I can't. I don't want you to even imagine…" Oh yeah, Carson could probably imagine just fine. All the blood that should have been in Tim's dick went to his face. This was so stupid, but… He'd get eaten alive at home if he couldn't claim virtuous indignation at not doing what he wanted to do so badly.

"I should leave. I'm sorry. I'm really sorry." Tim babbled apologies at triple time, dashing to the bathroom to retrieve his clothes, pelting downstairs to his shoes left at the door. He was all fumbles and hunches getting them on, skipping his socks in his rush to take his mortification out the door.

"It's okay, Tim."

So soothing, but so wrong. Maybe it was okay here, but Tim had bigger problems waiting. "I wish it was. I'm sorry. I do want to, but..." He had to get out of here before he either died of embarrassment or changed his mind. He was fucked either way.

Carson followed him downstairs, still gloriously, dangerously nude. "Do you want me to drive you home?"

"*No!* I mean, no thank you." Another good idea that would jeopardize Tim's safety. "I need to be really, really sweaty when I get there. I'll run home the long way around the lake, it's about eight miles, that should do it."

Tim paused, his hand on the doorknob. "I'm so sorry, Carson. But..." Hell with it—he threw himself into Carson's arms. "This is for today. But..." He pressed his mouth to Carson's, not knowing if he'd get an answering kiss or a recoil. Carson responded, kind of, maybe it was a recoil. "I'm sorry."

Tim bolted, his vision blurred with tears.

———

Watching Tim flip out was like watching time lapse photography. Scurry, scurry, get dressed. Scurry, scurry, put on shoes, scurry, scurry, gone.

They'd been enjoying themselves in every way, and then, like a switch. The wrong thought. The cockblocking bitch might as well have materialized in the bed.

If he wasn't naked, with the last languor of what they'd

been doing, Carson could swear he'd never had company. Except the door was unlatched.

Nude or dressed, Carson never left the door unlatched. He opened the door wide enough to reach the deadbolt on the safety door, because getting that door latched was more important than his neighbor not getting an eyeful. Then the main door could be latched too. There. Locked down tight.

Carson leaned his forehead against the door. They'd been doing so well, and then, poof. Nothing.

He could understand it. And still hate it. Guess if only one of them was done with sneaking around like high school kids, then they weren't done sneaking. Carson thumped his forehead against the door, more for the thud than the pain.

Then he thunked himself twice more.

I will see you in hell, Lorraine Ratliff.

CHAPTER TWELVE

Gotta get out, gotta get out made a chant to set his pace by. Tim turned north on Alkire Street, the lack of sidewalks making this country lane just as dangerous as the games he'd been playing in bed.

Damn it, he'd been so close to getting what he wanted with Carson! Nothing keeping him from it, except fear. He had to get out of his parents' house, today. Yesterday. Long enough ago that Carson would never know him except as the guy with a future who wanted to get together.

He had to get a different job, he had to! Something in his field would by definition pay better than fast food, then he could move out of his parents' house, hand them back all the strings they used to keep him in line and go rip Carson's clothes off!

He passed the eagle tree on the west side this time, when he and Carson had come to it from the east. There had to be another approach to his job search. But what? He'd filled out on-line applications, he'd sent résumés by the score, and nothing was coming back!

Not even a "don't call us, we'll call you" rejection.

Nothing.

By the time he'd rounded the last corner on the approach to home, Tim was well and truly sweaty, hungry, and mad. He should have stayed where he was, flat on his back with his dick up, and let Carson have his wicked, lovely way. And where was Tim headed instead? Back to the house where She Who Must Be Obeyed could be waiting with snark and accusations.

What. The. Fuck. Was. He. Doing?

Caving in, that's what he was doing.

What was he going to do? Oh yeah, Tim was going to make some changes.

He pushed into the house, wiping the sweat off his forehead with the back of his wrist. Shower, food, job search.

His parents weren't back from church yet. Great. His extra eight-mile run hadn't been necessary, but better safe than sorry. Tim bolted through the kitchen, inhaling a breakfast that staved off the bonk. He could plan now, not just rail against his situation.

A shower, clean clothes, and action. He'd been doing the same things for weeks and expecting different results than the nothing he'd been getting. So, time for advice from a trusted quarter, and one he could scram to before the parents returned.

There'd be a fight if they found out, but that would be a welcome distraction from any Carson-based or gay-based fights.

Tim headed to his brother and sister-in-law's apartment.

Paul and Miyoko greeted him with open arms. "Timmy! Long time no see!"

No, not since his graduation ceremony three weeks ago,

when Mom had pretended not to notice Paul, and Dad brushed by with barely murmured greetings. They'd never had much to say to Miyoko, though much to say about her, and said even less to her at commencement.

Tim had hugged both his brother and sister-in-law, even daring to thwap his brother in the head with his diploma and tell him, "This is thanks to you." And of course that got snorts about who paid the tuition, but seriously, Paul, six years older and a cover-to-cover experimenter with *The Dangerous Book for Boys*, had been the one to help build batteries using lemons and quarters and write messages in invisible ink, not the parents.

"Hey, Miyoko!" Tim smished his sister-in-law's slender frame until she squeaked.

"What, you're not going to call me 'Bad Influence' anymore?" Miyoko almost looked affronted. Poor kid, she'd tried so hard to get Mom to like her at first and had finally dropped the rope before the wedding. Instead, she'd taken Mom's term as a badge of pride.

"If you want, but it doesn't seem so funny these days." Mom probably had a similar nickname for Carson. Tim turned Miyoko loose with a smile that went flat.

"Oh ho! Someone's hanging around with an undesirable companion." Paul pulled his wife against him back to front, his arms clasped around her waist.

Tim's face went hot. "Is it that obvious?"

"Face it, bro, anyone Mom doesn't hand-pick for you is going to be an undesirable companion." Paul rocked Miyoko side to side, his chin on top of her head. "So, come on in and spill the tea."

Tim followed them into the kitchen, tidy, minimalist in a way that meant every object in it was wanted and chosen. A rustic wooden panel with "Welcome" in navy calligraphic script beckoned him to sit down in one of the four chairs at the pine table. Something smelled of cinnamon.

The vibe was a lot like Carson's place. Was that why Tim felt so at home?

Paul poured iced lemon-water from a pitcher foggy with condensate, serving a tinkling glass to Miyoko first. Not because she'd demanded or expected, but with his smile saying it was his idea and his pleasure. Funny how the difference was clear.

Tim really should spend more time over here. With the nice people in his life.

Paul slid in beside Miyoko, resting his hand on her shoulder. Seemed like he couldn't not touch her, even in this heat. "So, baby bro, tell us all about your undesirable companion."

Not all, not even close to all, when Tim still burned with the flesh-memory of Carson's tongue. "It's not even the companion, so much as..." He hadn't thought this through. But Paul would be cool with him. And Miyoko... Wouldn't they? After all Mom and Dad put them through? His fingers heated trails into the glass he clutched too tightly. "Um, I came out to the parents."

Paul whistled a dying note. "How'd that go?"

"I suppose it could have been worse. I suppose it will get worse, too." Tim was glumly certain of that. "They haven't had a lot of time to get used to it, and I haven't been making it easy for them, because my only defense is a good offense, and I'm being as offensive as possible. They aren't entirely sure I'm not pulling their legs."

"Bold move, young Padawan." Was Paul surprised at the news or at the tactics? "I take it you're not pulling legs here?"

"Nope." Tim braced himself.

Paul pursed up his mouth, looking terribly like their mother.

Tim stopped breathing.

"Pick a good guy then." Paul barely unpuckered his face, but his focus wasn't on Tim. Didn't matter, oxygen was back on the menu. "I'd offer you shelter from the fall-out, but we're a little cramped here, and it's going to get worse before it gets better, since we're moving soon."

"Really? I thought you guys were comfy here." Tim glanced around: Paul had put his "fling things in piles" aesthetic away in favor of Miyoko's "everything in its place" décor. Even the pile of music on Paul's digital keyboard was neatly stacked, with his beloved *Indispensable Chopin Collection* on top of the blue-covered *Well-Tempered Clavier* and the spiral-bound *Piano Classics*.

"We are, but…" Miyoko smiled and dropped her eyes. "We bought a house."

"Oh, okay. Wonderful." Mentally scratching off one source of refuge, Tim went back to his worry. "So you guys are okay with me…?"

"Of course, you big dope." Paul looked at him like he had two heads, which was not reassuring. "Why wouldn't we be?"

"Um, because you're our parents' son, and learned…" Everything that Tim had.

"Learned that our parents are often full of shit." Paul curved his arm over Miyoko's shoulder. "You know what they put us through when we started dating, and how much worse it got. You think we're going to pass that along? Fuck, no."

"I'm sorry she wasn't nice to you." Tim had been forcibly removed from best man duties. "I really did want to stand up for you."

"You were eighteen. I don't see you had a lot of choice." Paul grinned. "And we did get Mom under control. Eventually."

Eventually took a while and control was a relative thing. Tim drummed his fingers against the table. "That's what I came to talk to you about. Getting Mom under control. I really don't know how much longer my current tactics are going to hold. Now that the cat's out of the bag."

"First priority is cutting any strings she can pull. When are you moving out?" Paul had been thrown out, when he'd made it clear that Miyoko wasn't "just a phase."

"Right after I get a better job. And that's… Paul, I don't know what's wrong, but I've sent out at least a hundred résumés, to places that are hiring, and—nothing. Not one single response!" All Tim's despair at the state of his inbox came out as a wail.

"Not even an auto response?" Miyoko asked.

"Nothing. I don't understand." It couldn't be his grades, or his references, or his work history, when even a cheese manufacturer with listed openings didn't think him worthy of an interview.

"That is weird." Paul resumed tapping the table. "Tim, which email address are you sending from?"

"The usual one, TRatliff@comment.net. I have makeit-goboom@gmush.com now, but that's not very profession-al." What, in all his documentation, looked so unprofessional that he couldn't even get told to get lost?

"Tim. Who set that email up?" Paul's voice was soft.

"Mom, way back when." It had always worked fine, too.

"Who's the administrator on all the comment.net profiles?"

"Mom." He'd never really thought about it. What could she do, anyway? "I think. Maybe Dad."

"What computers show on the household network?"

Another duh question: everyone on that router showed up on the network. "All of them."

"So you can get into Dad's laptop? Or Mom's?"

"I don't know. I've never tried." What could either of them have on their laptops that would be worth snooping through? Even if he dared commit the breach of privacy?

"Do you think that goes both ways?" Paul's voice was really, really soft.

"I... don't know." A cold pit opened south of Tim's sternum.

"Here's what you do know. Mom likes power and control. Dad backs up Mom on everything, without hardly thinking about it. What's Mom's plan for you?" Paul pulled Miyoko even closer; her chair squeaked across the floor.

Tim didn't have to think on that one. "She wants me to work at Monument Pharma, meet a nice Christian girl, and, I guess, eventually get married and have a family?"

"Are you doing any of that?"

A bark of sour laughter forced itself through Tim's throat. "I'd love to work at Monument, but it's the one place I haven't applied to. Can you imagine Mom with HR superpowers? 'No, dear, you don't get vacation time in June, you get it in August, so you can go to Grams's cabin with us.' At the very least. Girls, Christian or otherwise, not happening, and any of the rest is just... can't imagine how that would go." He shook his head.

"Nothing about 'you be happy and live your life, and Dad and I will go to Hawaii just the two of us now that you're grown'?"

Tim shook his head. "She doesn't even let me do my own laundry."

Paul sighed. "Now that I'm the black sheep of the family, you know all her dynastic hopes are pinned on you, right?

"Dynastic..." Tim's brain zotted out. Nothing in his mind had ever associated that with himself. He'd mentioned the white picket fence life Mom expected only because it was her expectation, because any real-world application to himself was so theoretical that the equations to describe it didn't exist. "Paul, I can't even imagine that. Um, me?"

"Yes, you. Someone's got to give her the grandbabies." A chuckle grew into a guffaw from the other side of the table.

Grandbab... grandb... gra... Him... Whah?

Even Miyoko giggled. "Oh, Tim, you should see your face."

He struggled to find words. "No. This isn't happening. We aren't discussing this. Grandbabies are your department."

"You know that, and I know that, but I don't think Mom's on board with that, given how she refuses to accept my wife. Since arguing with brick walls wastes your time and doesn't convince the wall, it's kind of a moot point." Paul's face went somber. "Her loss though." He squeezed Miyoko's shoulder. "And we're veering off topic. Back to your computer. Are you doing all your job search from home?"

"I started before I left Fort Collins, but yeah, mostly. All on my laptop." Man, was this an out of the frying pan and into the fire conversation, whichever way it went.

"Then Mom did something before you started your

search in earnest. Something that doesn't require active intervention every time you send out a résumé. You need to find it, and kill it, and then you'll get somewhere. There must be dozens of places that need you. You'll find something great. But there's something blocking you." Paul went serious, and Miyoko's lips thinned.

Something sure was. Someone. A lump of ice grew in Tim's belly. "I don't want to believe Mom would…"

"Neither do I, but Tim, she's done other stuff we didn't want to believe, either." Paul twined his fingers with his wife's.

She had messed with the wedding party, and worn the next thing to black to the wedding, but this?

"Mom wouldn't do that… Would she?" Tim clung to shreds of hope. Wasn't she supposed to be her son's biggest cheerleader? Not his biggest stumbling block?

"If she thinks she's guiding you down the proper path, do you think she wouldn't?" Paul had suffered for her guidance. So had Miyoko—Mom had tried "guiding" her into going away.

Carson might be in for some rough sailing. Some more rough sailing. Or not, if Tim got hired at one of the half dozen New Jersey chemical companies he'd sent résumés to. One fabulous morning in bed wouldn't be enough to relocate for. So at least one person would be out of guiding range.

"Earth to Tim, earth to Tim," his brother called. "What does she want you to do, jobwise?"

"Work at Monument Pharma," Tim replied mechanically.

"And she's done what to encourage you to do that?"

"Emailed me the job website addy about a million times, and dragged me into the office for a paper application." Meeting Carson had been the best thing to come of that display of power.

"So, do you think pushing you from one direction means she won't also pull from the other side?" Paul persisted. "This is Mom we're talking about. The same mom we predicted might wear black to our wedding. Tim, you've known her a long time. Yeah, this is bigger than not letting you to go to college in New York, but you know how hard she fights for what she thinks is right. Or wants, which to her is basically the same thing."

"Yeah, I know."

What Tim didn't know was how to get far enough away she couldn't keep fighting him, without first winning on all things where she was fighting him.

————

There was, of course, hell to pay when Tim got home, long after dinner. Mom and Dad were waiting, angry.

"I had other plans," he mustered the courage to say, when there was a break in the tirade about disrespect and going to church. "Paul and Miyoko send their regards."

Their regards weren't exactly warm, but Tim didn't have to mention that part. Not when the bare sentence brought both parents to a screeching halt.

Made a nice change from posturing and lisping about "hith virthinity" though he had entire scripts prepared to uncork.

He used the lull to escape to his room, where the chair under the doorknob kept his parents from barging in, though not from screaming though the door. He ignored them best he could while sifting through his email client, searching for the breach in his communications.

Nothing job-related turned up in his spam file. Nothing in the deleted files. Nothing in the handling rules, where Tim feared he'd find instructions for "divert [chemist] [chemistry] [pharmaceutical] [pharma] [laboratory] [interview] [job] to junk file."

Tim pulled Outlook apart in ways even Microsoft hadn't thought of, and—nothing. Not a trace of why his job search was coming up zero. Nothing.

Paul had to be overreacting. Understandable, considering, but still, overreacting. Mom wouldn't do that. No, the flaw had to be in himself. He'd somehow managed to underwhelm every lab director and HR officer in entire industries, from pharma to food. Except at Monument, and that only because Mom was the HR officer. She'd find him a pity job.

Maybe he should take it.

CHAPTER THIRTEEN

LORRAINE RESTRAINED herself to glowering when her path crossed Carson's Monday morning. Carson smiled back ever so sweetly. She might be enraged, but she kept her mouth shut.

Guess Dave had been quite convincing.

Perhaps Dave had not been quite convincing enough to keep her quiet if Carson provoked her more actively. Killing her with kindness would have to do.

Even when she snarled at him, Wes, and Angie on their way out the door. "Eat your lunch somewhere that isn't Cluckets."

Might be a good idea anyway: Carson couldn't talk to Tim about anything substantive while he was at work. Last night's texts had been *Are you okay?* and *Yes* without embellishment. It wouldn't be kind to tease by sitting there with his friends, talking about the man who'd catch hell for joining the table.

Which didn't keep Carson from replying, "I do like the

extra crisp thighs," before the door shut on her popping eyes.

They had shawarma for lunch.

"So, Lorraine doesn't love you any better this week?" Angie asked over her flatbread sandwich.

"Doubt it," Carson told her, and dove into the lamb and tzatziki without more explanation. Wes did not need to know how his little matchmaking adventure was going. Not that Carson could actually determine how things were going. His head still spun from the whirlwind that flew out his door yesterday.

Damn but what had started as a campaign to make Lorraine go crazy had turned into something else. Not that the Lorraine end of things wasn't satisfying, but Carson hadn't reckoned on getting fond of the guy taking the brunt of her shit.

He'd give Tim a call after work.

He'd give Tim a call and be extra sweet after the little spat at 5 p.m., when he bumped into Lorraine on the way out the door. Bitch had to have timed her exit perfectly to catch him outside the office, because Carson thought he'd waited long enough to at least see her coming across a mostly empty parking lot.

She still managed to surprise him at the car.

"You need to stay away from my boy!" she spat. "He doesn't need to have any truck with the likes of you."

"Or what?" Carson unlocked the BMW, with one fingertip on the panic button. He'd let the car's commotion startle her into backing off if he needed to. And he could slide in a sharp dose of the truth. "Have you even noticed he's not a boy anymore?"

"He's my boy, and you keep your filthy mitts off him!" she nearly screeched.

Carson admired his fingernails for a brief, sarcastic moment. "Nope, not filthy. Although..." He gave her a side-eye. "He's probably safe enough from getting his balls fondled because they're firmly in your purse."

He shut the BMW's door on her reply before she could splutter out more vileness.

Damn. Either Tim would find his spine and break free, or he wouldn't.

If Tim wanted help locating his backbone, and backup if he used it, Carson was his man.

———

Maybe Tim had rediscovered a vertebra or two, because Carson's phone rang ten minutes after he arrived home.

"Hey, Carson? Mind if I come over after work? I get off at seven, after the dinner rush."

Carson paused, half out of his dress slacks. "Sure. Anything particular in mind?" He could hope for something smoochy, but this back-away-closer guy might still be too skittish for even a hug.

"Maybe we watch a movie?" Tim sounded tentative, like he expected to be brushed off.

Not hardly. "Sure." Carson got his other leg into his basketball shorts and his mind in gear. What could he offer that Lorraine would have forbidden? "Anything you want to see in particular?"

"I... I don't really know. Something with humor, or fantasy?" Tim's relief gusted through the phone.

Had he expected to hear, "Sex or nothing?" Which would be his fear talking and not what Carson had said yesterday. "I'll rustle up a couple of choices, you pick, okay?" He had just the thing for a guy who'd only lately read Harry Potter.

"Great! Should I bring some chicken?" That sounded less enthusiastic. Well, Tim had been smelling it all day.

Carson already had his daily allotment of grease. "Um, no, that's okay. Unless you're hungry for it."

"No, not really." Tim laughed wryly. "I could..."

"I'll have snackage for us." Carson needed food that looked like it started in nature, and he couldn't think of anything Tim was likely to bring that met that requirement.

"Great! I gotta go. See ya!"

Carson smiled at the phone going dark in his hand. None of this sounded like he'd asked Mommy for permission to come over and play.

———

The munchies Carson had ready when Tim arrived were certainly not the chips and dip he expected. Note to self, Carson liked fresh veggies and hummus to snack on, and only the pita chips pinged as junk food. Barely. Tim scooped another dollop of hummus onto a celery stick.

Maybe if he reached for the pita chips, on the lean back he could bridge the six inches of couch separating them. If they both propped their feet up the same direction, Tim might recline against his host's chest while they watched computer-generated beasties create havoc in 1920s New York City. And not one more scene would make an impression after that.

Which would be okay, more than okay, they could watch the rest of *Fantastic Beasts and Where to Find Them* some other time, especially if Carson diverted his attention to

Tim. Since Tim was almost brave enough to do something fantastic to Carson, starting with a kiss and involving unzipping.

He still hadn't made his move when Carson casually rested his arm on the back of the couch, and with a smile invited Tim to lean against him.

Heaven. Even if his brain did short out.

He reconnected in a hurry when a spotlight just outside the sliding glass door lit up. "What was that?"

"Hmm." Carson cocked an ear in time to catch the scream. "Guess that wasn't a stray cat."

Dear Lord, no. That was Mom, and she screamed again. With words this time. "Damned plants!" Not even her atypical curse penetrated past *Oh fuck, she's here!* Tim froze.

"Damned plants just earned their keep." Carson rose and took the five steps to the slider. He kicked a dowel out of the door and flicked the lock. Through a six-inch opening he bellowed, "You okay there, Lorraine?"

"I've been cut!" she shouted back.

"That's what you get for trespassing." Carson re-secured the slider and swiveled the vertical blinds shut.

Oh man, if he thought drawing the drapes on Mom was going to make her anything but angrier, Carson was so wrong. Tim's heart banged against his chest. He should get up, he should let her in, he should— He shouldn't— What should he do? "Carson..."

What could he even say that would help?

"Don't worry, she can't get in." Carson threw him a wry smile. "And I'm not going out there. Did I miss much? Should I back the movie up?"

How could he be so calm? Especially when the doorbell

blew up with rapid-fire chiming? Every *bong* signaled a bigger explosion when she finally got her way. She always got her way.

The chimes gave way to furious pounding. And yelling, things like, "Open up this door immediately!"

Carson stayed on his feet, his raised eyebrow defying Tim to get up and answer *his* door. "If she keeps that up, the next-door neighbor will call the cops."

Dear God, Carson would let things get that far? Tim buried his face in his hands. "Could we not take it to the cops stage?"

"I won't call, but John next door likes his peace, and she's disturbing it." Carson didn't move.

"Maybe open the door?"

"Sounds like rewarding bad behavior to me." Carson reached for the remote. "If I go back about five minutes…"

"If it keeps him from calling the cops…" How could Carson not see how unthinkable that was?

"Actions have consequences. Even hers." Carson cranked the volume, which didn't drown out her commotion.

"Please, Carson? Open the door." Something inside Tim's chest broke and squeezed with every second he delayed obeying.

Why was he asking, when Mom was screaming, "Send my son out here immediately!" Wouldn't that be the stupidest thing he could do?

"Is she going to say anything you want to hear?" Carson paused the movie, which mercifully dropped the ambient decibel level below "need industrial ear protection." "Because as far as I'm concerned she can stay out there 'til the boys in blue haul her away if she's not smart enough to figure out nobody wants to talk to her. You don't have to go out there just because she demands it."

"There'll be consequences if I don't." Of that, Tim was horribly certain.

"She's going to ground you?" Carson sat down and backed the movie up a couple of scenes. "Or what?"

"She'd...." She'd what? Tim didn't know, but he didn't want to find out. "She'll think of something."

"About the only things she could do besides scream and threaten would be hold your documents hostage, which you can replace, or throw you out, which solves your going home to catch hell problem. Unless she has access to your banking, which you could have taken her off at eighteen." Carson paused to let a particularly loud bit of pounding on the security storm door pass. "Or I guess hold your computer hostage. Turn off your phone. If she hits you, you call the cops and push it through, but don't hit back. Anything else is pretty much dependent on the power you give her."

"The power I—" got interrupted by a shout from outside, deep, male, and pissed off.

"Knock it off!" brought silence.

For a moment.

Then a sobby plea: "Please, mister, you have to help me, he's holding my baby against his will!"

"Hey, Carson, you okay in there? What the fuck is going on?"

That did get Carson off the couch and to the door. He opened it but didn't reach to the deadbolt on the glass and wrought iron security door. A man about Mom's age, tall, muscular, and with Mom hanging off his arm with both hands, scowled down at her. Drippy red slashes marked her bare forearms, dark against pale skin in the porch lamp's light.

"Hey, John. Aside from the delusional kumquat on my doorstep, everything is peachy. The baby looks like a grown man to me." Carson stood aside and gestured to Tim on the couch.

In the face of Mom's screaming Tim didn't feel all that grown, but he'd fake it for Carson. If Tim didn't stand up, nobody'd see his knees shaking. He managed as nonchalant a wave as he could muster, and tossed a pita chip into his mouth, the only gesture he could think of that said, "Here because I want to be." If he dared chew and swallow, he'd choke for sure.

"What's the kumquat's problem?" The neighbor lost his scowl into something he needed to stroke his mouth for, once he jerked out of Mom's hands.

She glowered at being brushed aside. "I told you, he's holding—"

Carson interrupted her, something Tim never dared, even if his heart wasn't pounding hard enough to stop his voice. "Mommy here doesn't like admitting little boys grow to be men and make their own friends and decisions. Too bad, so sad, but they do, Lorraine."

Damn it, why couldn't Tim have said that for himself? Except that his voice would have come out as a squeak. Tim tried to swallow the boulder in his throat and found the pita chip had gone mushy enough to go down. Carson couldn't be the only one to stand up for him: he had to stand up for himself. He swallowed again, trying to find words.

"Okay, lady, you need to leave. I hear any more racket and I call the cops." John folded his arms across his chest. "Even if Carson's too nice to do it, I'm not."

She didn't respond to a word he'd said, though it sounded like promise, not a threat. "Tim, you come home right now!"

Tim found a voice, now that he had backup on both sides of the security door. "Movie's not over."

"Be home in ten minutes!" she shrieked. "That movie is not okay for you to watch!"

"At this point you're trespassing, Lorraine. Go away." Carson shut the door in her face. Dear Lord. He really shut the door in her face.

"Ten minutes, you hear me!"

"Damn, lady, seems like the only one trying to hold that guy prisoner is you." John's voice boomed through the doors. "Cops. Now."

"All right, I'm leaving, since you're on that pervert's side!"

"Us perverts gotta stick together against the likes of you!" got chopped by the slam of a car door and the gunning of an engine. Tires squealed. Something thudded, bouncing into silence.

Two quick raps on the door and Carson opened: he hadn't taken his hand off the knob during Mom's big dramatic exit. John stood in the doorway.

"She tried to kill your trashcan. What a bitch." He glanced past Carson to Tim, and his face went from "meant it" to "oops." "Sorry."

"You aren't the first one to say that." Tim rubbed his temples, while Carson let John in and made introductions.

Damn, why did Mom have to offend everyone in her quest to be in control? And why did she need to be in control over every little thing? Or was it just over him? And Paul? And Miyoko, and weddings, and jobs, and universities, and…. And. And. And, and, and… Every damned thing.

"Carson, dude, what's with you attracting crazy screamers?" John helped himself to a strip of red pepper and dipped it into the hummus.

"Just lucky, I guess." Carson made a face. "And being willing to tell them no, in spite of potential screaming." He glanced at Tim. "Long story."

"It can wait." Tim had all he could manage with the screamer who'd busted up their evening: he wouldn't push Carson into talking about anything that sounded like it went with his we're-not-going-there past. He couldn't think past the throbbing in his temples. "What am I gonna do now?"

"What do you want to do?" Carson gazed evenly at him. Like he had nothing but casual interest in the answer. Like he had nothing but casual interest in Tim.

Tim dropped his own gaze to the veggie platter. "Stay here and finish the movie."

"Works for me." Carson pointed the remote at the flat screen. "John, wanna watch with us?"

"Sure." John helped himself to a celery stick and dabbed it in the hummus.

"But—" Damn it! Another person to witness his humiliation hanging around.

"But what?" Carson remained poised with his finger on the button.

"I meant for longer term."

"I thought we covered that already." Though Carson did put the remote down. "Except for working out the logistics. Is your banking still connected to hers?"

"One account." The account she'd helped him set up when he was twelve and had dog-walking money. "I mostly use the account I set up in Fort Collins." He pondered. "I don't think she knows about that one. Maybe. I get paperless statements." His brother's concern rose in his mind—did she have access to everything because she could tap into his laptop through the home router?

"Is there enough money in there to hurt if she moved it to where you can't get it until you fall into line?"

Nice of Carson to not say "steal it." Also nice of him to not say, "Why the hell haven't you changed this?" But he could probably guess—easier to not rock the boat. Tim's unwillingness to face his mom's *Don't you trust me?* could cost him now.

"Mmm, yeah." Any sum would hurt to lose at this precarious stage. "I guess I better transfer everything, huh?"

"I would. Want my laptop?" Carson scooted to the edge of the couch.

"Mine's in my car." Tim had sent off another two résumés today, hoping that using the library's router would bypass the mysterious black hole he'd fallen into.

"Your car..." Why did Carson sound so concerned? "Any chance she'd show up with a tow truck? She spins a likely story about it being hers."

"I didn't think she'd show up here." Great, now Tim had another reason to bite his nails. "At this point, I have no idea what she'd do."

"Then put the Corolla in the garage. It'll look like you aren't here, and nobody can put it on a hook." Carson made a beeline to the back door.

"Um, maybe I should just leave? So you don't get dragged in? Um, dragged in more?" Unhappily certain his presence painted a target on Carson's back, Tim tried to think where he could go. Home? To appease Mom? Or could he claim a night on the couch with his brother? Did Mom even remember where Paul and Miyoko lived?

Carson paused in the doorway to hit the garage door opener. He turned to speak over the rumble of the mechanism, a dark figure against the sudden brightness in the garage. "Tim, I am as thoroughly dragged in as it is possible to be, and nothing short of moving to Nepal without a forwarding address is going to get me out. Leaving is only going to drag someone else in, unless you go home, and that's going to be a funfest, isn't it?"

Tim groaned. Would he get one hour of screaming or two? Or three? "I guess you're right."

"Hey, John, give me a hand with the dresser?" Carson called.

Everyone was doing their best to help, Tim told himself, while Carson and John wrestled a partially dismembered highboy to the side, and slid the drawers back in. A leprous thing, three colors of chipped paint and some sort of floral paper stuck to one drawer. Nothing that looked like it belonged in Carson's pristine home. Tim pulled into the second bay, next to the BMW.

He cut the engine and slumped. How had his life come to this? Hiding from his parents?

Hadn't he always known he'd have to hide from his parents? Who he was, what he wanted from life? That cat was out of the bag for sure. Now he'd taken refuge in someone else's home, because his own was a battleground.

If he had to make a tactical retreat, at least it was to someone who understood.

John left after a commiseration or two, and Tim opened his banking profiles, making money disappear from one and reappear in the other.

"Now change your passwords and associated email

accounts," Carson advised from the kitchen, where he stowed the food no one felt like eating now.

"Don't you think changing the emails is going overboard?" Passwords Tim could see, sure.

"Better safe than sorry." Carson stuck his head out into the living room. "Be a shame to find out you could have prevented a problem and didn't because it was an extra step."

Carson didn't know he had email issues already, and not for lack of trying to fix them. The last thing he needed was his money disappearing into the same black hole that ate his job search. Tim switched to his makeitgoboom account and went through the two-step authentication process, entering the codes that appeared as texts. "It's gonna be awkward if she shuts off my phone."

"Yeah, that's a possibility. Can you get your own account?" Carson returned to the couch to run a hand up and down Tim's back.

"Probably not without changing phone numbers. I think the account admin has to sign off on that, and Mom's in no mood to do me any favors." Her ten-minute deadline passed half an hour ago. Tim was afraid to stick his head outside, lest a fountain of sparks in the north mark her explosion.

"You're going to need a number you control for your two-factor IDs, so this can't wait. When do you need to be at work?" Carson's hand ceased its spinal journey.

"Not until one."

"You need to do this ASAP, Tim. Before you get locked out of anything. Has she ever tried stuff like this?" Carson sounded grim. "That might give you an idea of how long it will take her to think of things to control."

"Not that I knew of." Pulling him out of the wedding

party didn't seem like the same thing. "My first task in the morning, then." Together, he and Carson googled up a pre-paid plan with a free, if dated, phone, at a price he could swing without wincing, much. "I guess I can't tell her about this."

"I wouldn't. That would be giving her the power to do something about it." Carson pulled Tim back into the position they'd been in when the ruckus started, what, one short hour ago? "You want to finish the movie? Or another night?"

"Some other night." Tim scrunched his eyes closed. Maybe they could recapture the mood on a day Mom hadn't popped out of the woodwork, shrieking. "I guess I should go home."

"Daniel." Carson gusted out a sigh to ruffle Tim's hair. "Do you really want to go into the lion's den?"

"No, but…" He really didn't know what else to do.

"Then stay here." Carson squeezed him. "You know that bed's big enough for two."

Tim tensed. Hadn't that sparked half the problem?

"Or you can have the couch. But the bed's more comfortable, and we don't have to do anything you don't want to do. And if you don't want to do anything, you get a goodnight kiss and the sound of me snoring." Carson kissed the back of Tim's head.

"Oh man, you snore?" Tim reached for the only bit of levity he could find tonight. "That's a deal-breaker."

"Couch it is." Carson laughed.

"Nah, you can't be worse than my old man. He rattles the house." Tim thumbed out a quick text to his dad. *Staying with a friend tonight, see you tomorrow.* He turned the phone to *Do not disturb.* "Let's go to bed."

Carson peeling down to nothing but silky blue bikinis

was almost enough to chase the cold chunk of ice out of Tim's belly. Cuddling up with his head on Carson's chest felt like the most natural thing in the world, and almost enough to silence his mother's screams in his head.

He could almost believe he'd sleep tonight when Carson mumbled, "Wonder how she knew you were here?"

CHAPTER FOURTEEN

THE HOUSE BEING one degree away from a fortress let Carson conk out in spite of his question, though he wouldn't swear Tim had slept as well. Poor guy, such dark circles under his eyes.

He made enough coffee to fill the carafe, all four cups of it, and dressed for confrontation. Crisp white shirt, green paisley tie, which would likely be the only one in the office, and gray microfiber slacks all looked professional—just let Lorraine try to take him on.

On the other hand, why was he putting a grab-handle around his neck? Carson ditched the tie.

He kissed the top of Tim's head, bowed over his untouched coffee, his face in his hands. "I'll text you about whether or not your mom is in the office this morning."

"Why?"

Maybe Tim should drink that coffee and then he could figure it out himself. Carson tried jump-starting the uncaffeinated brain cells. "Anything you want or need out of the house, you can get it without a confrontation."

"What would I need to get?" Tim bleared at Carson.

"Your birth certificate, your passport, your Social Security card, the title to your car. Your diploma. Checkbooks, any credit cards, insurance cards, and such that don't normally live in your wallet." Just in case Tim was too sleep-deprived to remember, Carson added, "Clothes. Your treasured clarinet."

"I don't play the clarinet." Tim sipped at the coffee.

"Your violin, then. Or Gameboy DX, whatever. My point is, anything you can't do without, or replace easily, or need right away if replacing it takes a while or more money than you want to spend." Maybe Tim was too sleep-deprived to think this stuff through, but Carson was on high alert. He'd answered his own question last night as "Doesn't matter, it happened," but it had come back twice as hard this morning.

"I live there. My stuff is there. You're talking like I'm never going home again." Tim's knuckles whitened around the coffee mug.

"I didn't say that. But you have a window of opportunity here to make sure you aren't stuck there if you do go back. We talked about this last night, remember?" Frustration leaked into his voice, though Carson tried to remain calm. "That's why you're going to get that other phone."

"We talked about a lot of things last night, Carson. And this feels like pressure." Tim's lips went thin. "You said you weren't going to do that."

Oh. Not what was on his mind at all. Or not much. "Tim, you can have half the bed, an air mattress in the other room, hell, we can put you in the garage, far away from my lecherous grasp in the night. Or you can keep going back to your folks' house, as long as you won't get held prisoner by important stuff." Carson needed three cleansing breaths but dared not take more than one. "This has nothing to do with me, and everything to do with you. You need that phone."

"I'm not sure I need it." Coffee slopped over the rim of the cup. Tim set it down at enough of an angle to splash the placemat. "This is my mom we're talking about, not some crazed kidnapper."

Do. Not. Scream.

"I know. She's your mom and you love her. But this is the same mom who's blown up so hard that two different people have threatened to call the cops on her and that's just since you and I met. I don't know what you told yourself in the night that you're abandoning your sense of self-preservation, but I'm pretty sure she hasn't abandoned her belief that you being gay is wrong, and you being with me even for something innocent like a movie is wrong, and that I'm evil and dangerous for existing." Carson drew in a deep breath and let it out slowly. Oxygen had to help.

"So this is about you staying safe?"

"It's *always* about me staying safe!" Carson smacked the table hard enough to make the cups dance. "Why the hell do you think this townhouse is such a fucking fortress? Why do you think I planted Spanish bayonet around the patio and beneath every window? Do you think they're pretty? Or do you think sword plants might be intended to keep intruders from getting in? Motion detecting spotlights—are they just for show? Have you noticed that I lock doors as a matter of course, and that I drive the next best thing to an Abrams tank?"

Carson stopped to draw in a sob of breath—he'd never laid out his defenses to someone like this, never expected to. Not to someone who stared at him with horror. "Yes, I keep myself safe. And I'm trying to keep you safe now too, because I forgot the first fucking rule of staying safe, which is fly under danger's radar." He tried to rub the sudden throbbing in his forehead away with one hand.

"My mother's not dangerous, Carson." Whoa, did that carry an edge. To go with the delusion. "She's opinionated and thinks she's right all the time, but she's not dangerous."

"Has she ever been successfully challenged on anything important? If she's so not dangerous, why are you dancing the crazy dance trying to either hide from her or keep her happy? Why aren't you just applying to Monument Pharma like she wants you to? They'd take you in a heart-beat, you know." Ghat damn, the kid was dense!

And so was he. Carson should have figured someone like Lorraine would escalate. "And you never did say why she thought to look for you here."

At least Tim's wrinkled brows signified thought, or the need for thought, though it might be a buzzing confusion under those tousled waves. At last he said, "Well, of course she'd look for me around you."

Maybe his brain was engaging at last.

"Not what I said. Why did she think to look for you *here.* At my address, which isn't precisely a government secret, but close. An address which she should not know." Lorraine's knowing where to find him dripped a chill down his spine. "Did you tell her?"

"No, of course not."

"Then how, Tim? If you have Facebook check-ins acti-vated, you want to deactivate that ASAP." Not that Carson's house should even register like a business that desperately wanted to be found, but still....

Tim shook his head.

"Do you have a tracking app on your phone?" Carson threw out his next best guess. "A Friends and Family thing?"

"N-n-no, I don't think so." Said with no confidence at all.

Carson pounced. "But you don't know. You need to check, and if you do, you need to delete it, and if you can't find it, better assume it's there and you can't find it. Which is why you're going to do the smart thing and get a different phone. That you control and only you."

"Geez, Carson, you act like Mom knowing where you live is some big deal," Tim scoffed. "It's not."

Arrogant little shit didn't know the half of it. "It's a big deal to me." Forget taking the little prick to bed—Carson itched to kick his gay-virgin ass.

"But you're not going to explain because we don't go there, right?" Tim took another swig of coffee. "You're kind of paranoid, you know that?"

"Not paranoia if they're really out to get you." Had someone turned Tim into a fucking pod person overnight? Did Lorraine have him that brainwashed that he could only assert himself twenty seconds at a time? "We're going to check your car for trackers. It could be stuck inside the wheel well. Or in the glove box."

"No, we're not, Carson." Tim snorted. "My mom is not sufficiently techie to even know what to buy."

"That's what I said about my step-father." *Whoa, Eddinger, cut that off right now.*

"Well, Mr. Paranoid, you're making this way too complicated." Tim got up to pour a second cup of coffee, looking much too good in nothing but jeans to be such a bonehead. "She's HR where you work. She probably just looked in your file."

His file. His ghat damned file. Of fucking course.

———

159

Carson shot through the front door, past Lorraine's closed door and the cubicle farm, and down the corridor to Dave Pfeiffer's office. Through tight lips, he asked, "What are the rules about accessing employees' personal information?"

"Only for company-related business. Why?" The Human Resources director frowned at something not quite on his screen.

"Someone threw a lawn tantrum at my home last night. Someone who had no reason to know where I live. Is there any way to know who looked at my file recently and why?" Carson didn't sit down and wouldn't have even if Dave suggested he stop looming.

"Hmm." Dave tapped away, bringing up screens Carson couldn't see from his narrow pacing path on the far side of the desk. "Who threw the tantrum?"

"Do you even need to ask?" Carson snapped. "I was watching a movie with a friend, minding my own damned business, and your pal Lorraine showed up to peek in my windows and pound on the door. Screaming foul things at me and my neighbors."

Dave sighed. "You know I can't do anything about off-site incidents." He flicked his glance between Carson and his screen.

"I know. I'll let the cops handle that part. What I want to know is—who accessed my information and why? When?" Carson kicked the Chair of Tears, Manager Edition, hard enough to stub a toe. He came to a vibrating stop. "Because there was no easy, legit way for her to know where I live."

He'd kept that information out of circulation long enough that it was a habit more than active fear. Until he'd been given a new reason to look over his shoulder every seven minutes.

"This isn't proof, Carson." Dave tapped his mouse with one finger, staring at the screen.

"I'm not due for any training, I'm current on my certifications, which mostly fall in January anyway, and I haven't requested PTO. Who's accessed my information in the last week?" Carson would flip that screen 180 degrees and look for himself in four more seconds.

"Lorraine. Twice." Dave clicked. "Log says once last Friday and again yesterday."

"And I had her screeching ass on my doorstep last night." Carson leaned over the desk to get in Dave's face. "This is harassment, and she's using company resources to harass me. Get a muzzle on her, Dave, because I will take this as far as I need to in order to make it stop."

CHAPTER FIFTEEN

THIS WAS MOM. This was Mom. Who loved him. And yet... She did this.

Crazy.

Crazy to think someone who loved him would do... This. Yet he hadn't imagined last night. Had he?

But Mom beating on a door, yelling, was so far out of his comprehension that Tim had to ask himself if he was the crazy one.

He hadn't imagined the lying down in Carson's bed part, because he'd had to drag himself out from under the man's arm to toss and turn.

But the rest?

The world had turned inside out.

It was just too fricking much.

And now Carson was talking like Mom, his mom, who loved him, was some deranged—he couldn't even think of a word.

None of this computed.

Except here he was, barefoot and shirtless, drinking

coffee in the kitchen while Carson accused Mom of terrorist activities or something.

She wouldn't do that. Would she?

No.

Not possible. None of what he thought he remembered could possibly be possible. Moms didn't do that stuff.

Bossy, yeah, and protective, but this?

Carson's urgings were so much *wah wah wah* in the background while he fought with the concept.

"I gotta go, Tim. Use the keypads to shut the garage when you leave, okay? There's a phone store at 92nd and Wadsworth, I think they open at ten." Carson's palm rested warm on Tim's cheek—he opened his eyes at the shock of the contact.

"Get the phone. At worst, you've spent thirty bucks. At best, you've protected yourself." Carson came in for a kiss on Tim's forehead.

"Do you know how long it takes me to earn thirty bucks?" Tim had spent that on the car because he needed the car. In the light of day, a new, prepaid phone looked like a stupid extravagance.

"Not nearly as long as it will take to rebuild all your two-step authentications if that number gets turned off." Carson pulled his wallet out of his pocket and dropped a couple of bills on the table. "Humor me. Get the phone."

"Oh, all right." At least Tim could get *someone* off his back.

"And don't be surprised if she's super sweet to you for a while."

"She's my mom. Why would I be surprised?"

Carson really shouldn't scrunch his face up like that. "You have been paying attention to her behavior for the last week, right? 'Sweet' was not it. And it wasn't getting her what she wanted. So she's likely to change tactics. You have to be aware that it's tactical, and that her long-term goals haven't changed."

"I still say you're paranoid." Tim shoved the bills into his pocket. "Good thing you're cute."

Carson enveloped Tim in strong arms and a hint of citrus cologne. "Cute, accurate-not-paranoid guy here has to get to work."

Too bad Tim was still angry about all the shit-talking on Mom. He didn't hug back.

Not even when Carson said, "I'd like to be wrong, Tim. I really would."

————

His phone trilled the all-clear text from Carson. Proving that his phone still worked.

For now.

Dang it, Carson was rubbing off on him. Tim was pretty sure he had an accurate read on Mom, and now he was waiting for her to do the underhanded things Carson speculated.

But he'd waited to head home until he knew where she was for sure.

Dad, well, he was a reasonable sort, aside from backing Mom up 98.5% of the time, and he'd already used the 1.5% for this week. Would he stay home, lying in wait?

Apparently not.

Tim's keys still worked, a point he'd make to Carson.

Of course, it was still only nine o'clock.

Hating himself for doubting, Tim dug through his files, looking for his car title. Wouldn't hurt to know where that was. Whew, in his desk drawer, right where it belonged.

Maybe, just maybe, it would be safer somewhere else.

He chose the most unlikely to be examined, unlikely to be used spot he could think of, tucked into the yellow-bound *Indispensable Chopin Collection* in the piano bench. Mom didn't play, nor Dad. Tim's single year of lessons had ended in tears when he refused to count *one-y-and-a-two-y-and-a three-y-anda four-y-anda* out loud while his fingers forgot what they were supposed to do.

Paul was the pianist. He'd rolled the bass-heavy storm of the Raindrop Prelude from this very book while Tim lolled on the floor, playing quietly and wishing he could coax that music out of the gleaming oak upright that had belonged to their late grandmother.

Paul had his own home now.

His piano was here.

Made sense, really. Not easy to get a piano into a second-floor apartment, and it would take up most of the living room. Maybe when he and Miyoko moved into their new house. Tim would happily spend an afternoon helping his brother schlepp the piano across town.

Of course, then Paul would have duplicate Chopin music, and duplicate Bach, and duplicate...

Duplicate everything, of nice portable piano music, that no one here needed.

Maybe he should go find his Social Security card.

Halfway up the stairs, Tim's phone rang.

"Tim, my daycare just called. The baby's vomiting." Gail sounded near tears. "Can you please come in and run the shift? I have to go, like, five minutes ago."

Bet she made other calls first; the extra time would put him perilously near the forty hours Cluckets never scheduled. But this was Gail, and he owed her one. And the extra hours would cover the new phone, if he decided to get it. "Be there in twenty. Hope the baby's okay."

Oh well, everything would still be there when he got back.

Man, Carson had to be full of it—Mom was happy to see him when he came back after an overfull day of feeding the customers.

"Hi, honey." Mom smiled brightly across the Formica-topped island in the kitchen. "Are you hungry?" She flipped greens with two big spoons, as if last night had never happened.

"I had dinner at work." He'd been on his feet so long he'd gobbled down the extra crisp poultry he'd grown tired of after five years. "Thanks, though."

Here was the mom he'd always thought he had, who'd had some hiccups around important events but was really a great human person, who'd had a moment or afternoon or a couple of afternoons....

While he slid out of his uniform and into some jeans, he decided how he'd let her know his plans. Since she sounded so chill.

"Headed over to a friend's," Tim offered on the way out, instead of sitting down at the table with Mom and Dad. "Might be real late."

"Have fun, dear," she said.

What the...?

"That means you won't..." How could he give the short version of last night so his father could understand how big a breakthrough he witnessed, instead of accepting the salad and pleasantries at face value?

"Silly," Mom smiled, but there was a hint of tension in her jaw. "I may have been a teensy bit upset, but have some faith in your mom, please."

If that wasn't the biggest spin ever to be put on an altercation.

"'Kay," seemed like a better idea than fighting out the discrepancies of last night versus right now.

"I'm not even asking where you're going, dear." Though she gave him that arch look that meant *As if I don't already know.*

"Because we don't want any more of your gay histrionics." Dad snorted.

Tim pressed the back of his wrist to his forehead. "Are you thertain?"

"Yes!" in stereo, and not another word did either of them say about it.

If she was going to be pleasant— And ask for trust—

"Can you dig out my passport, please?"

"Why ever do you need that?" Mom shook some seed and dried fruit topping onto the salad.

"I thought HR always asked for citizenship documents for new hires." Tim held his breath.

"Oh that, yes. I'll just make a copy and take it into the office." She smiled over the salad bowl.

"I have other interviews, Mom," Tim lied, planning to make it the truth. If he had to be TRatlif-f95784622@gmush.com, he was going to have other interviews.

"I might not be able to get by the bank tomorrow. We'll see." She leaned down to peer into the oven.

"It's important, Mom." Tim kissed her cheek as usual, hoping that would be enough to buy her continued cooperation.

He wanted to kiss a lot more vigorously once he got to Carson's place, but Tim's recounting of his exit from home didn't relax Carson much—he kept glancing to the door.

They managed to see the end of the *Fantastic Beasts* movie, which wasn't nearly as interesting as kissing Carson, but the tension restrained Tim, too. Their clothing stayed on. Dang, Mom could cock-block him by being on her best behavior!

The smooching didn't improve after the movie, when the conversation turned to, "Did you get your papers? How about that phone?"

No, and no, and Tim could get a little pissed that Carson wouldn't let it drop. He didn't stay late.

Carson was really making mountains out of molehills. Why shouldn't Tim try a polite request?

Next morning, he picked up a call. "Hiya, Mom." Inspiration struck before she could tell him what she wanted. "Can I take you to lunch?"

"What a lovely idea," she purred. "Dress nice."

Did she expect a pricy repast at the white-tablecloth Italian restaurant on the other side of the main road? "It'll have to be someplace casual. I thought maybe the pho place? It's close to the bank. We could drop in and get my passport." Tim held his breath: how would she play this?

"That's fine," she agreed. "Be here by eleven thirty. And I meant it. Button down shirt, dress slacks. It will be an incentive to keep the soup off your clothing. And iron the shirt. I will not be seen with a ragamuffin."

She was fricking nuts, but if a dress shirt got her into the bank and his passport into his hand, he'd dress for the occasion.

She never did say why she called. Guess he'd find out when he got there, not looking like a refugee from behind a fast food counter. Carson could get a look at him dressed professionally. Tim wouldn't mind teasing him a little, with lookie-no-havie the guy in the tie to add spice for tonight.

Eleven twenty-seven saw him buzzing in at the Monument Pharma admin building. Promptness was a virtue, as he'd been told at least a thousand times, and he had every reason to keep her sweet. Maybe it wouldn't last, or maybe it would. He could hope—he liked this version of his mother.

She met him at her office door. "Oh, you wore a tie, good boy!" Mom didn't acknowledge his cringe. Did she have to call him that when Carson sat not thirty feet away with his mouth hanging open? Tim pulled his shoulders back. *Confidence, dude, confidence.*

She shoved a sheaf of papers into one of his hands and grabbed the other. "Come along, dear."

The door to the parking lot was *that away!* Why was she towing him farther into the guts of the building? And why was he letting her? Because freedom lurked on the other end of this lunch, with his passport in his hand, and he dared not rock the boat. "Mom—"

"You're meeting with Dave Pfeiffer, my boss, and Ron Altieri, the head of the Product Development lab. You're interviewing for a Chemist I slot, and don't you dare embarrass me. We'll have lunch when you're done." She smiled sharkily at him, daring him to contradict her in any way, and shoved him through an open door. "Gentlemen, your 11:30 appointment is here."

After that, there was really nothing else to do besides put his hand out and say all the right things. *Think of this as rehearsal for all the interviews to come.* He could mess up with these guys because he wasn't going to work here. He'd run twice as fast for this being a stealth interview, set up without his knowledge or consent, but Tim refused to give it less than his best. *Practice what you mean to perform,* he told himself, and spoke easily about his 4.0 GPA and his part time job in a professor's lab. Not caring kept the butterflies out of his stomach.

At last, the lab director rose and offered another handshake. "We'll be making a final decision soon."

Dave also rose for his exit. "One thing, do you think you can maintain a professional demeanor when you have family working here? You'll be in different departments, but I do have to ask."

With perfect sincerity, because he intended to never put it to the test, Tim replied, "It won't be any problem for me."

Welp, that explained why Mom called this morning, and he'd walked right into it. She'd have to admit he needed his documents if they offered him a job.

Tim pulled into the bank before taking her to lunch, because Mom couldn't deny he needed his passport now, not when she burbled on and on about how he'd aced the interview.

Before she even got out of the car, Mom peered into her handbag and made the errand useless. "Oh dear, the safe-deposit box key must be in my other purse."

CHAPTER SIXTEEN

THE SCENT of new-mown grass filled Tim's nostrils as he and Carson ran through one of the parks that threaded the neighborhoods like green jewels on the string of the concrete bike path. Children shouted and tumbled on the playground equipment in the fading heat under the evening sun. Parents pushed little kids on the swings or supervised from the picnic tables, one eye on their phones.

The trouble with running side by side with someone was that it was impossible to ogle their ass. Carson had on those microscopic red shorts again, and Tim remembered a jockstrap this time. Strictly for the run—he had every hope of getting admired and then peeled out of it. A lot of things had gone right today, including Mom not questioning him when he left the house with his running gear.

So maybe he could get another dose of this non-devirginizing gay experience. Carson understood what the issues were, he'd been really understanding last time. If Mom got on his case again, Tim could tailor any necessary crudity to avoid their specific activities.

"I caught it once, do I still get to pat it?" Tim asked.

"After your freak-out the first time, do you still want to?" After two miles, Carson still spoke without huffing and puffing.

"Yeah, I'm sorry about that." Tim had some time to think things through, and besides, this new, sane edition of his mother might not need his gay virgin spiel. "And yeah. I would love to do some patting."

"I didn't expect to see you at Monument this morning." Carson swiped at his forehead, never breaking stride. "What happened?"

They still had another mile to run, guess they had to talk about something. "Mom set up an interview for me and didn't mention it. Went pretty good, too, so it's kind of sad I can't actually work there."

Mom might have calmed down, but Tim still didn't want her knowing his salary or scheduling his vacations.

"A surprise interview, huh. She filled out the application for you?"

"I... I guess so?" Damn. Tim hadn't even questioned that—steamrolling him into the interview seemed so in character for her that he hadn't contemplated her methods. He'd handed over the paperwork she'd thrust into his hands, the same information he'd sent around the country in a hundred emails. "She had a copy of my résumé, so she probably got the info right."

"Where'd she get that?" Carson swung around a curve and took them back to the sidewalk along a deserted street.

"Hah, she wrote most of it." A quick glance at the sheets he handed to Ron Altieri confirmed it was her version, not his.

"Dude." Carson's disapproval positively dripped.

"I mean, I asked her to proofread what I'd written, and

she, ah, really got into it." His mom might drive Tim berserk, but he wasn't going to let Carson throw shade on her, or on him. "I've been using my own version for everything else."

Maybe he should have used her version. His own sure hadn't brought any results. Had the two applications he'd made today disappeared for good like the rest?

———

Running with a companion was a whole different workout than running solo. Carson almost always ran alone because none of his friends could keep up.

Tim could. On the running paths at least. As far as seeing the bigger tactical picture of his life, he still limped along.

Hard to see when you were still in the FOG. Fear, obligation, and guilt made a pretty dense smokescreen, hard to see how bad things really were. At least he was trying to get out on his own.

Carson stopped them at the edge of his townhouse's development to scan for cars that shouldn't be there, or anyone prowling around trying to get past his lovely spiky clumps of Spanish bayonet. The sun hadn't dropped far enough that the spotlights would respond to movement.

All clear.

For now.

Locking the door behind them, Carson suggested, "Shower?"

That got an enthusiastic, "Yeah!" Tim trotted up the stairs. Guess he knew the way now and was ready for a little britches-off activity.

Carson followed, liking the view. He started the water

and stepped into the shower to be embraced. Tim wasn't shy this time, starting kisses and initiating a little tongue.

A noise loud enough to penetrate the running water jerked Carson out of the moment, tension thrumming though him.

"Garage door," Tim said, and tried to reengage.

"Whose garage door?" Carson left Tim in the water—he had to know. Leaving a trail of wet footprints, he ran downstairs to peer out the back door. Tim's Corolla sat next to his BMW, undisturbed, with the garage door down. Someone—John—called out, "Damn it, Leon!" on the far side.

Neighbors. Okay. False alarm. His heart rate could come down now. Slower rhythm and more volume would fill his cock again.

Back in the shower, he tried to lose himself in Tim's attentions. Soapy hands and dancing tongues, all good, and their bellies slipping together. Carson slid a hand between them to grasp their erections.

"Feels good," Tim groaned, thrusting into Carson's grip.

Yeah, did. Only take Tim to orgasm now—he'd be up again before long. Twenty-two and no refractory period to speak of. Carson remembered those days. He shifted them to get the spray off the back of his head.

The clatter at their feet killed the moment. Carson jerked away, his heart leaping. Nobody came through the bathroom door.

Tim picked up the shampoo bottle. "I must have knocked it over."

"Let's take this to bed." Carson would bypass the towels just to be in a surprise-free zone.

Rinsed, dried, and shy again, Tim let Carson kiss his way down. Maybe he'd let Carson kiss all the way down tonight. They had time—they had all night. He could spend quite a while on Tim's neck, nibble an ear, flick a nipple. Make Tim want the heat of Carson's mouth on his cock.

A shriek from outside—oh, a child's laughter. Carson slumped his head against Tim's chest, panting. Just let him catch his breath, he'd go back to that nipple, or the other one…

"You are really jumpy tonight." Tim rose up on an elbow.

"You're weirdly calm." Carson spoke to Tim's pec. Recovering from the jolt got harder and harder, and his cock went the other way.

"It's like you think M—someone's going to leap out at you." Tim folded his arms into a pillow behind his head.

"Recent evidence suggests that, yes," Carson agreed. Damn, she didn't even have to try to break in again—she was already in his head.

"Okay, she was weird once." Tim snorted.

Carson rolled to his back, not touching Tim. "Once? Tim, your normal meter is broken to shit."

"What?" Tim sat up, glowering. "It is not."

"Yeah, you've normalized her behavior until you can't see the waving red flags." Carson sat up too, to glower. "You're seeing the other night as just her being her, a little worse than usual but no big deal.

"But it is a big deal. Nobody just falls into the Spanish bayonet, everyone who *isn't trying to break into my home* stays away from it! That's why it's there! So, yeah, I'm jumpy. And I don't understand why you're not."

"Mom's just the way she is." Tim dismissed his

concerns with a flick of his wrist. "But she was really nice last night, and this evening."

"And you think she's had this big change of heart."

"No, she probably hasn't, but she's maintaining. Honestly, Carson, give her some credit!"

Tim's erection was wilting to limp as his own. Maybe the guy could think better that way?

"When someone shows you who they are, believe them the first time. Lorraine's shown herself, and then she pulls back to normal behavior and you want to believe that so hard you're ignoring everything else."

"You can quit shit-talking my mother." Tim swung his legs out of bed and grabbed his jeans. "I mean it, Carson. I had my sexuality on hold until I met you, I can hang on a little longer until I find someone who—"

"Who won't ever stand up to your mother? Who can't help you stand up to her? I'm not shit-talking her, I'm pointing out the cold, hard reality of what she's doing. Which you seem bound to ignore, like you don't want to know." Carson sprang to his feet as well. "Tim, I understand wanting to believe a parent isn't really doing what they're doing, and I even understand holding on to that belief until reality hits you in the face."

"Your sad history that we don't talk about, yeah, yeah, yeah, I get it." Tim fought his way into his shirt.

Damn it! "Try 'voice of experience.' Would you at least learn from my mistakes and not repeat them?"

Shoving his running gear into his bag, Tim snarled, "Since you won't actually tell me what those mistakes are, because we don't go there, I guess I'm shit out of luck."

Clenching his fists against his thighs would keep Carson from using them. "I am telling you what the mistake was! I believed my mother and the shitstain she married wouldn't escalate, because she was my mother and mothers don't do shit like that, and mothers don't let their husbands do shit like that. And I kept believing that right up until—" The memory of a fist growing huge, the pain, stole Carson's voice. "Right up until they did."

"I'm sorry about the escalation, whatever it was, but my mother isn't them." Tim slung the bag over his shoulder.

"I know that, but I also know she surprised you with an interview you didn't request, for understandable reasons, and that she *tried to break into my house.*" Ghat damn it all! Could Tim not step back for one minute to consider that a crime for anyone else was a crime for her too? "You said it yourself, you have no idea what she might do next, but you were nervous enough to park in the garage. And you think two civil encounters lasting, what, an hour total, cancels out the rest?

"Close the garage door after me, Carson." Tim marched out the bedroom door, headed for the stairs. "I have a job search to work on."

CHAPTER SEVENTEEN

YES! Tim needed to get out from under his mother's thumb. YES! He needed to stand up to her, and no, he didn't know what she'd do next, but couldn't she get all reasonable just as well as she could get worse? Mom had to have reevaluated her approach since Monday: she'd looked stupid in front of John and Carson, and she hated looking stupid. Of course she'd be nice after that.

And after getting a couple of savage burns about how she treated her son, she'd reevaluate that too. Right?

No, Carson didn't get to talk about her like she was some kind of maniac. Bossy, yeah, controlling, but that was for Tim to say, and Paul. Nobody else.

Maybe he should just shut down this whole "hang with Carson" thing until he'd scored a job. Which was the same as shutting down on Carson completely, because most of the jobs he'd applied to were out of state. He could email the cheese manufacturer again. After he quit seething about the way Carson talked about his mom.

Guess he wasn't going to do quality control on mozzarella.

He waved good night to his folks, who were camped out on the master bed, watching Jimmy Fallon writing weird thank you notes. With his bedroom door shut, he opened his laptop. Maybe Glass Door had some new listings.

Still no responses to his other queries. Why the heck...? Something would come up soon.

Nothing tonight though, and Tim was way too wired to sleep yet. Forget whacking off to relax: he'd only think of Carson and how sex that looked headed to his first ever blow job fell completely apart. And if his thoughts strayed to their fight.... Nope, tonight's stiffy was gone for good.

Might as well make sure he had his Social Security card and birth certificate handy. Though why hadn't he seen them when he found his car title? They should be together. Mom wouldn't have taken them to the bank with his passport, would she?

Tim's breath came short while he clawed through the hanging files in his desk drawer and found nothing. Last time he remembered seeing it was when he applied at Cluckets. No, it was after that, when he'd taken it in to the financial aid office, last fall. Mom went with him, and she'd taken the pile of documents home with her....

Well, he didn't need to keep important papers in a dorm room, where people meandered in and out.

Bet she put them in her paperwork. In her desk. Which meant they were about as far as the moon. Mom's desk was in the master bedroom, and she and Dad had the door closed.

They'd still be there in the morning.

———

Fixing Mom a to-go cup of coffee just the way she liked it didn't really qualify as sucking up. Even though he handed it over with "Please don't forget to go to the bank, Mom. Do you want me to come with you?"

"That won't be necessary, dear. And thank you." She accepted the cup with a smile.

His dad poured his own mug. "You slept at home last night. Trouble in paradise already?"

Tim couldn't do anything about the flush on his cheeks, but he could fix the cringing. With an overly-dramatic wrist to his forehead, he announced to the ceiling, "Oh Father dear, there ith no paradithe to trouble."

"Ugh! Will you stop that!" Dad barked.

"Oh, don't worry about it, Glenn. This gay thing's just a phase. Over soon." Mom swept out, mug and purse in hand. "Have a good day, fellas."

Tim watched them leave for work, shaky inside over the truth of his campy performance. If his and Carson's fight last night hadn't killed off their chances, distance would, soon.

But meantime: Carson had a point, even if it came with a whole bunch of other nonsense.

Time to find his papers.

He checked his own desk again, and no, not lurking, nor had they gotten tucked into any of the notebooks he'd dragged home after graduation and couldn't bear to toss just yet. Looking amongst his college remnants let him stall on going into Mom's desk. He wanted absolute certainty she wasn't going to appear, leaning against the doorjamb with crossed arms, saying, "Just what do you think you're doing, young man?"

She was darned organized: even Carson would have to be in awe of her tidy desk with labeled files. Tim reached for the one marked with his name to leaf carefully through old standardized exam results and immunization records. His birth certificate should be in here too.

Wasn't.

Tim leafed through the folder again. Still nothing.

Maybe she misfiled it into Paul's folder.

Jackpot! Hah hah on her, not that Tim would dream of teasing her—her desk was more sacred even than her purse.

Except—that wasn't his name. Paul's birth certificate and other paperwork were all there, but not Tim's.

He pulled out his phone. This was important enough to call his brother at work. "Hey, Paul. Need your passport?"

"What?" came sharply. "Wish you'd asked me that before I spent the $135 to replace it as stolen. Where'd you find it?"

"In Mom's desk, in your file." Tim rifled again, imploring the file to cough up his documents as well. Though why wasn't Paul's passport in the bank with his?

"Wasn't there when she told me I could look, 'cause she didn't have it. Did you find any other important papers?" Paul sounded angry, not desperate.

"Social security card, and birth certificate." Only Paul's, not his own. Damn it.

"You might as well put them back where you found them, because I've already gotten duplicates. And Tim," Paul growled, "if you find yours, hang on to them, because they're a bitch to replace. You need one to get another. You do have yours, right?"

"No," was a choked admission. "I'm looking now." His brother always had been a superior strategist. Now Paul echoed the man Tim had dismissed as paranoid.

"That sounds like they aren't in her desk, then."

"I haven't gone through the whole thing yet. There's a

lot." A daunting number of files, but he could pull each hanging file for a quick zip without removing the contents.

"Do yourself a favor. Ask yourself 'Where is the last place I, Tim, would think to look for anything?' and look there. Then tackle the desk if you have to."

Tim shuddered. "I can't rummage through her underwear drawer."

"Don't. It's the first place you thought of. First place everyone thinks of, it's a cliché. So is the freezer and taped to the bottom of desk drawers. Where is the *last* place you'd think of?"

"If it's the last place I'd think of, I might be a while getting to it." Damn it, he needed more concrete help. "What do you think?"

"Think fast," his brother advised. "The last place I'd think of might not be the last place you'd think of, though I'd check for anything taped to the wall above the closet door, inside where you can't see and nobody has reason to look. Did you solve the mystery of the emails yet?"

This morning Tim would have thought those two things unrelated.

"I found a bunch of things that weren't wrong." The icy fist around Tim's heart tightened. Mom was more ruthless than he wanted to believe, but more cunning as well? More cunning than Tim was, or could hope to be?

"Sounds like push is coming to shove, Tim." Paul paused, and Tim could practically hear the gears turn. "If you need a place to stay and don't mind moving boxes, I can offer you the couch. Then the couch moves. You could move with it. Because I don't want her doing to you all the things she did to me."

"Thanks, Paul. You don't know how much that means." Tears prickled behind his eyelids. Not everything it meant was good. Meant Carson was right. That he couldn't tell himself Monday night was an aberration, or that he'd imagined it in a movie-induced dream.

Meant that he really couldn't trust the one person he thought he could always trust, and he didn't have time to cry about it.

He ran the flashlight over the inner walls of all the closets, and about had a heart attack when he found a manila envelope on his father's side of the master closet. Then he did have a heart attack over the contents, a couple of yellowed photos that had to be taken pre-Paul. Dear God, eye bleach, STAT!

He never, ever, wanted to see that again.

And then he knew where his documents might be.

A white, letter-sized envelope hid under the sink in the master bedroom, behind a blue plastic packet of a product he'd never need and never thought about. An envelope that made it impossible for him to lie to himself.

An official green certificate folded over the stiff blue passport booklet and his Social Security card. Everything he searched for, things he needed for his life as an independent adult, tucked away where the sanitary products lived, defended by a guy's never wanting to think about *those* and his mother.

His passport, which could not possibly be in the bank vault, because it was here in his hand.

She might have been mistaken, but... Tim went back to her desk, checking the drawer where the keys and unused credit cards lay in a shallow tray. The blue tagboard packet with the bank's name and *Box 2457* sat on top of a JC Penney's credit card and a Blue Eyes White Dragon card she'd taken from Paul for safekeeping fifteen years ago.

No. This couldn't be true. Tim leafed through the passport. Yeah, that was his face and scrawled signature, the few stamps within matching up to his high school trip to Spain.

He put everything back where he found them. Everything. Because Mom had to be so secure in belief he'd never go into her vanity, let alone rummage through the cotton balls and makeup and girl stuff that she hadn't even sealed the flap.

Two could play at this.

Let her think he didn't know or that he couldn't figure it out. Let her be confident that she'd outwitted him. That she'd win any battle that required his documents as a weapon.

A ghostly Carson whispered at the back of his mind that he could take the contents and leave the envelope, but Tim dared not give her any reason to think up worse tactics than she already had.

Nope, he put everything back, except the Social Security card, which he tucked into his wallet. She could freak about what she'd done with it if she even thought to check, and he had the major building block to replacing the rest.

Next stop, phone store.

———

The acid built in Tim's gut with every hour he spent behind the register or assembling chicken dinners. Apologizing to Carson would be the easiest thing, and most heartfelt thing, he'd do all night. He'd left the laptop in the Corolla's trunk, parked three lots over in the employee area of a barbecue joint. He couldn't disguise his license plates, but he could pull the Purloined Letter method off as well as Mom could.

By the end of the dinner rush, he'd almost decided how

to handle things tonight, home and elsewhere. Though no strategic plan ever survived contact with the opposition.

Need to talk, can I come over? he texted Carson. *Off at 7.*

K was his answer. Not welcoming, but not *fuck off, stupid* either.

Because he deserved that. He could only hope to make amends.

Fifteen minutes after clocking out found him walking through the front door of the place he'd always considered home. Home was where you should feel safe. Home was where you should feel welcome. Part of the life there.

Not scared. Not wondering which landmine you'd stepped on today.

Not taking a change of clothes to work was just flat out stupid, but Tim would plead high anxiety and not thinking clearly in the face of shock. Not that Mom was ever susceptible to those arguments when it conflicted with her preconceived notions.

He absolutely had to maintain perfect control of his face. No matter what. He made it through the evening pleasantries okay, and barely stumbled when he set his trap. "Did you bring my passport home, Mom?"

"No, dear." She didn't miss a beat. She never even bobbled pouring her coffee. "I took a copy of the necessary pages at the bank and put it back. It's in your file at Monument."

Tim went numb. He'd touched his passport this morning. Shock was an accidental ally—he didn't blurt, *"The master bath vanity is a safety deposit box now?"* "I'm going to need it for other interviews."

"Nonsense, dear. You've had the only interview you need." She added sugar to her after-dinner cup. "Ron was quite taken with you."

He waited until he was a block away to scream, "Liar!" and beat the steering wheel.

His shaking hadn't subsided when he pulled into Carson's empty drive. Of course he'd have the BMW in the garage. It might be a tank, but it was a pretty tank and no sense making it an easy target.

Tim rang the bell, holding up the new phone for a greeting.

"Do you want to put the Corolla in the garage?" Carson didn't unlatch the door.

"Please." If Monday night was "a teensy bit upset" then the Corolla might become scrap in a smoking crater. Or Mom'd be a grease spot if he had to deal with her before he'd gotten himself under control.

Tim came through the back door with his laptop clutched to his chest. "I'm sorry about this morning. That I didn't believe you. You were right."

Carson didn't try to hug him, but hitched a hip against the kitchen counter. "About anything in particular?"

"About enough of it that you're probably right about all of it." There wasn't enough air in the kitchen to fill Tim's lungs. He had to set the computer down before he cracked the case. "She had my documents hidden. She had Paul's. I didn't know she'd done that until I found them and called him."

"You have yours now, right?"

"I left the bigger ones hidden, it's a real good hiding spot and I didn't want her to think I knew." Maybe asking for them, drawing attention to them, hadn't been his best idea. "And she said my passport's in the bank, when I saw it myself. She lied to me, Carson."

"You had to see that for yourself. I'm sorry you had to see it at all." Carson opened his arms.

189

Tim threw himself against this rock of a man who'd called his mom's every move. He shook until the tears came. "Why would she do this?"

"Power and control, boo." Carson held him tight, patting. "Power and control."

CHAPTER EIGHTEEN

COMING out of the FOG hurt.

Carson remembered—he'd been there himself.

Fear. How much of Tim's pain came from being afraid of his mom? Or from feeling the obligation to be a good son as she defined it? Or the guilt from wanting not to disappoint her?

Man, but the FOG had to lie thick for Tim to have flipped so hard overnight.

The fog over the Denial River, longest river in the world, the hardest to cross.

Words alone couldn't have burned that FOG away: Tim had to see it for himself. One thing to know his mom was controlling and embarrassing in her pursuit of keeping him in line, and another to find out the depths to which she'd sink to keep her power and control.

Carson held Tim through the storm, offering no duck-billed platitudes about *"It's going to be okay,"* because it wasn't. Nothing he could say or do would make her betrayal less painful. Maybe time would—Carson was okay holding Tim for as long as that would take. With appropriate breaks for meals and sleep, preferably with some sex and things to laugh about in there, because it would take years.

His own betrayal lay far in the past and could still rise up to strike him in the face. Three times since he met Tim. Now a fourth, because he knew the heartache of wondering why his mom would....

Damned shame he and Tim couldn't average their mothers out and get nice, healthy relationships.

Eventually Tim wound down to the hiccupping stage. He spoke into Carson's shoulder. "I didn't want to believe she'd go that far."

"Even after Monday?" Carson spoke softly.

"Yeah. I thought she'd just come a little unglued, but... She's usually not aggressive, just... in charge and you do it her way. I just didn't want to believe she'd go so far. I've been wanting to get out of the house and be on my own, but she didn't want me to. And now I know she *really* doesn't want me to." Tim hiccupped again and rubbed the back of his hand across his eyes. "So now it's super important that I find a job and get out of there."

"You can get out first." Carson refused to think about the state of his T-shirt, dragging it off ever so carefully. He balled it up, wet one side, and offered it to Tim. "I told you, you have a place here."

"You don't really want me here, Carson. You want to be safe, and having me around isn't safe. How long before Mom's back to pounding on your door?" Tim wiped his face, red from his breakdown.

Carson wouldn't have offered if he didn't mean it, so he skipped to the prediction. "Maybe not long, but she won't be doing it long." He couldn't keep the satisfaction out of his voice. Lorraine would look so *good* in the back of a cop car.

"I'd still like to keep the law out of this, Carson." Guess Tim could read minds, even if he didn't realize the hamper he was looking for was behind the louvered doors with the laundry machines.

Carson relieved him of the messy bundle. "If she don't start none, there won't be none."

Tim sighed. "I don't know what she'll start. I didn't think she'd do…anything she's already done. But she was awfully nice yesterday and today."

Just as Carson called it. "I would like to say she's had a change of heart, but more likely she's had a change of tactics. She spent some time in Dave's Chair of Tears yesterday."

"Maybe it made her reconsider what she was doing?"

She'd emerged seething more than chastened, and good thing the lightning bolts shooting out of her eyes couldn't actually fry Carson on the spot. "You're contradicting yourself. Please don't talk yourself out of looking at reality again."

"The reality sucks pretty bad." Tim glanced at the laptop on the counter. "Not only is Mom acting like… like she's acting, I've sent out a million résumés and gotten nothing back. Not even an auto response. I've checked every configuration in Outlook, and—nothing. I get the junk just fine."

That did not sound like it happened by accident. Not after the week they'd had with The Harridan from Hell™. "Let's open it up and see what's going on."

While Tim set up on the couch, Carson drew all the curtains shut and twisted the vertical blinds to closed. "We respond to nothing from outside, okay? Now, let's see what you have."

A depressingly accurate assessment of the state of his email, that's what Tim had. Carson leaned back, scowling, with nothing to show for punching the buttons and twisting the dials. "This doesn't make sense. Comment is a huge company. Their emails should work fine."

"Except I've been emailing résumés into the void," Tim pointed out. "And every online application might as well have disappeared once I hit 'Submit.'"

"What did Sherlock Holmes say? When you have eliminated the impossible, then whatever's left, however improbable, must be the truth. Or something like that. And we've eliminated Outlook as the problem, there simply aren't any rules to cover this." Would rubbing his temples ward off the blooming headache?

Ward off…

"Tim, when was the last time you looked at your email on the Comment.net server?" Carson jolted bolt upright. "Not through Outlook?"

"I don't even remember. Maybe never. It dumps into Outlook, it works great, I never have to go…" Tim trailed off. "Shit. Mom administrates the Comment account."

Tapping furiously, Tim plunged into the ISP portal. "Nothing in the inbox I haven't already seen…"

"Check the junk file." Carson held his breath.

Might as well not have bothered. Offers for sunglasses and designer handbags for screens going back only as far as the auto-delete date.

"What about Trash?" Tim clicked another folder. "It's got to be…"

Lines upon lines of emails spread across the screen,

with addresses like Dupont, Regency Pharma, Pilot Chemical and FerroCorp.

"Dear God," Carson muttered. "Nothing ever got to Outlook."

"This can't be," Tim croaked, but opening the "Routing" instructions revealed line after line of "Direct [*pharm*] to Trash," "Direct [*chem*] to Trash," "Direct [*interview*] to Trash." "Everything she could think of."

"She's thorough, I'll give her that." Carson watched with fascinated horror as Tim scrolled through the wreckage of his job search. Auto responses, requests for online applications. Requests for interviews.

"Nothing, I mean, *nothing*, got through." Tim's breath caught, and Carson had to grab the laptop before it toppled off Tim's knees. "I knew she wanted me to work at Monument, but to sabotage me everywhere else?"

"This is… fucked up." Carson could say a lot more, but not to Tim. Poor guy was reeling as it was. He'd say it if Tim showed signs of talking himself out of believing the evidence of his own experience again.

"How do I…." Tim waved a hand helplessly. "How do I even start to recover from this?"

"You have a spreadsheet or a list, right? With dates submitted and who and how?" Carson's answer to most of his job was a spreadsheet. He had fifty states, five territories, and twelve foreign countries to track for licensing and keep current in order for Monument Pharma to sell their wares legally: if he didn't keep detailed spreadsheets updated, they could lose accreditation and market share.

Lorraine ought to kiss his ass a little bit more: Carson didn't just keep the copier functioning, he made it possible for everyone in the company to draw a paycheck. Perhaps she'd forgotten that, or never known, just as few besides Dave Pfeiffer knew that Angie didn't have licensing authority in all fifty states, let alone the rest of their markets.

"Um, no...." Tim curled up in himself, the picture of misery. "I figured, they'd respond, I'd get a job, no worries about the rest..."

"I got this." Carson risked pulling his poor miserable hedgehog of a sweetie close enough to land a kiss somewhere. Hair, sort of, maybe neck. Contact, anyway. Didn't seem to make much difference.

No wonder, with weeks, months even, of effort shown to be floating in the toilet courtesy of the person who should have been Tim's biggest supporter.

Carson generated a basic spreadsheet with headers like Company, Date Applied, Contact, Email, Date Responded, Y/N, Action Needed. He'd make a second sheet when they knew what Tim had to work with. Maybe Tim's way out lurked in the jumble of the trash folder. Which needed to be transferred: Carson selected all and copied it into folder he named School, marking them all Read. No sense putting up a neon sign that they were on to her.

"This is gonna be a huge project," Tim fretted. "I should have done this from the beginning. Probably would have realized there was a problem earlier, too."

"Done is done. Don't beat yourself up about it." Carson tapped away. "I'm building this in Google."

"Huh? Not Excel?" A bare spark of interest, but enough to let Carson hope for some brain function lurking in the misery. "Why?"

"Multiple users. It is a big project. But doable." Carson left off setting sort instructions to rub Tim's shoulder. "I'll help."

Tim leaned into Carson's hand. "You've done so much

already. I'd be so screwed without you. I mean, I *am* screwed, but now there's hope."

"There's more than hope. It's all going to be different going forward." Carson changed some settings—Tim's computer no longer recognized the router named "Ratliff_-Family" as a home network, but a public network with no snooping allowed. One less avenue for control could only be good. "I'm going to leave the commands as is, no sense in her thinking to look and finding it's changed. Do you think changing the password would make her look?"

"Maybe." Tim chewed at a cuticle. "And she can change it to where I can't change it back, so… I'm just as screwed if she notices. Guess this email account is dead to me."

"Not necessarily." Carson grinned without mirth. "We're not going to alert her to any changes. We can hide in plain sight for a while if she has no reason to look." And he added one more command below the lines of routing instructions that had fucked Tim over so completely. *Forward [all Trash] to makeitgoboom@gmush.com.*

———

Hours later, Carson yawned until his jaw creaked. "Tim, I need to be at work in the morning. Come to bed, finish this in the morning? Later this morning?"

"We're almost done. And I'm—" Tim caught the yawn. "—off tomorrow. It'll kill me to wonder how many more interview offers are hiding in here."

So far they'd found nine, two rescinded for non-response, some old enough that the position was likely filled. Some from companies Tim had genuine interest in. All of them outside Colorado. With every addition to the spreadsheet, Carson could feel Tim's future diverging from his.

At least now the guy had the hope of a future out from under his mother's thumb.

———

Carson woke alone. Like always. Except for Tuesday, and he better not get used to that.

He found Tim sprawled on the couch, his cheek resting on the keyboard, the screen dark. Carson coaxed the laptop out from under him and covered him up with the turquoise throw.

Man, when the guy went in on something, he went all in. Carson liked that in a man. Just one more thing to draw him to Tim. Smart, sexy, able to absorb a shock and rethink —an attribute less common than it should be. Fast. Sweet. Able to find wonder in the world. Everything Carson could want, all rolled up in one. Everything Carson felt himself falling for.

He'd thought Tim was the worst possible choice because of his baggage. And he was. The baggage he was going to pack and leave the state with.

He kissed the sleeper's hair and slipped away. Would be his luck to meet the man he could love, just in time to kiss him goodbye.

CHAPTER NINETEEN

Tim woke to an empty townhouse, a dead laptop, and an aching heart. He'd stayed up much too late, finding the evidence of his family's betrayal.

Say, it, dope, say it to yourself. Your mom's betrayal, because she was the one spouting "one true life path."

Which didn't mean he could trust Dad, though, because Mom told him what to think and he said, "Yes, honey."

His phone still had juice. Texting Carson and finding out Mom was miles away gave Tim the courage to head home.

Home. What a funny word: now it meant more like *prison*, because he'd certainly been blocked from leaving.

Not anymore.

But it wouldn't do to show his hand too explicitly, when he still had financial strings she could pull. He'd really hoped not to have to buy his own car insurance until he'd hit the magic age of twenty-four and his rates went from sky-high to merely horrible. Bad enough just paying his share of the family policy. Maybe Carson had some ideas on that, since he'd found a financially feasible way to put a phone in Tim's pocket that Mom couldn't cut off.

Health insurance? Stuck with the parents playing nice there, until he got a job. Guess he'd better be careful crossing the streets.

Job had to be first priority—he couldn't impose on Paul, and Carson, well, he'd already led trouble to the man's doorstep. Probably Carson couldn't wait to get Tim sorted enough to get out of his life and take his lunatic mother with him.

Tim stuck the laptop and phone on their chargers while he ran through the shower and plotted his strategy. Respond to everything he could respond to, accept everything offered for interviews until he had a better idea of his marketability.

Monument would take you in a heartbeat, Carson had said.

Yeah, and he'd take Monument in less than a heartbeat, except that his life's goal was to get to where Mom couldn't pull his strings. Alaska might be far enough.

Email alerts slid in from the side of the screen. "Autoresponse: Thank you for your interest in…" "Autoresponse: Thank you…"

Right away. The real person emails would take longer to come in, probably, but Tim was on his way at last. Interviews, here he came, with documentation in hand.

———

Come to lunch.

Carson texted Tim before he realized they wouldn't have a lunch date, more of a 'meet the gang' meal, because Angie and Wes wouldn't let him out the door unescorted.

Of course, right in front of Lorraine's office was no place to shake them off, not when she glared daggers at him already.

He played nice until they got all the way outside. Shooing them away didn't work. Nor did pleading to be left alone for one meal. Not even failing to unlock the passenger doors of the BMW deterred them: they pressed their faces to the glass and made sad eyes, and of course, he couldn't drive off without risking an injury.

Outmaneuvered, damn it. "You guys get your own table!"

"Aw, why you gotta be that way?" Wes batted his eyes.

"Because you put nose prints all over my car."

"You love us and you know it." What happened to Angie being the voice of reason?

Outside the burger joint across from the mall, Tim paced like a caged tiger. He brightened at the sight of Carson, and gave his companions an eyebrow.

"Tim, meet Angie, who's in licensing with me, and Wes, who will be divided among six digesting canisters and reduced to his component atoms once he gets back to his lab." The threat made zero impression on the future victim. Carson needed to find a more attainable threat.

"Is dressing like that a requirement for your group?" Tim didn't quite laugh, but the brilliant turquoise and magenta lizards dotting Wes's foliage-patterned shirt certainly deserved it.

"You should only hope to be this stylish." Wes exhaled on his fingernails and buffed them against his shirt.

"If we ever need to rob a bank, we're going to send you in first, and then we poor drab people will make off with the cash while everyone's staring at you." Carson ushered everyone through the door, hoping against hope to ditch his colleagues in favor of a private table and the most current updates from Tim.

Instead, he got, "You're here, you must have thought Carson's cute too," while they were still in line. The only available table was a four top, so the inquisition didn't stop until Carson took control of the subject.

"Wesley." A pronouncement of gloom. "You've mistaken Tim's life for Comedy Central. Your quote/unquote 'little prank' has caused him and me a whole lot of trouble. You owe him an apology."

Wes paused in mid-bite. "Nonsense. I facilitated the two of you sad, lonely creatures finding the love of your lives. You should thank me." He chomped into his burger like the subject was closed.

"How about, the trouble is real, the need for an apology is real." Damn, this was not the time or place to address the "love of his life" issue. Whether or not Tim had any real feelings for Carson beyond *Hubba hubba!* and *Help!* was so mixed in with the shit he shoveled with the rest of his life, Carson couldn't begin to know. And how did he really feel about Tim? How much was genuine affection? At least part was *Fuck you, Lorraine.* A not-insignificant part was *The guy is hot.* Which dovetailed nicely with the rest, but…

He'd fight with that later.

Looked like Tim had the same battle going—the poor guy was red enough to cause heat ripples around his face.

"We're waiting." Carson refused to let this pass.

"Oh, all right." Wes scrunched his face. "For all your troubles, which you'd have to face eventually, minus all the glorious benefits of you two finding each other, equals the amount of apology, which is 'Need me to jump start any other aspects of your lives?'"

"You're going to be walking back to the lab at this rate." Carson warned. Why did he hang out with this jerk?

Tim pinched a French fry into mush. "I could have gone forever without provoking Mom like this. You know, just move away?"

"Without Carson?" Wes tried the stern look, which mostly made him look constipated. "He's your destiny."

Carson choked. So did Tim. Maybe Angie too.

"Your destiny is about to be 'rectal insertion of footwear,'" Carson snapped. "You owe Tim an apology, no matter how this turns out."

"You made trouble, Wes," Angie pointed out. "Doesn't matter what your intentions were or what good you think you've accomplished."

"Very well." Wes composed his face and took a deep breath. "Tim, I am very sorry for provoking your mother, and not at all sorry for bringing you and Carson together. Is he good in bed?"

"That's an apology?" sounded like a group scream.

"Close as you're gonna get." Wes smiled beatifically and rose with his tray of trash. "Grab his ass for me. Oh, and I hear you're joining us in the product development lab." With a wink and a double cluck of conspiracy, he left a stunned silence behind.

"You are?" Carson recovered enough to say. Wasn't that exactly the opposite of getting out from Mommy's thumb? Even if it meant a better class of lunch companion?

"I am?" Tim twitched. "I mean, I did interview, but I haven't accepted... Haven't even been offered formally. Besides, I have interviews all next week. I wanted to tell you, but Wes..."

"Was being Wes." The guy better start walking—it was

a ways back to the lab. "So, interviews? Stuff you found in those emails?"

He shouldn't be surprised: he'd helped Tim sort through the dozens of emails, picking out the occasional expressions of interest, some of them quite warm. From all over the country.

"Yeah, I'm talking to FerroCorp, Catalystics, Lokicia Pharma, and Amraine Labs." Tim turned into a whole new man, shining with hope and gazing into a future full of possibilities.

"I recognize two of those." As not being local, as far as he knew. Carson's burger turned to lead. "But not Lokicia or Amraine. Where…"

He didn't want to finish that sentence: he didn't want to know for sure that Wes's stupid idea of destiny was headed for the scrap heap. He couldn't bear that what had started as a prank had become real. For a couple brief shining moments that had no real chance of a long-term success. He knew, but he didn't want to know for sure.

"New Jersey."

Now he knew.

Carson forced the words out past a mountain stuck in his throat. "Need me to drive you to the airport?"

CHAPTER TWENTY

MIYOKO BUSTLED AROUND THE TINY, half-in-packing-boxes kitchen making Tim an after-work, late evening snack: he should be a good enough guest to eat it. Instead, he used the carrot stick to paint lines of ranch dressing on his plate while he told her and Paul what they'd discovered.

"I am really sorry." Paul patted Tim's shoulder. "I wish I could say I'm surprised, but this is the woman who tried to cancel all our wedding vendors."

"She what?" Tim jerked to upright.

"After we got a concerned call from the florist, we password-protected the caterers, the venue, the photographer, everyone. Mom called them all, trying to cancel. Like that would keep us from getting married." The carrot stick Paul bit into took his wrath.

"That's what I got for trying to involve my mother-in-law in the wedding planning," Miyoko added sadly. "She knew who to call."

"Dear God. That's terrible." Were there no depths Mom wouldn't sink to? Would she fulfill Carson's every awful prediction? But still, this was Mom, who should be on their side. And yet...

"I just can't believe Mom would do this." He must have said that out loud thirty times and thought it another hundred. "I mean, what mom would do this? Any of this?"

"The ones that like power and control, Tim." Paul sighed. "Most of them wouldn't. We got stuck with one who does."

Miyoko sipped at her lemon water and set the glass down on a coaster. "Good that Carson had some additional ideas. Do we get to meet him?"

Dear God. Carson. Tim's groan started at balls-level. "I have so fucked up with him. He's been nothing but wonderful, and I basically told him I'm leaving him already. To go to New Jersey, for fuck's sake."

The expletive made him flinch once it came out of his mouth, but if ever he needed to say *fuck* out loud it was now. Nether Paul nor Miyoko batted an eye.

"I take it long distance isn't on the agenda?" Miyoko looked grave, leaning into Paul's shoulder. "You haven't been seeing each other very long."

"Not nearly long enough to ask him to come with me, and we haven't talked about anything. We haven't had time. I dropped the bombshell on him at lunch." Tim pulled his phone out and texted a quick *Am at brother's place. Can I come over and stay the night?*

Carson knew they needed to talk: he'd be texting back any second now, something like *Yes* or *Okay* or, if he was thinking about last opportunities, maybe *Bring condoms.*

But the minutes ticked on. The phone mocked Tim with its refusal to ping, and he wasn't tracking Paul's words all that well.

Then he did get a chime.

If brother has a bed for you take it.

———

The beauty of doing the Ratliffs' next door neighbor's lawn care meant Carson could legitimately wake that bitch Lorraine up as early as seven on Saturday morning. Rage-mowing was the least she deserved.

Of course, that meant rousing Mrs. Hedstrom too, but that lady was already up with a brewed pot of coffee when Carson pulled into her driveway. Tim's Corolla was nowhere to be seen, which, good, he wouldn't get the slop-over noise, and he hadn't come home to deal with his horrible parents.

On the other hand, Tim also wasn't around to share the task, but since Carson had turned down a night's company that could have easily turned to sex, doing the yard work alone barely registered.

Yeah, Tim was coming out of the FOG, all right. Carson hadn't planned to be collateral damage, but there he was.

Mrs. Hedstrom greeted him with a smile that quickly turned to the wrinkles of concern he remembered from botched homework and calls to Child Protective Services. "Carson, dear, come in, have some coffee before you start, and tell me why you're wearing storm clouds."

He settled at the kitchen table with a steaming mug, not knowing what to tell her. "Your neighbors aren't my favorite people right now" covered everything from that bitch to the boyfriend who got away.

She clucked aloud, bustling up a plate of muffins wafting of apple and cinnamon. "I thought you and Tim were getting along swimmingly."

"We were." Carson took a bitter sip and made a mental note to get Mrs. Hedstrom a bag of proper arabica beans, maybe with a bag of chocolate chips so she'd take the gift under the guise of being put to work baking. "Maybe too well. Lorraine's livid over it, little though I care what she thinks, after what she did to her son."

Twenty years fell away—Mrs. Hedstrom stiffened into her mandatory reporter mode. "What. Did. She. Do?"

"Down, ma'am." Carson patted the air with his free hand. "It's fixed now. She'd sabotaged his job search. We found out how, we fixed it, and she doesn't know it yet, although him leaving for three days for interviews is going to be a big tip-off."

She relaxed minutely, barely enough to stop vibrating. "Going out of state, I take it?"

Carson nodded—the words balled up in his throat. He swallowed them down with more coffee, shaking a rivulet down his chin. "He wants to get out on his own, so yeah."

Reaching out to place her wrinkled hand over his, Mrs. Hedstrom nodded thoughtfully. "Which leaves you…"

"Behind." Carson set the coffee cup down before he spilled any more. "It's not like we have anything to even break up. We've known each other barely two weeks, so how do I know there's even something there? Something big enough to pull apart my life to follow?"

She didn't withdraw her hand, but squeezed instead. "Joined against a common enemy, that makes you allies. But you wish…"

"Yeah, I do. I really do." He'd told this lady much more awful stuff than his love life woes, though— "Didn't we have this same conversation about seventeen years ago? Over Tony Bianchi?"

She chuckled. "I don't recall his name, but yes, I think we did."

"I guess we're having a repeat. You got me out of a situation, now I'm paying it forward to him. Maybe we'll end up as friends after the shouting dies down." Carson recalled the feel of Tim's body against his a whole lot too well for friendship alone to have much chance. "He's way younger than I am, and in a different place in his life."

"You two will have to talk, and even if your relationship doesn't progress, you'll have done something good and worthwhile for him." Mrs. Hedstrom cocked an ear. "You may have that chance very soon, because I think I just heard his car pull up."

"Time to mow, then." Carson rose from the table, extricating his feet from the forest of legs that must spread this table into a flat surface big enough to perform surgery on.

She rose as well and hugged him. "You're a good man, Carson Eddinger, and Tim would be lucky to have you."

Grandmother-type hugs didn't come along so often in his life that Carson would turn one down. He hugged back. "Thank you. Let's see if he thinks so after I rouse the neighborhood."

He met Tim at the shed, jerking the mower into snarling life. Impossible to talk through, and maybe they'd already said everything.

Or maybe not—when front and back yards had been mown, whacked, and yanked into proper suburban order, Tim said, "Come on over while I clean up."

For anyone else, that would be an automatic okay. "I don't think so. I'll hang out with Mrs. H if she'll have me."

Tim took a deep breath. "I understand, but I want to make a point to Mom."

He could play along better if he knew what to back up.

"Which point would that be?" Because Tim had removed his T-shirt. Distracting.

"That you're not going away." Tim wiped his face with the soggy cotton he'd sweated through front, back, and pits.

Maybe Carson wasn't, but Tim was. But the chance to tweak their nemesis? Had to grab it. "You do know she can trespass me and I have to leave, legally speaking."

"I know, but if so, come back to Mrs. H's and I'll meet up with you. But if you can deal with a couple minutes of the parents, I'd appreciate it." Tim didn't reach out in any way—they hadn't touched each other or even made much eye contact. All work this time, not like last week. "And if you could just play along with whatever I have to say to make this work?"

Oh, that could be such fun! "You got it."

CHAPTER TWENTY-ONE

Intent to agitate or no, stepping through the Ratcliff front door still made Carson's stomach flip. Lorraine's silver Cruze sat next to an SUV of uncertain parentage in the drive—he wouldn't let on to his unwitting hosts how much he wanted to be headed the other way. Tim had to be a mess of nerves, but his face wasn't showing it.

"Hi, Mom, hi, Dad," Tim called.

"The prodigal returns!" The unfortunate who'd shackled himself to Lorraine came around the corner. He didn't *look* insane. "Who's this?"

"Dad, this is Carson Eddinger. He's a friend of mine. Carson, my dad, Glenn Ratliff." Tim couldn't know how much that description hurt, but they'd wandered into the lions' den, so best not to pull their manes. Carson held out his hand.

"Pleased to..." died a whispering death when the gesture wasn't returned.

"*The* Carson Eddinger?" came with a glare.

"That would be me." Carson remained mild. He'd

211

taken a lot worse than this and come through the other side. Glenn wasn't swinging, and Carson could outrun him without breaking a sweat.

Footfalls sounded on the wooden stairs, letting Lorraine into view, her hair in a bandana and a basket of laundry in her arms. "Oh, there you are, Tim, high time you came back. You're treating this house like a hotel and that's not acceptable. When exactly are you planning to va —" She stopped short when she made eye contact with Carson.

Felt like getting hit with a taser, that much hate.

"What are you doing here?" she snapped.

"Mom!" Tim interrupted. "He's my guest. Be nice."

Whoa, that was some serious ballsiness. Amazing what a little betrayal could do for retracting testicles from Mommy's handbag. Carson let the corners of his mouth turn up ever so slightly at Lorraine's double take.

"To *him*?" she snapped.

"Are my friends no longer welcome?" Tim stared her down. Wow. That was hot. "Come on upstairs, Carson. You can hang out in my room while I clean up."

That was even hotter—too bad he had no chance of taking Tim up on it. Cue the shrieking.

"Oh no, you will not go upstairs to my son's bedroom!" Were her eyeballs actually popping? "There will be no gay men in my son's bedroom!"

Too late for that, since Tim slept there. *Follow my lead and don't be surprised at anything,* Tim had said, but how the hell was he supposed to respond to that?

"Then make him welcome for ten minutes down here, Mom." Tim took Carson's arm and steered him to the kitchen where he opened the fridge for a frosty pitcher. "Have some iced tea, and my parents will make polite small talk while I shower." Under his breath he added the not-reassuring reassurance of "I'll be real fast."

"I will not." Lorraine could face down tigers with that scowl.

"Then bring your tea upstairs," Tim countered.

"You will not touch my son!" Lorraine shrieked.

Tim transmogrified.

If Carson hadn't seen the dramatic re-enactments, he would have lost his mind at Tim's metamorphosis.

"Oh, Mother, Carthon hath yet to toutth me, but he hath kept hith handth to himthelf." Tim pouted hard enough to be seen, make that *theen*, from space, swinging his clasped hands from one theatrical pose to the next. "Do you think he'th going to throw me down on my virthinal bed and ravith me?" He switched to offended-teenager voice. "Reaally, Motthhhhhherrrrr."

Even running his hand over his mouth couldn't keep the smile off Carson's face, and his shoulders might dislocate from the shaking. Dear lord, but Tim worked it hard!

"You stay where we can keep an eye on you, young man," Tim's father commanded. "Timothy Neil Ratliff, that is enough nonsense."

"I'll stop if you'll stop." Tim dropped his posturing. "Ten minutes of minimal politeness, and Carson and I will be on our way."

Follow his lead, okay. Carson pulled out a chair. If he waited to be invited to sit, he'd be there a long time.

"You have chores to do!" she yelled at Tim's retreating back. "You need to vacuum!"

"I'll help!" Carson yelled too. "I want to see your dust bunnies!"

"You will do no such thing!" Lorraine snarled. "You know you're not welcome here. Why are you here?"

"Tim invited me." Replying mildly would only make her look like more of a loon, though she wouldn't recognize it in herself. Who knew what kind of *wah wah wah* her husband heard when she opened her mouth. Carson took a sip of his drink.

"Agh! Since you're here, keep your butt in that chair and don't move." She stomped out with her laundry basket, leaving Tim's father goggling hopelessly between him and her.

Carson lifted his glass in a toast. "To new friends." Funny, Glenn didn't respond.

The rush of water from upstairs filled the quiet, soon cutting off and giving Carson hope for a speedy escape. Being eyed by Tim's dad like some six-legged specimen made him want to fidget, but he wouldn't give the man the satisfaction of seeing him squirm.

The silent beady eye was a lot more tolerable than conversation, though that seemed inevitable when Lorraine marched back into the kitchen. "Since you're here, you can explain how you're surviving in debt up to your eyeballs."

Carson choked on his tea. "What kind of question is that?" Besides fucking wrong. Not that he expected polite chitchat from this quarter.

"I don't want you teaching my boy any more of your filthy habits, like extravagance. You're living quite the life-style, with your fancy townhouse and your luxury car, and there's no way you can possibly afford that." Lorraine hitched her hip against the counter and folded her arms across her chest.

"With all due respect, Lorraine——" Which was no respect at all, but he'd let her fill that in for herself. The phrase brought him a moment to recognize she was baiting him. "——that's none of your business."

He deserved at least two points for keeping his voice even.

"If you're hanging around my boy, it's my business. I don't want him thinking it's acceptable to declare bankruptcy because you like flashy toys." Her mouth went back to a thin, tight line.

"There's so many unwarranted assumptions in there, I can't even begin to unpack it, even if it was your business." Carson took his hand away from the glass, because throwing the tea in her face was entirely too tempting. "Suffice it to say that I am nowhere near what you're suggesting. It's rude to count the money in someone else's pocket."

"You forget, I already know what's in your pocket." She smirked. "It isn't BMW money."

Carson smirked back. "Didn't Dave discuss accessing employee information? Or should I mention this conversation to him?"

She quailed for the barest instant—if Carson hadn't been watching for it, he'd have missed it. He drove in harder. "And yes, it obviously is BMW money, because obviously, I drive a BMW. Perhaps I know something about buying cars that you don't."

"Mind your mouth to my wife."

Carson twitched—he'd forgotten Glenn standing like a statue in the corner. "Your wife has an interesting notion of hospitality, sir." He let his polite words carry the contempt. "I think I've had my fill of it."

He timed standing to the sound of Tim's footsteps on the stairs. "Shall we be off?"

Tim stopped short, like he'd smacked into a palpable wall made of hostility. "I asked for ten minutes, Mom." He shook his head, wet hair flipping. "See you later, folks. Come on, Carson."

Best idea he'd heard since walking into this house.

"You're very mouthy when you've got your 'friend' with you," Glenn growled at their backs.

"Relax, Glenn. It won't last," the bitch gloated, following them to the door. "We'll make sure of it."

CHAPTER TWENTY-TWO

Tim pulled into the second bay of the garage, appreciating Carson's castle with electric drawbridge. Maybe one day he'd have something like it, and in the meantime, when he wasn't under this fine man's protection, stealth and distance would have to do.

First he'd have to tell Carson about the distance part.

He followed Carson into the kitchen. "What were they giving you shit about?"

The grimace returned to Carson's face. "Lorraine accused me of drowning in debt to finance my 'extravagant lifestyle,' which is A, bullshit, and B, none of her damn business. She's determined to find something horrible about me, even if she has to invent it."

Tim wouldn't have dreamed of questioning Carson's finances—this was a guy who planned ahead. Plus they hadn't managed to get to the full blowjob stage, let alone the 'compare bank accounts' stage. "I'm sorry she was rude."

"She's the one who should apologize, but I'm not

holding my breath on that one." Carson whirled back to the door. "You know how I have nice things? Let me show you."

He flicked on the overhead light just as the garage door opener light clicked dark. Tim followed, pulled by the magnetism of Carson's passionate declaration. "I find pieces, cars, houses, furniture, whatever, usually used, and usually with some flaw. People can't see past flaws, or they don't know how to fix them. Look at this dresser."

Yeah, the abomination with the leprosy paint and the shelf paper glued to one drawer. It didn't look any better than it had the other day when the neighbor, John, helped them move it out of the middle of the stall. "That's ugly."

"It is now." Carson pulled out one drawer with the facing stripped down to bare wood, dull and swirly. "It won't be when I'm done with it. This is burled maple veneer on solid wood, and a good piece of burled furniture can run four or five thousand bucks. Some asshole painted over it. Stuck contact paper on it, like it was a piece of particle board crap." Carson ran a hand over the bare wood. "I bought it for $25 at a garage sale. Didn't know what was under the paint and paper, just that the dresser had good lines. The burl was a nice extra. The case might not be burled, a lot of times it's a different wood. I won't know until I finish stripping it, but if I end up with a painted case and burled drawers, it's still a nice piece, very trendy, and worth a lot more than I paid for it. All because I invested some time and effort."

He turned to gaze at the BMW, all glossy black reflections in the harsh fluorescent light. "Same for the house. It was a foreclosure after the meltdown of 2008, and the old owners wrecked it pretty bad before the bank took it back. I bought it for a fraction of what it's worth now. I couldn't afford what I could sell it for, the market's gone so nuts in Denver, but I already own it."

"You don't have to tell me your private business, Carson. And I won't repeat it." Tim ran a soothing hand down Carson's arm, or he meant it to be soothing, but Carson jumped like he'd been burned.

"Thanks. I don't know why her accusation pissed me off so bad." Carson led the way back into the house. "Well, yeah, I do. Because it's the opposite of who I am."

Knowing what he now knew, Tim could see the house with a different eye—imagining Carson kneeling to lay the wood floor strip by strip, screwing in a new faucet, or painting the walls. "I guess I'm one of your fixer-upper projects."

That got his sweaty host to turn around fast. "Um, No. I don't think you need fixing. Unwrapping, maybe. You're so new you still have the manufacturer's tags on. Haven't even been shipped, really."

Tim warmed under that considering gaze. He wanted Carson's eyes on him, his hands...

"I think you should unwrap me." Tim took the few steps closer, enough to bring his own heated stare to eyeballing range.

Carson didn't blink. "You want me to shower first?"

"You might want me to shower first." Tim chuckled deep in his throat. "Or we could scrub each other's backs. Or shower after." He drew a deep breath and nearly drowned in the fresh sweat and hot man scent.

"I thought you did." Carson combed his fingers through Tim's slightly damp locks. Then he sniffed. "You were wet."

"This stealth thing is rubbing off on me." Tim could hardly contain himself and put his arms around Carson's waist. "I turned on the water and packed. Changed shirts, stuck my head in the spray, and voila, everyone, including you, thinks I spent my time naked and wet."

"I like naked and wet too much to think past it." Carson grinned and finally, *finally* bent his head for a kiss. "You sly thing."

"You bet I am." This wonderful, prepared man's approval was as good as a hug, which, yeah, Tim got too. "Made my parents think about preventing naked and wet and together, so while they babysat you, I got my stuff packed. Unfortunately, I didn't get it all the way out the door. My backpack's sitting there in the front foyer, where everyone's used to seeing it, but I lost my nerve about grabbing it when Mom chased after us. I can't imagine the shrieking if she thought I was moving out without saying anything." He shuddered in spite of himself.

"So asking if you've informed them about the trip is a real dumb question." Carson's chest expanded and deflated in the world's biggest sigh. His cheek rested against Tim's hair, his mouth way out of kissing range, though he hadn't pulled away. "Do you have a plane ticket?"

Tim's turn to sigh. "Yeah. It ate a good hole in my bank account, being last minute, even on a budget airline."

"As long as they let you sit inside the plane." Gentle fingertips played against the nape of Tim's neck. "When do you leave?"

"Tomorrow, about one. Guess I need to be there..."

"Around eleven. Security can be real fast or stupid slow, you never know." The pressure from Carson's cheek increased. No pressure at the groin though. "We'll need to be on our way by ten-thirty at the latest."

"About that..." Nothing for it but to bite the bullet. "Carson, I'm sorry. There's just such a heavy concentration of chemical industry in New Jersey, and there were so many places that replied positively, and…"

"And you needed to be as far away from your parents as you could get." Carson sighed again. "I can see it."

"New Jersey was about as far as I could go without leaving the country entirely," Tim mumbled into Carson's neck. He couldn't tear away—this might be the only time Carson's skin lay beneath his lips once this conversation ended. "But I don't want to leave you."

"You've hardly even gotten together with me," Carson pointed out. "And you're nearly out from under your mom's thumb. That has to be the biggest thing in your life right now. More important than me."

"It's not!" Tim jerked back to look into this frustrating, highly prescient man's eyes. He didn't have to know everything Tim was doing, or why, one step before Tim did, that was a whole lot like his mom—

No—Carson was nothing like Mom. Carson had done nothing but help.

Damn it, why couldn't Tim feel just one thing at a time, instead of this horrible muddle of stay/go/run/stand fast next to—next to a guy who expected him to leave.

"I want it all, Carson, I want freedom and you and a good job and a place to live where I have some privacy and feel safe, and—"

"Then what you want isn't with me. Privacy, well, you've seen how big this place isn't, and your mother knows exactly where it is, so I guess I better increase my homeowner's insurance in case she Youtubes 'How to make a Molotov cocktail'."

Dear Lord, Carson's mind went to some shitty places! Mom would never—

Yeah, Tim had trouble believing Mom would undermine his job search, but all evidence pointed that way. After what she did to Paul and Miyoko. Maybe "Mom would never…" could only end with "apologize" or "be supportive of Tim and Carson together."

"Then come with me." Even as he said it, Tim knew he asked for too much.

"You aren't there yet," Carson noted.

"I was so mad I couldn't see past getting away, and… FerroCorp has a real sweet position open. A salary that blew my mind." Once again Tim saw the high five figures dancing on the screen. "More than my dad makes."

"An East Coast budget might make that seem a little lean, but if you need to get away from here, take it and we'll figure out how to make it cover everything and then some." Carson did kiss Tim's hair this time. "And you won't have to watch me do what I have to do to your mom to make her leave me alone. Because she might take some convincing. Especially since she knows I'll cover your tracks."

"I'm sorry, Carson. I should have applied at local places first, but I was so…"

"I'm not going to hold you back, Tim. That's not what someone who loves you does." Carson went to solid stone in Tim's arms. "I'm sorry, that's not what I meant…"

"That you love me, or that my mom doesn't?" Tim had to let go—this conversation had so much truth and sucked so hard he had to pace around the living room, stomping over the ocean-colored throw rugs and slipping his socks against the laminate floor. "Because I think she does love me."

"I'm sorry, I wasn't trying to tear her down. It sounded bad, I'm sorry." Carson stood back, out of Tim's way. "I wasn't talking about her, but… I know something about how a mom can love you as 'less than'. It hurts."

"Yeah. It does." Tim flung himself into the embrace of the soft couch. "Being loved like a well-trained dog, or a possession. I do the tricks she commands, and she's happy, and if not…"

"Yeah. It sucks. At least Lorraine's required tricks are things society approves of."

Well, Mom might never be happy with him again. If Carson knew how to deal with that… "I'm still not supposed to ask about that?"

"No, Tim, you should know." Carson landed heavily on the couch, a good two feet away. "My dad left when I was little, and I was about fourteen when my spawn point got together with a man who… didn't like anything about me, from the way I breathed to the way I cleaned the house to the fact I liked guys, which I sure never mentioned to him, but… He knew, and he tried beating it all out of me. And she let him wale on me. Remember I said Mrs. Hedstrom was the teacher who changed my life?"

"Yeah." Better not stare, hard though it was, because Tim could not imagine anyone striking Carson and getting away with it. Tenth-grade Carson wouldn't have had that same aura. "You said."

"Mrs. H worked out what was going on, and stopped it." Carson twisted his hands together, staring at his fingers and not even looking at Tim. "It's real hard to talk about, because…."

He paused so long Tim thought he might not keep talking. And what could Tim say? "I understand?" Because no, he didn't, not really. His mom might have her own brand of awfulness, but she didn't lay hands on him, or support someone who did.

Carson jerked his head up, still not looking at Tim. "Because, look at me." He didn't wait for an acknowledgement. "I'm a big guy, I got my height young. The shithead was shorter, and lighter. He still hit me. And everyone who knew wondered why I didn't just hit him back. Around three a.m. *I* wonder why I didn't hit him back."

"I don't wonder at all." Tim knew exactly how a small adult could rule. First you have to believe they'd really do it. Then you have to believe you could fight back. "Big power imbalance."

"Yeah, well, it's gone now. Except sometimes in the wee hours there's a weird sound from outside, and I spend the rest of the night reminding myself I'm not still sixteen." Carson rocked back and forth, clenching his hands again. "It was humiliating then, and it's only better now because I've had a lot of counselling and have the means to fortify my life."

So much made sense now. Everything from Carson's situational awareness to the near-prescient way he could call Mom's next moves. Tim asked softly, "What finally happened?"

"Aside from my broken nose? The asshole went to prison, and good riddance." Carson scrubbed his face with one hand, not looking at Tim, and ended up with his fingers covering his nose. "But not for all that long, and when he got out, my spawn point took him back. Which is why I spent my senior year of college couch surfing and eating a lot of oatmeal. And why I have Spanish bayonet for a garden and locks on stout doors. Asshole holds a grudge."

"That's...horrible." Tim had to choke down a lump. "That's way worse..."

Was that a chuckle? "Comparatively speaking, your

mom is a piece of cake." Carson took his hand away from his face and smiled square at Tim. "Not for you, of course, but I have dealt with worse."

"And you didn't move far away?" Carson had to be local if Mrs. Hedstrom had him for math.

"Nope. That would be letting them win. I have friends here, I have a nice life, and I won't let them take that away from me." Carson could frighten sharks right out of the ocean with that smile. "Living well is the best revenge. Living with caution is how I continue living well."

"Is the asshole still after you?" A guy could hold a long grudge over going to prison, especially if he thought he was entitled to do whatever sent him there.

"Not actively," Carson said after a moment. "At this point it's as much for me as them. All my moats and alligators keep me from getting close enough to beat anyone's face in. Much better all around to laugh at them from behind a locked door. When John mentioned crazy screamers on my doorstep, he wasn't joking. They didn't stop until I transferred the townhouse to a limited liability corporation, and they thought I moved."

"That's horrible." Wow, that was way worse than Tim had imagined, even after Carson had shied away from discussing his past. "Sorry you got caught up in my family drama too."

"Like I said, I've coped with worse." Carson leaned back into the couch and pulled Tim to his chest. "Yours got exponentially worse because I got involved."

"It was bound to happen sometime." His previous plan of sneaking away seemed ludicrously naïve, now that he'd seen how hard his mom would fight for her version of his life. "Lot of things were bound to happen sometime. Including this."

Tim turned against Carson, wrapping his arm around a muscular, sweaty chest. He pressed his mouth to Carson's, letting his lips part. Carson tasted of tea and effort, of freedom. And he kissed back, oh, did he kiss back.

Softly at first, with all the wonder that went with this newness, and then with rising heat.

They toppled over into the throw pillows, slipping half of them to the floor, and who cared? Not when Tim lay on top, his entire body pressing into Carson's. Nothing else mattered but thrusting into Carson's groin, hard as his own.

Then it was all hands and lips and knees and clothing getting shoved out of the way. Underwear fouled on one foot didn't matter when Carson pulled Tim over him, his big hands on Tim's hips, urging him up, over. In.

Oh fuck, Carson licked.

And sucked.

And Tim could *see*.

See how his cock disappeared between Carson's lips and feel how his tongue played over head and down the shaft. The pop of suction breaking when Tim pulled too far away and the gasp when he came back farther than Carson wanted. He had to let his partner direct traffic—Tim didn't know where he was going, except that he was going to come.

No way he could last, not when he was getting everything he'd yearned for, in the heat of Carson's mouth, the dancing pressure. Everything he'd imagined, everything he'd yearned for. Everything he'd treasured more for having denied himself before. Now he knew what he'd missed, and how ardently Carson wanted to give it to him. Hands, lips. Joy.

"Not gonna take much..." Tim gasped, and when

Carson shifted his grip to Tim's butt, it wasn't going to take anything more at all. His world went incandescent.

Carson held him through it, not letting him collapse until he finished pulsing and the jets of come dwindled to drips and then stopped.

Dear God above, that was...

And into Carson's mouth, where Tim had only been imagining. Before.

Before he made his strike for freedom, with this amazing man at his side.

Carson let him go and swallowed. He let Tim settle back on top of his chest for some snuggles. "Let me know when your brain comes back."

"Guh." Might be a while. Especially since he had to wrap his head around the wonder of what they'd done. What Carson did. And enjoyed. Every slurp, every noise, every grip said he liked what he'd just done for Tim. With Tim.

Didn't even have to see him smile to know, but Tim looked all the same, and smiled back.

"I should reciprocate, huh?" Tim hugged Carson more tightly. "'Cause wow."

"Wow is good." Carson rubbed his cheek against Tim's hair. "Reciprocate is nice. Only what you're comfortable with."

Yeah. Carson made it plain that he wasn't holding Tim to any checklist, but after action that wonderful, he really ought to do something. Maybe start with what little was familiar, and keep going?

"How about we jump in the shower, get the lawn off us?" Not that Tim wanted to move all that much, but after they got clean they could fall into bed without grinding chlorophyll into the sheets. Guess the couch got to take its chances. Tim didn't bother zipping his shorts—one hand would keep them from falling off on the stairs.

Sexy times in the shower—Tim was feeling almost confident this time, with big handfuls of round butt, and more tongue than he knew what to do with. Maybe he should figure that out—he transferred his attentions to Carson's neck, to be rewarded with deep groans of, "Yeah, like that."

That had Carson rock hard, and Tim was on the rise again before they'd rinsed off the soap.

"Ah, youth." Carson cupped Tim's balls in a gentle hand. "No refractory period to speak of."

"Not around you," Tim dared to say. Not with his wet dream come to life and twice as interested.

"Flattery will get you everywhere." Carson sucked Tim's earlobe into his mouth.

"Will it get me into your bed?"

"If that's where you want to be," was a warm puff in Tim's ear and everything he wanted to hear.

Oh yeah, the things he wanted to do to Carson.... He didn't half know where to start, except by falling splat on the mattress with this amazing man. "Let's go!"

Comfy flat surface with Carson sprawled on it—best place in the universe. Tim set to exploring, with hands and mouth, and frequent checks to make sure Carson was still smiling.

He was.

They had all the time in the world, but Tim was tired of waiting. He rushed the last eight inches of Carson's belly to reach the root of his cock. That beautiful, hard cock that he let Tim examine and handle to his heart's content, but that needed to be licked. Like now. With Tim's very own tongue.

The smell of Carson's groin, man mixed with soap, heady stuff. He was really nose to cock with another man. Carson. All he had to do was stick out his tongue and he could taste...

Tim drew a slow, wet line up the ridge of Carson's cock. Ohhh... The groan might be his. Or Carson's. Probably both.

Carson tasted like every hope Tim had. Salt and flesh and utter sexiness—he didn't know whether to savor or gobble, maybe both, spread out over days and weeks and months and years, but never again to be the first taste.

Carson moaned again when Tim flicked the tender cord near the head and sighed when Tim rubbed his lips along its ridge.

Oh, man, he was really going to put Carson's cock in his mouth. Ready, oh yeah, he'd only waited his whole life...

Thud! Thud! Thud!

"What the fuck?" Both Carson and Tim jerked upright.

"Police! Open up!"

CHAPTER TWENTY-THREE

CARSON JUMPED TO HIS FEET, staying to one side of the window. Tim looked frozen.

Damn, that really was a police cruiser parked on the street.

"Get dressed, come downstairs, bring your wallet. Follow my lead." Carson dove into a shirt and yanked his shorts up halfway out the door. "Coming!"

Ghat damn it, he should have seen this one coming. Carson opened the door but left the wrought iron and glass security door deadbolted. Two cops stood on the porch, one close-clipped ginger with freckles and the other bronze with equally short black hair. Carson tried to read names off badges and gave up in preference to eye contact. "Good afternoon, officers. What's going on?"

Staying calm and collected, first priority.

"Just responding to call for a welfare check. Are you Carson Eddinger?" asked one of the officers.

"I am. Who's concerned for my well-being?" Nope, keeping the cops on the far side of the door was first priority, because he just knew who skulked around the corner, waiting to come rushing in to make a scene and throw guilt trips and demands.

Tim materialized behind Carson, staying quiet and out of sight. Only his ragged breathing betrayed his presence.

"Not yours. Is there a child named Timothy Ratliff here?" the officer asked.

"There is a Tim Ratliff here, but he's hardly a child." What the fuck had Lorraine told the cops? Carson opened the door wider, exposing Tim. "How old did the caller say he was?"

"I don't think she did." The officer turned to his partner. "Did she?"

"Ah, no." The second officer quirked his mouth. "Mind if we come in and check?"

"Do you have a warrant?" Carson minded very much if they came in.

"No."

"Then we can keep talking like this." Carson was not about to open that door.

"Are you Tim Ratliff?" The officer spoke past Carson.

"Yes, sir." Tim already had his driver's license out—he held it to the glass. "I'm here because I want to be here, and I'm doing quite well, thank you, aside from having an overbearing mother."

Oh, good—Tim held his license horizontally. If he'd left his license in the vertical orientation of the under-twenty-one, they'd have more explaining to do. But he'd clearly updated and couldn't be mistaken for a minor.

The officer leaned to the glass, glancing back and forth between the picture and the man. "Looks like a match."

"Is there anything else we can tell you, officer?" Carson asked. He was skirting the edge of what the cops would consider cooperative, but he wanted them gone, along with any trailer they'd picked up.

"No, I think we're good here." The officer exchanged glances with his partner. They turned.

"One more thing." Carson wouldn't let this go without more ammo. He did open the security door for this. "Can I please get your business cards?"

"Certainly."

Both officers extracted cards and handed them over. Carson read them carefully. "Officers Mario Diaz and Isaac Anderson. Thank you. Is there going to be an incident number for this call?"

Officer Diaz glanced at his partner. "No. Do you need one?"

"Possibly. I like to keep good records. It makes getting the inevitable restraining order so much easier." Carson ignored the gasp from behind. "But we've had issues with the person who called this in, and if she happens to be lurking around the corner, please remind her that she's been trespassed from this property. Lorraine Ratliff, age about sixty—" He deliberately added five years to his estimate out of sheer aggravation and hoped she heard him. "—about five feet two, streaky bottle blonde in a Karen cut, last seen in a red bandana. We'd just like to be left alone. So if you encounter her, kindly suggest she mosey along."

Officer Anderson's lip quirked, though he didn't break a smile. "Not a problem."

Carson dashed upstairs to watch from the bedroom window while the officers headed to their patrol car. Sure enough, a third person, short, and with a red head scarf, walked between them.

"Damn." Tim shadowed him here as well. "Did they arrest her?"

"Doubt it. Her arms are swinging, they aren't touching her." Torn between disappointment and not wanting to see Tim hurt, Carson said, "Looks like a little friendly escort to her vehicle."

"She just doesn't stop." Tim flumped to a seat on the edge of the bed, still watching the three marching down the sidewalk.

Carson could only pat Tim's shoulder and say words he'd never imagined stringing together. "Maybe moving to New Jersey is the best idea after all."

———

The mood was well and truly trashed. Nothing else for it—if even Carson agreed he should get out of town, Tim was going.

Leaning together over the laptop while they hunted for restaurants near the budget hotel Tim had booked with Paul's help, activating the Uber app on both Tim's phones, downloading his boarding pass, and looked at apartments and "roommate wanted" ads in a state Tim had never really imagined living in wasn't even close to what he'd almost had.

Damn it.

Sometimes cussing was the only possible response.

Because making sandwiches for lunch, and working on a project together, even this one, and then scraping paint off the leprous dresser together, and fixing some dinner and watching a movie with Carson was exactly how he wished his weekend would go. Without the looming elephant in the room.

They did end up in bed together, in each other's arms.

Hesitantly, like someone would break if they squeezed too hard. Seemed like forever until they got to the handsy stage.

Finally Carson said, "Tim, you don't have to do this with me. You can wait."

"I don't want to wait!" Tim protested. "I do want this with you. Why would you even think otherwise?"

Carson only sighed. He brushed his lips against Tim's brow. "Because all the kisses taste like goodbye."

CHAPTER TWENTY-FOUR

CARSON PULLED the BMW to the curb around the corner from the Ratliff house. The neighbors' lilac bushes thrust their purple blobs of flowers between their parking spot and the house, filling the air with their perfume. Sweet floral fought with sun-warmed leather inside the car, though the air conditioning and deeply tinted glass were winning the fight against the spring morning.

"Even if your folks are at church, a little extra caution doesn't cost us anything."

Tim sighed. "I know. And sorry, but you do understand why I'm having such a hard time applying your level of vigilance to my parents." The people he should be able to rely on. Instead, he had to dodge them like his life depended on it.

"Even having seen what you've seen? We had cops at the door just yesterday." Carson caught Tim's eye and glowered. "I swear, 'But faaaaaamily!' has gotten more people into more trouble than any other two words in the English language."

"I know. All cognitive dissonance aside, I'm doing it your way. I will run down the block, grab my bag, and run back." Like a thief in his own home. Why couldn't he do this openly, with his parents' support and good wishes? Tim patted Carson's hand, resting on the gear shift. "If I'm not back in four minutes, something's gone dreadfully wrong."

"It's going to be real awkward if I have to come extract you," Carson grumbled. "Sorry, I know this should be a quick in and out, but I am one giant ball of acid reflux right now. What if your key doesn't work?"

"I know two other ways to get into the house, Carson." Tim hoped he wouldn't have to use either of those routes today. He'd probably never use them again. "I'm not such a goody two-shoes that I've never sneaked."

That got a laugh. "Go to it, then."

Tim stole a kiss. He wanted it for kissing Carson, but he needed it for luck. "This kiss better taste of 'be right back'." He pushed the heavy door open on its silken hinges, not looking back at Carson. They'd stopped even heavy groping after Carson's gloomy description, but Tim hadn't given up yet. Carson *would* be more than the driver on this stage-coach headed out of Dodge.

He jogged down the street, each step bringing him closer to his backpack. He'd filled it with dress clothes, good shoes, and two ties, one borrowed from his father's closet, since he owned but the one, and a change of casual cloth-ing. Just enough for four interviews over two days plus trav-eling. Not enough to trigger a baggage fee.

Mom's car sat alone in the drive, not unusual on a Sunday morning. They usually took Dad's little SUV when they went somewhere together. Tim sprinted to the front door, quickly sliding his key into the knob. This should be fast—Mom didn't always remember to latch the deadbolt on her way out.

In! All he needed was to reach around the doorjamb and he'd have everything he needed for his trip.

No backpack.

Tim stuck his head all the way around. No black backpack sat among the pile of shoes at the front door.

Why—? He'd left it right there in the "ready for school" position it had occupied since he was six. He *knew* he had.

Maybe Mom put it in the coat closet.

Nope. His heart started racing. Where—? He *needed* that pack.

Shit. Maybe she'd carried it upstairs, its place repurposed in her head now that he graduated.

Tim tiptoed upstairs. His heartbeat in his ears drowned out the small creaks of the stairs. The house didn't feel empty. Had to be his nerves jangling. Mom and Dad always went to church this time of day. But his backpack wasn't on his bed or in his closet, or anywhere it normally landed.

Carson had to be sweating bullets by now. If Tim had the spare bucks for it, he'd go without the pack and replace everything new in New Jersey, but that was rich man's thinking.

He should run.

And not face first into his mom. "Oh hi."

"Hello, dear." She sounded awfully normal, confident with a dash of triumph. Why the hell wasn't she at church? Services started half an hour ago!

He'd have to risk it. "Have you seen my backpack?"

"Of course, dear. It's in the car. Do come along." She took his arm and started walking him to the front door.

"Why is it in the car?" Wrong car!

"Because we're taking you."

She didn't normally speak in half sentences. "No, you're not. I need my pack."

"Of course you do, and it's in the car." She led him to the sedan.

He could outrun most everyone, certainly his mom. He just had to grab his pack and go. If it was in the back seat. Which was empty.

Until he landed in it. Face first.

The unexpected tackle knocked him halfway into the car. "What the hell?" Tim yelled, but his father shoved him in the rest of the way and slammed the door.

The latch pulled but the door wouldn't open. His mouth dry, Tim yelled, "Let me out!"

He pounded on the glass, but neither parent reached to the handle.

Fuck, the child-proof latch had been thrown.

On both sides.

Tim pounded the glass with his fist, yelling and got told, "Shut up," when his dad got in the driver's side. Diving at the passenger seat bought him an elbow to the mouth.

Tim spat blood. "I need my pack and I need to get out of here, damn it! I'm on my way to the airport!"

"No, you're not. Shut up." Dad stretched his arm across the gap between the front seats and turned to see where he backed down the drive. "That meddling old bag!"

God bless Mrs. Hedstrom—she stood behind the car, her phone to her ear. They weren't going anywhere—unless Dad stopped being squeamish about crushing old ladies.

She bought him enough time to fling himself halfway into the front passenger seat. They couldn't child-lock the front doors—if Tim could just worm the rest of the way into the front, even if he ended up head down in the footwell, he could get the door open.

Dad brought a fist down on his head. "Get back there!"

No, he would *not!* Tim flailed for the door handle.

The Cruze accelerated backward, hard. For half a second.

They stopped with an almighty crash.

———

Two and a half minutes ticked off into three, taking half a century to do it. Carson watched the clock with one eye and tried to see around the corner of the lilac bush. Tim was fast—he'd be here any second. He left the BMW idling. A fast getaway might calm the volcano in his gut.

His phone warbled—Carson ignored one ring, but anxiety made him pick up on two.

The voice was Mrs. Hedstrom's, but the words were disaster. "Carson, they're taking Tim! They've forced him in the car! Agh!" The sounds of an engine filled his ear.

Oh shit. Anywhere Lorraine and her enabler wanted to take Tim was no place Tim should go.

He gunned his purring monster, squealing a right around the corner. Lorraine's silver broom backed down the drive.

Mrs. Hedstrom sprawled in the grass while Lorraine ran to the passenger side.

No. Just no.

The BMW reached the house next to the Ratliffs' when Carson stomped the brakes hard. He screeched to a stop in front of the Ratliff driveway.

The BMW lurched sideways three inches. The side curtain airbag punched Carson in the face.

CHAPTER TWENTY-FIVE

THE SCREAMING STARTED while Tim was still upside down in the footwell. He opened the passenger door and oozed out, shaken. What had they hit?

Oh, shit. The trunk of the Chevy jammed into the passenger side of what had been a sweet ride and was now so much crumpled steel.

Mrs. Hedstrom sat on the ground, with Mom looming over her. Of course she'd scream—the right response was to give Mrs. Hedstrom a hand up, so screaming it was. Tim hauled the little old lady to her feet. She wasn't so shaken that she didn't yell back.

Carson! Was he okay? Trusting that Mrs. Hedstrom had bounced rather than broken and would stay on her feet, Tim dashed for the driver's door.

Carson emerged, one eye swelling shut and blood pouring from his nose. "Are you okay?"

"You're asking me? You're the one bleeding!"

"So are you." Carson pinched his nose, making the fresh rivulets stop. "Mouth."

"Oh, huh?" Tim put his hand to the wetness at his lip. "No big. Is anything else on you damaged?"

"Not sure. Shoulder maybe."

The screaming came their way. A cacophony of "You idiot! What do you think you were doing?" and "Tim, don't you even think—" and more. Worse. Much worse.

Where was a cop when you needed one? Maybe on the phone with Mrs. Hedstrom?

Carson started yelling back. "What the fuck do you think you're doing? Where were you taking Tim! You killed my car!"

Everyone else could bellow. Tim still needed his backpack. Since the rear of the Cruze was imbedded firmly in the passenger side of the BMW, he needed Plan B.

The whoop of a siren silenced all the shouting. A cop car had pulled up unnoticed, until the driver uncorked the single blast. Two officers emerged.

Familiar officers, one ginger and crewcut, the other with a deeper complexion, and both twitched when they saw Tim and Carson. Or maybe Mom. Or all of them.

"Want to tell us what's going on here?" from Officer Anderson cued the babble, which he shut down. "Stop. Driver of the Bimmer first. What happened?"

"I was driving down the street when this maniac came shooting out of the driveway and T-boned me," was a pretty succinct description from Carson, who handed over his license, registration, and insurance form.

"Had some speed to cave in the side that bad," observed Officer Diaz. "Who was driving the Cruze?"

Funny how neither Mom nor Dad wanted to own up. Tim broke the silence, pointing. "He was. Glenn Ratliff, lives here, he's my father." Dad glowered at being ratted out, but if he wasn't willing to admit to driving, maybe he fucking shouldn't have been doing it.

"Mm hmm, and where were you?" Officer Diaz took the documents Dad grudgingly extracted from the car and his pocket.

"I was in the back seat, and *I couldn't get out.* Because I was being *kidnapped.*" Tim aimed the venom toward his parents. "Until I got flung upside down into the passenger footwell."

"Oh really." Both officers went alert.

A sheet of paper fluttered from the open passenger door. Mom pounced on it like it was gold, folding it quickly and aiming it toward her pocket.

"Ma'am, let's see that please." Officer Anderson held out his hand.

"It's nothing. Just trash," Mom spluttered, clutching the paper into crinkles.

"Then you won't mind me looking." The officer motioned "give it here" with his upturned fingertips.

"I mean, it's a family document. Personal. Nothing to do with the crash." She shoved it into her pocket.

"Ma'am, you can hand it over, or you can lean against the car with your feet apart while I remove it from your pocket," he warned. The bright spring day went suddenly cold.

Actions have consequences Carson had said. *Even hers.*

Oh gee, Mom was about to get a sharp dose of consequence. Tim inched sideways to stand shoulder to shoulder with Carson. His heart thudded; he could draw only shallow breaths. Mrs. Hedstrom limped to his side and slid her hand into his.

Good idea. Tim groped for Carson's hand and felt the answering squeeze.

Officer Diaz leaned into the open sedan. "Wonder if it's part of this?" He brought out a white folder with a red and black logo, shaking the half-escaped papers into the pockets. "Exodus Way," he read aloud. "Return to the path of righteousness." He looked up at Mom and Dad. "Any particular form of righteousness?"

"No!" Mom blurted, but she held out the folded sheet like it was going to burn her.

"Do you have a warrant?" Dad tried bluster.

"No, but I do have probable cause to search." He turned back to the Cruze.

"If you find my backpack, I need it, sir," Tim said, and refused to look at his parents.

He shouldn't be surprised. He shouldn't. Carson had called it, that day back on the rock in the mountains. Not after everything he'd already seen from Mom, and how Dad went along with her, chirping, "Honey's right!"

Not after hearing Mom say, "It's just a phase" and "We'll make sure of it."

She'd do that. She'd really send her son to conversion therapy. Who was this woman who looked like his mother? His dad agreed? He really didn't know these people.

Carson's horrible question had been answered—Mom had pinned the meter on never accepting her son. Tim could only clutch Carson's hand harder.

They watched as Officer Diaz went through the Cruze, compartment by compartment. He did notice the activated child locks. When he got to the back seat, he flipped down the folding rear seat to access the trunk. He pulled out a familiar black backpack.

"Is this the one?" he asked.

Tim nodded. He'd made it so easy for his parents to bundle him up and away to Camp Hell.

"The big suitcase is also full of his things," Mrs. Hedstrom piped up. "Lorraine loaded it into the car."

What big suitcase?

"He's going to visit his grandmother for a month, of course the suitcase is full of his things." Mom spoke with the utmost certainty.

"No, I'm not! And she lives five miles away," Tim burst out. "I'm going on a short trip for job interviews!"

"I thought you had that locked d—" Dad stopped short at Mom's glare.

Fucking great. Not even a hope for allegiance there.

The officer extracted the big blue wheeled case they always used for family trips. "Is this your stuff?"

With a last squeeze on either side, Tim approached the case. He unzipped it, knowing with horrible certainty what he'd find. Jeans, shirts, socks. All the underwear he couldn't find yesterday. "Yeah. These are mine. Can I take them, please?"

"Depends. Did you want to swear out a complaint?" Officer Anderson's voice was level, offering no clue if he should do it or not.

If he looked to Carson, would he see *Do it!* all over his face? Nope, that was as neutral an expression as he'd ever worn.

Mrs. Hedstrom, though—if ever a woman wanted to take a big legal bite out of someone's ass, it was her. The way she glared, Mom and Dad should burst into flame. But she said nothing to influence him.

"Um, is this something I have to decide right this instant?" He should—he really should, but he had a plane to catch, and—this was Mom and Dad. As awful as they were, they were his.

"Best to do it while everything's fresh," observed Officer

Anderson. "Since we're sitting on the evidence at the moment."

"How about when I get back from my trip?" Anything to buy some time. Some leverage.

"Would you really do that to your parents?" Mom demanded.

What fucking nerve! Tim rounded on her. "Considering what you've done to me? To both your sons? Do you really want to go there?"

She took a step back, her face nearly purple.

"Tim—" came from behind him. Carson. "This is your last, best chance to get everything you value out of the house. While the officers are here to supervise. If you would, please, gentlemen."

"Certainly." Officer Anderson nodded to his partner. "I'll go in with you. Officer Diaz will supervise out here."

"That'll give me time to write Mr. Ratliff his ticket." Officer Diaz pulled his pad out of his pocket.

"I'm going in, too!" Mom screeched. "To make sure they don't steal anything."

"As long as you stay calm, okay." The cop escorted them to the door and up the stairs.

Carson patted Tim's shoulder on the way up the stairs. "We can throw everything on the bed and use the sheets as hobo packs."

Good that someone was thinking—his brain had gone numb.

There wasn't much, not near as much as he thought. His life had been here, and now it was down to a couple of makeshift bags of clothing and shoes. Boxes of books, leaving a lot more than he packed. He could leave a lot of stuff behind. Academic awards he sorted into the keep box, church awards stayed where they were. Those were important to Mom, not him.

Carson carried his sortings out of the house, though to where, Tim couldn't say. The BMW wasn't going anywhere. He returned empty handed.

The officer regarded their packing quietly. Mom shot lasers from her eyes with every item he selected.

"What am I forgetting?" The lime jello in his skull wasn't providing any answers.

"Winter coat, boots." Carson held his arms out for the cold weather gear in the front closet.

"I think that's it." Tim wouldn't bother hunting for the second glove and dropped the loner into the string bag with the others.

Carson wasn't done. "Documents. The title to your car."

"Oh shit." Tim would have walked right out the door without them. "Thanks."

He trotted to the living room. The Chopin book from the piano bench fell open where the title nestled inside. He handed it to Carson.

"So that's where—" Mom cut herself off.

"Yeah, that's where." Her admission cut right through his fog. "Officer, my other documents are upstairs."

"Lead on." The cop cast a quelling look at Mom before Tim led their little parade up the staircase.

Tim turned right at the head of the stairs, not the left into his bedroom.

"Oh no, you don't!" Mom shrieked. "There's nothing of yours in the master bedroom! Don't even think of going into my desk!"

"Officer, I don't plan to rummage randomly, but yes, some of my possessions are in the master suite. I'm going to get those and nothing else, okay?" Tim wouldn't even look at her. Didn't want to hear her lies. Wouldn't grant her last bid for power and control.

"I'll look at them before he takes them, ma'am." Officer Anderson gave her a "shut the fuck up" glare. "So far he hasn't taken anything that wasn't in his room or didn't have his name on it."

With the policeman to keep her in check and Carson for moral support, Tim steeled himself to invade the parental sanctum. Only knowing what he knew let him steer past the vulture-sized butterflies in his gut. What if she'd moved the envelope?

Wouldn't matter. He had his driver's license and his Social Security card, thanks to his brother and Carson. He had a phone he controlled, and if he went in and didn't find what he sought, oh well, he'd apologize for the intrusion and show her how it was done.

"Are you really letting him go in there?" Mom snapped.

"Yes, and so are you. Stay where you are." The cop followed Tim into the bedroom, stopping where he had line of sight to the bedroom door and the bathroom, where Tim headed.

He knelt at the vanity, pushing past the cotton swabs and the extra shampoo to the lady stuff. The white envelope lay where he'd seen it last. Please let it not be empty....

He reached a trembling hand. The envelope hefted of paper inside—yes, oh thank God yes, his passport and birth certificate nestled right where he left them. Resting his head against the vanity for just a moment wasn't weakness, it was relief.

Which he couldn't indulge in here or now, not with Mom ready to tear him limb from limb faster than Carson could intervene—or she might go for the 'troublemaker' first.

The mixed Mom-and-Dad scents, the cologne, the deodorants and hand lotions, should mean comfort, but no, not now. Probably never again. His mother's signature scent would forever smell like betrayal.

"This is everything," Tim handed the envelope to the cop. "Please check it."

"Passport, Timothy Neil Ratliff. Colorado birth certificate, Timothy Neil Ratliff..." The officer double checked the documents. "Yep, that's your name. Nothing in there without it." He handed the envelope back. "Good job on remembering those. A lot of people don't and have to go back. It's never pretty."

No, it wouldn't be.

Tim met his mother's eyes and read nothing of remorse in their cold depths. "My passport's in the bank, huh." He pushed past her to Carson. "Let's get out of here."

They emerged to flatbed trucks loading both vehicles. The BMW was a crumpled echo of its sleek beauty. Tim stood with Carson and Mrs. Hedstrom, watching the car get winched onto the flatbed. Oh fuck, Carson's car. His beautiful car, a dented wreck—because of Tim. Would Carson ever forgive him? "Guess the folks' insurance is paying for your wheels until the BMW's settled."

"We're done here. I think it's best everyone heads in their own direction now. Unless Tim has decided about pressing charges." Officer Anderson glanced pointedly from Tim and his allies to the parents.

"I've decided." Through the churning in his gut and a silent cry for the fucking waste of it all, Tim made his decision.

Mom clutched Dad's arm, like he was going to protect

her. Yeah, let them think they'd get to enjoy some time at the Graybar Hotel.

Tim took one step from Carson and Mrs. Hedstrom. His parents should see him alone as the one who decided their fate.

"I'm not pressing charges. For now." Nope, don't let them relax. He took a deep breath and closed his eyes. He knew what need needed to do, what he had to do. What they'd pushed him to do. Still, claws slashed at his heart. Once the words left his mouth, no taking them back. He opened his eyes, sure of his course.

"The price of my leniency is that you leave me alone. Both of you. Don't ever try to contact me, not by phone, or text, or in person, or Facebook or Twitter or skywriting or carrier pigeon or anything at all." He stopped, forcing eye contact with his mother, still defiant, but deflating as she realized how much he meant it.

He spoke straight to her, because his jellyfish of a father could at least do what he was told. "Parents who loved me would want me to live my best life and be happy, not control me and make me into their little puppet. I'm done letting you pull my strings."

No, he'd never again plan around Mom's wishes or Dad's demands. They wanted him to change the most basic element of himself, and proven they'd go to any length to get him to be just what Mom wanted, in every way.

"I know what that Exodus Way place does, and I would never voluntarily go there. I'm not ever giving myself into the hands of the torturers, and the fact you would means you value your idea of me more than you value me. Go ahead and disown me. It'll be mutual."

Tim pulled himself taller. "In the unlikely event I want to see either of you again, I'll contact you." He pulled his old phone out of his pocket. "This belongs to you. I don't need it anymore."

"Sim card."

The two words from Carson reinforced Tim, and still gave him a jolt. He'd just come too damn close to handing them the keys to his life. "Right." He extracted the tiny chip with all the crucial data and contacts from the device and tossed the phone at the parents. "All yours."

His father made a half-hearted attempt to catch the phone, but it bounced off his fingertips. Too bad, not like Tim was getting into touching range when his lip was fat from his father's last tender caress.

"Am I forgetting anything?" Tim asked Carson, not caring if anyone else heard. This man was his lighthouse in the shitstorm of his life. Mom already blamed him for Tim's breaking loose. Asking him out loud couldn't make things worse.

"Mail. Change your address, and oh, Lorraine?" Carson shifted his focus to the woman who had somehow, magically, been silenced. "Tampering with someone's mail is a federal offence, and the post office maintains inspectors who investigate it, and take it very seriously. So seriously that they'd consult with our good officers here. So, don't even think about it."

"Get off my property. All of you." Her words were weak but venomous.

"Gladly." The asphalt wasn't her property—Tim guided Carson to the sidewalk and on to the street. With one hand behind Carson's head, Tim drew him down for a kiss, tenderly and without regard to the blood on their faces. Mindful of his fat lip and Carson's swollen-shut eye, Tim whispered, "Thank you," and kissed the man who'd helped him break free.

CHAPTER TWENTY-SIX

THANK GOODNESS FOR MRS. HEDSTROM: turned out Carson had parked all of Tim's stuff in her car. She drove them straight to the neighborhood post office, where Tim marched past the silent walls of post office boxes to grab a blank change of address form. He'd hand it back thirty seconds after the counter opened in the morning. No good could come of waiting.

She dropped them at Carson's place, quiet and deserted as it should be. Both Tim and Carson hugged her. Poor lady—her neighbors were not going to be very neighborly for a while.

Tim's backpack lay to one side of the new pile in the living room. "Oh hell. My flight."

"Don't think you're gonna make it." Carson rummaged for bags of frozen vegetables in the kitchen. He handed the peas to Tim and applied the corn to his own eye. "Since it's going to take off in less than forty minutes."

"Can I reschedule?" Paying for a second last-minute ticket would bring his reserves perilously low, and he had no hours at all scheduled until after he was supposed to be back—he'd cancelled his Cluckets shifts for the trip.

"Call the airline." Carson leaned back to drape the hand not holding veggies to his face across Tim's shoulders.

Best not think about that right now. He had to stay calm and manage practical matters.

"Same flight tomorrow? That's as soon as I can get reticketed?" didn't feel much like managing matters, but that was the best he could coax out of the airline. Wearily he dialed the hotel to change those dates too.

"Crap, I'm supposed to be in the FerroCorp offices tomorrow at 9:30." Tim leaned wearily into Carson's shoulder. "Gotta email them and reschedule. If they'll let me."

"Tell them you had a family emergency and they might let you do a phone interview at the same time." Carson sighed. "I'm sorry shit went down like it did, but I'm not sorry you got out of there. Especially not sorry you got out of there before...."

"Yeah. Before." Mom was probably burning his baby pictures now, gnashing her teeth at being foiled. Because it was too much to hope that she'd seen the error of her ways. "Maybe I should have pressed charges?"

"That had to be your call, Tim." Carson squeezed his shoulder. "I understand why you didn't. Been there myself. But if you got her off our backs with a little generosity, you did good." That assessment felt almost as good as the second arm wrapped around Tim's chest. "Not to mention, a kidnapping attempt that doesn't get all four wheels out of the driveway might be hard to prosecute."

"Glad the cops didn't even hint about that." Tim didn't think they could have pulled any of today off without the officers' assistance. "Guess them showing up yesterday was a blessing in disguise. They already had a good idea of what was going on. That was genius, you asking them to supervise me grabbing my stuff."

"I found out that was a thing after it was too late to do me any good," Carson said. "Though I've replaced everything she kept—or sold after I left—except the Pokémon cards."

"Damn, I forgot Paul's Blue Eyes White Dragon card!" Tim had thought only of himself, damn it.

"If it wasn't yours, the cop shouldn't let you take it. It's somewhere safe and unlikely to attract her wrath?"

"Yeah. I should tell Paul what's going on." In a minute. The adrenalin hangover was setting in. If he had to move away from Carson for any reason, he'd fall over. Good thing the sofa was nice and soft, with wide cushions. Even if he and Carson both fell over, there'd be room. "I'm really sorry about your car."

"Don't worry about it." Carson sounded way too calm and sincere.

"It was beautiful, and now it's wrecked, because of my dumbass parents." Tim *loved* that car—so did Carson. Why was he so relaxed about it?

"Tim, yeah, I'm a little bummed about it, but think— that car did exactly what I bought it to do." Carson kissed his ear. "I bought it to defend myself, and anyone I saw fit to defend. Which is you. Maybe I should have just chased you through town, yodeling for help, and risked losing sight of the car and not knowing where they were taking you. But I couldn't risk that, not when Mrs. H said they'd forced you into the car. She's very precise with her language."

"Yeah, Dad did a rugby tackle on me and they had the child-locks set. I had to escape through the front." Which he couldn't have done had Carson not ensured the Cruze stopped. "But I'm still sad about the Bimmer."

"Remember what I said about things with flaws?"

"That car was flawless." Nothing at all like the leprosy dresser, though it was looking better with less paint and no contact paper.

"Not when I bought it." Carson snuggled into a better position, with Tim leaning against his chest. "The second owner was panic selling, and I was in no hurry. It popped a valve gasket. Oil everywhere. He was ready to bail because a greedy mechanic told him it was a $3500 repair, so he sold it to me for about half of what it was worth at the time. Three hundred bucks and some grease under my nails, and I had a car that everyone made assumptions about. For about four grand more than you paid for the Corolla."

"Wow. Maybe you should help me upgrade." Or maybe that was a once in a lifetime steal.

"You bought something pretty near bullet-proof, you did good, especially for not having any mechanical background. The problem we fixed was basic maintenance, easy once you knew what to look for. But if you want fancy wheels, yeah, we can keep a lookout for a bargain." Carson offered automotive heaven, and then took it away again. "Though insuring it in New Jersey may cost you a small fortune."

"Shit." One thing after another. "I suspect my car insurance is eighteen hours from cancellation."

"If she thinks of it."

"Now who's depending on luck?"

"Not me, boyo. You need to decide what you want to do, whether it's get your own policy, or piggyback on your brother's if he's agreeable. Or off mine." Carson twined his fingers through Tim's and rested their hands against Tim's belly.

"You'd do that?" No question but that it would be advantageous for Tim, but it seemed so much to offer. More than a bed for a week or a month. More like an offer that went with a bed for life.

"We're in this together." Carson's words were a soft baritone puff in Tim's ear. "Didn't stop once we drove away today."

"You're awfully good to me." If he turned around, he could take this cuddle of relief into a full-on expression of appreciation. Maybe even one that required nudity.

If Carson didn't still think the kisses tasted of goodbye.

Shit.

"Yes. Yes, I am. Which is why I'm reminding you to call your brother. Before Hurricane Lorraine makes landfall on his doorstep. If she's prone to doing such things." Carson was just full of cheery ideas. Which so far, had mostly come to pass.

"I wouldn't think so. She doesn't talk to Paul much." At all. "He married someone she disapproved of, and she was awful to Miyoko, to the point where Paul doesn't want to talk to her either. It can get real tense when we're all together." Not that whole-family get-togethers were a frequent feature. Tim's graduation was the first in how long?

"So I'll fit right in."

Carson's wry joke sounded like truth to Tim. "Yes. You will. You'll like Paul, and Miyoko's sweet."

Why shouldn't Carson fit in? And why shouldn't he see that Tim had family that weren't complete jerks? He dug his new phone out, the functional phone that he controlled, thanks to Carson's push, and punched his brother's number.

"Heya, Paul, how's the packing going?" Tim blew through the chitchat about the new house fast. "You need to know, Mom's on the warpath, and it's kind of a long story. You've only heard chapter one."

"There's beer and pizza and a listening ear if you want to come over and give us a hand," Paul suggested. "We've got the truck for today and tomorrow, so…"

Tim glanced over his shoulder at Carson. "I should. But you don't have to." They'd been through plenty today—Tim wouldn't blame him in the least for saying *Sorry, gonna take three ibuprofen and a nap.*

Carson pulled the bag of corn away from his face to run fingertips over his swollen eye. "It's better than sitting around moping. Let's go. I'd like to meet them."

————

Not that he really wanted to move house for strangers, but sitting still with his arms around Tim was making Carson forget how much last night's kisses tasted of goodbye. A hard flavor to hold on to, when the man he wanted leaned against him, slightly shocky and in need of comfort.

And with a plane ticket to the East Coast. Humping boxes and furniture down a flight of stairs still seemed like a better idea than getting highly involved with a guy who planned to be a thousand miles away this time tomorrow.

Tim deserved better than an opportunistic fuck for his first time, and Carson needed to give more than a man headed to the East Coast could take with him.

Boxes it was.

Introductions were quick, and Tim brought Paul and Miyoko up to date with the fewest possible words.

Paul's "Holy shit!" said it all.

Tim wanted to think about anything else in the world

right now. "Guys, it sucks, and I need to process. Can we just move you?"

They paired off in teams: Tim and Paul attacked the furniture, while he and Miyoko carried packed boxes from the single bedroom down the stairs to the U-Haul.

"One at a time, babe!" Paul jumped up from disassembling the bed to remove the second box from Miyoko's stack.

"I'm fine. You're a big worrywart!" She hauled her remaining box out the door.

Carson took one at a time because he wasn't kidding about his shoulder. That side curtain airbag had knocked something lose. His swollen eye wasn't helping with depth perception either, and one box of bathroom stuff was enough to drop if he missed a stair. At least no one was making a big deal over it once he'd asked them not to fuss.

He caught up with Miyoko at the van, parked near the building's door in the shade of mature cottonwoods. He jumped in to stack her box and his in the cargo area.

"Oh, don't you coddle me too," she said.

"Wouldn't dream of it." Carson could use a little coddling himself by now. "I'm already up here."

"Okay." She waited until he returned to the ground. "You do look like you've been through the mill."

"Getting T-boned will do that to you." He hadn't dared look in the mirror. What he could feel was quite bad enough.

"And yet you're here, helping." She smiled at him. "I'm not sure if that means you're a really good guy or you hit your head."

Carson shrugged, sending a protest through his left shoulder. "Tim wanted to talk to Paul, and he wanted me to meet you guys. Not like we were going to do much except wait for his flight."

"He talks about you a lot. He thinks the world of you." Miyoko leaned against the rear of the van, in no hurry to go back for another load. The bright mid-day sun missed the van, dappling sunlight through the cottonwood branches.

Great, add some salt to the wound that is Tim leaving. "He's a great guy too, but you knew that." Suddenly hungry to learn more about Tim from someone who'd known him a long time, Carson leaned against the van beside her.

"He always has been, but the last couple of weeks, it's like he's really blossomed. More self-assured. I think it's you." Her smile invited confidences.

"I'm glad to know someone in this family thinks I'm a good influence," shouldn't have been so funny, but she laughed out loud.

He quirked a brow.

"It's just that my mother-in-law's nickname for me for the longest time was 'Bad Influence'. Never my name, which she pretended not to be able to say." Miyoko shook her head.

"What made her stop using that nickname?" If Miyoko had tactics to make Lorraine behave better, Carson wanted in on the secret.

"We stopped talking to her." Miyoko lifted an eyebrow, daring him to say something.

"Works for me." He'd had enough Lorraine to last a lifetime. "Tim made his stance on that pretty clear today. He told both parents not to contact him again."

"Whoa!" Miyoko recoiled. "That's pretty strong for right off the bat."

"It wasn't right off the bat though." Carson ran

through the events. "It was a lifetime of... everything it was a lifetime of, followed by a horrible escalation. Can you blame him for saying enough?"

"No. I suppose moving to New Jersey will enforce no contact." She looked thoughtfully at Carson. "Are you okay with that?"

"Yes. The no contact part." Surely Miyoko of all people would understand that. She'd stuck with Paul through whatever crap Lorraine had thrown at them, so maybe she wouldn't understand the rest. "And no. I'm really not okay with him leaving at all, but..." A lump rose in his throat. "But what he needs is more important than what I want. If he needs to get far, far away, then I have to suck it up."

"You're a rare man, Carson." Miyoko surprised him with a quick squeeze of his hand. "I hope you guys find a way to stay together."

"We haven't had a chance to talk about anything farther in the future than tomorrow, so...." Was he really looking at a future of Facetimed sex and flying visits? Or of calls that slowly trickled away into trivia until there was nothing left to talk about? "And I'm not sure we're together as much as we're united against a common enemy."

"You're an uncommonly good ally. At least you're not starting from 'trying to get potential mother-in-law to like you.' I spent a couple of years on that fruitless project." Miyoko snorted. "She wore dark gray to our wedding only because we told her she wouldn't get a corsage or sit up front if she wore black."

"That's Lorraine." Did they have to keep talking about The Harridan From Hell™? Carson uncoiled from his perch. "I hear boxes calling our names."

———

Tim unscrewed while Paul pulled the bed rails away from the headboard. "So you'd really take a job out East if they offered?"

"It's not what I want, but…" It looked like such a good idea on Friday, with all his stolen opportunities coming to light. When all the hurt was fresh. When hurt drove him to run, far, far away from the one who'd hurt him.

"But what?" Paul rocked back on his heels. "If it's not what you want, why are you doing it?"

CHAPTER TWENTY-SEVEN

PIZZA DULY EATEN, empty new house admired, Tim drove Carson back to the townhouse in the fading light. Poor guy looked worn to a frazzle and it wasn't even really his fight.

But he'd made it his fight, for Tim.

And they'd won. Even if this was only a battle and not the whole war, they'd won. They could keep winning.

So why was he even thinking of retreating? Now, when the whole world was open to him, and this amazing man had offered to share—well, everything.

Maybe it was only a temporary offer, or Carson thought it had an expiration date of firm job offer on the other side of the country, but what if it could be more? And how was he ever going to find out?

His Corolla sat alone in the garage with only the leprosy dresser for company. Carson sacrificed his beautiful tank for him.

What the hell was he doing?

"Do you want to watch some TV or just veg out?" Carson waggled the bag of frozen peas before applying them to his face. "Think I might take a shower and fall into bed to read for a while. It's early, but it's been one hell of a day."

"I have a couple of things I need to do." Tim fired up his computer. "I'll be up in a few."

"'Kay." Carson and peas trudged up the stairs.

Half an hour later, Tim stepped out of the shower stall, washed clean of the fear stink, sweat, and uncertainty. He wrapped the towel around his hips and headed to the bedroom, where a bedside light still burned. The ceiling fan hummed a monotone, wafting a cool breeze through the room.

"Got everything done?" Carson lay against the pillows, bare-chested, the silky blue sheet pulled to his waist. He glanced up from the whatever he was watching on his iPad, something that featured Elton John music.

Yeah, Tim was still standing too. Picking up the pieces of his life.

Carson had to be imagining how many more labs in New Jersey had a copy of Tim's résumé. "Almost. I cancelled my interviews, I cancelled my hotel and plane tickets, and now I need to cancel my ride to the airport."

"You what?" Carson let his iPad fall into his lap.

"And I sent off a couple of applications to local companies. There's a lot of them in Boulder, more in Denver and Commerce City. The ones who thought I was a flake for not following up a month ago probably won't recall that when they see the new cover letter." If it worked fine for New Jersey labs, it should work just as well in Colorado.

Tim took a step into the bedroom, sacrificing the support of the door jambs. "All the shit that went down today kept me from making a huge mistake. A mistake you didn't make, way back when."

"Which was…?" Carson's words trailed off. His lips remained parted.

"You didn't let bad people run you out of town. You said you had a nice life here, and you wouldn't let them take it away from you." Tim needed to swallow down a lump of emotion. "I—almost—let someone scare me away from the life I want. I won't give them that power over me."

"What is the life you want?" The iPad went silent, cutting the song off in mid "yeah". Carson parked the tablet on the bedside table.

Maybe Carson said they were in it together because of how they'd mixed it up with the parents. Maybe he didn't really want Tim except out of a sense of obligation. Maybe… maybe Tim could say what he meant and wait until Carson answered, instead of dreaming up reasons why he was about to fall flat on his face.

"I want to live well. Doing something useful, having a relationship with a man who…" How could he wrap everything into one small description? "Who does what he thinks is right, even if it comes at a cost to him, and is willing to help someone who needs it. Who's honorable and thoughtful, and sexy as hell.

"I want to do it in Colorado, where I have friends and family, and things I love doing." Tim took a deep breath. "What I want for my life is what I've had so far with you."

"But with less drama?" With every word, Carson's eyes widened.

Was that a yes?

"Absolutely with less drama. We might still get some, but we can shut it down together." Tim took another step toward the bed. "If you'll have me. I've moved in 90% of the way because I had to. And once I have a couple of paychecks, if you think we've rushed it, I can get my own place—"

"The last 10% is finding a place for all that underwear in the living room." Carson held out his arms. "How about, when we get that dresser completely refinished, you put your clothes in it?"

The extremely valuable, soon-to-be-not-leprous burled dresser? "Carson, that's one hell of a gift."

"Hah. It's a prettied-up $25 garage sale find."

Tim shook his head. "You're way generous, but that's not what I meant."

Carson interrupted. "What's your last 10%?"

"Filing the change of address form." Tim watched Carson's face carefully. "And fucking each other stupid."

CHAPTER TWENTY-EIGHT

THANK GOD, Carson smiled. No, he grinned, and his laughter came from somewhere near his navel. "Hell to the yes, boyo, hell to the yes. Come here."

Tim's towel hit the floor—he vaulted into the bed with a light sonic boom. Carson wanted him!

"I owe you the rest of that blowjob," Tim gasped into Carson's neck.

"Newp." Carson flipped Tim to his back, scrabbling the sheet out from between them. "No owing. No ticky boxes."

"How about, I want to suck your cock until you call my name?" got Tim an *Oh yeah* and a whole lot of tongue.

Wow but Carson felt good, all muscled hugs and hungry mouth. Nude as Tim, and just as hard. Demanding. Joyous. Generous. Finding all the funny places Tim didn't know were erogenous—the shell of his ear, the strap muscle in his neck, the dip of his collarbone. Anywhere Carson grazed with his teeth.

Tim would love to lie back and let Carson have his lovely way, but—they'd been doing this from the very start, all foreplay, all teasing and anticipation. Then—stop. But no fear now, and no interruption. Felt like they were picking up where they left off the first times.

Where Tim had broken off what he wanted. Not this time. Not when he could roll this amazing man to his back to take charge of what got kissed and where got touched, or licked, or nibbled, or stroked.

He could spend years exploring this man, but he had a destination for now. "Seems to me we left off right—" Tim buried his nose in the dip where Carson's close-clipped ball-sack met his cock and breathed in the heady, musky scent. "—about—" needed a trail of tongue up his firm column. Words were almost too tough, but Tim needed only one. "—here."

Here was the plum-purple helmet of Carson's beautiful cock. The crystal droplet leaking from the tip was bittersalt ambrosia. Tim licked it away.

It was time, and past time for this—the joy Tim would not let anyone take away ever again. He slipped his mouth over Carson's cock, and went down.

Hope Carson liked what he was doing—had to, the way he arched his back and dug his hand into the sheets. The other he rested on Tim's shoulder, and the sounds, oh, the glorious sounds. Wordless *mms* and quick gasps, and a full-throated *Ahh* when Tim cupped his balls.

He could do this forever, bobbing up and down on this marvelous cock attached to this marvelous man, rubbing the head against his palate and finding every vein and ridge with his tongue. Forever, or until Carson lifted him up and off.

"Let me come down a little, Tim," he panted.

"I guess I'm doing it okay?" Tim was a little concerned about what he'd do when Carson shot, but in the meantime, it was fun all around, and exactly what he wanted to do. What he'd waited his whole life to do with someone, and what he'd waited much too long to do with Carson.

"More than okay." Carson pulled Tim into his armpit to cuddle. "Gonna make me come at that rate."

"Sounds like a plan to me." Tim rubbed his hand up and down Carson's belly, settling it under the erection still wet with his saliva. Man, he'd had that in his mouth!

"It is, unless there was something else you wanted me to do with it," came with a squeeze. "Your choice."

Yeah, it was, Tim realized with a jolt. He was done hesitating out of fear, or because someone who wasn't in the bed with him had an opinion. Nobody else got a say in what happened in their bed.

Yeah, their bed, it was theirs because this marvelous man had offered to share it with him.

"Oh yeah, there's something else." Tim hitched himself up on an elbow to gaze into Carson's face. His poor, swollen face, that he hadn't uttered a word of complaint about getting for Tim's sake. "I want you to do me."

"You sure?" Carson blinked. "There's no rush."

"True, but I've been waiting my whole life for any of this, and now there's you, and I want to do it with you." Tim leaned down for a kiss. "Before the universe finds some other way to interrupt us."

"Yeah, we've sure had more of that than two guys need," Carson agreed. "But we have all the time in the world if you want to slide into it more slowly. Fingers are nice."

"Then you're going to show me that." Tim liked the stuff along the way, but he wanted some main events. "And we aren't going to let anything stop us, not even if—" What could he name that would make Carson believe him, without killing the mood? He might get a chuckle out of Tim's fears. "Not even if a mouse runs across the pillow."

"Pretty sure there won't be any mice running across the pillow." Carson chuckled. "But you have a point, the universe has a weird sense of humor. My bottle of lube might have turned to dust."

"Uh…" If practicalities stopped them now, Tim might scream all the way into his britches and to the nearest… What was still open after nine? Did Walmart even stock lube?

"Teasing. We're good." Carson kissed the tension out of him. "In a fit of excess optimism, I bought stuff."

"It's not excess if I'm here, right?" Oh man, things were about to get real. He'd asked, and been told yes, and now… Carson would really…

Tim's head got a little swimmy.

"Earth to Tim. You can say slow down or stop or change up, do something different." Carson kissed him again. "This is supposed to be fun, remember?"

It was gonna be fun. It was. Tim was sure of it. Almost. But—he wanted Carson, and first times were only once. "Has been so far. I trust you."

"I will be worthy of your trust. The idea is to have fun along the way." Carson untangled them and reached into the bedside table.

The bottle he produced sloshed, not puffed. Thank goodness. The foil packets were real, not Tim's imagination, and they'd use one. Um, in him. Even with how much he wanted Carson to enter him, Tim trembled with anticipation. "What do you want me to do?"

"Roll over kind of on your side, right leg up. Then I can kiss you and touch you and get you ready." Carson cuddled up to Tim's back, a warm comfort when the cool air licked him in places that didn't usually get exposed. He twitched, anticipating what his new lover—yes, lover—would do.

"A little fingers, a lot of lube." Warm lips against his shoulder, wet fingers touching…

And in, the tiniest press inward that became a slide. Tim gasped at the breach, but damn, that felt… "Wow."

"It gets better." Carson demonstrated. "Even better if I got a different angle on it, but I don't want to let you go." With his mouth on Tim's shoulder and his finger deep in Tim's ass, and he didn't let go.

"Feels good."

"We'll do an evening of nothing but this one day. Soon." Probing on one end and licking on the other, he drove Tim a little closer to brain meltdown. "And you'll do it to me."

"*Hnngg.*" Real actual words—gone from his head.

The pressure changed and the stretch grew—Tim took a bite of pillow to keep from squirming right off the bed.

"Still feeling good?"

Two fingers sliding in and out and he had to ask? Um, yeah, it was a question, but the answer was sidling up past yes and getting to hell yes. "Yeah," he breathed.

"'Cause you're feeling good to me."

The anticipation might kill him, if the occasional brush past the good button in there didn't do it first. "Carson…"

"Yeah?" Another lingering lick up his ear wasn't improving Tim's speech abilities any. Nor was the bump of Carson's cock against Tim's buttock. "Do you want a third finger or back to one?"

"Cock? Is cock a choice?" What Carson was doing was amazing, but Tim wanted the main event, now, before anything at all happened to stop them, even his orgasm. Or his fear. Did something you wanted desperately really make your stomach churn?

"Yeah, it's a choice. With more lube though." The choice came with no fingers at all for a moment, and then the cool swipe of goop on his hole fixed his emptiness.

"Lots for you. Some for me." The tip of Carson's dick danced a line on Tim's butt, until...

The rounded head of Carson's cock rested against his opening. He could say *Stop*. Carson would—even this close. Tim was sure of it, even if he had the jitters. Saying *Stop, wait, we'll try this tomorrow* would be letting fear win.

He'd won all his other battles and the prizes were worth the fight. He'd fought to get here, in this bed, with this man, and nobody, not even himself, could make him turn back.

"Still good?" Carson reached between Tim's legs to find his cock. "You're still hard. Erections come and go at times like these."

"Please, Carson!" came through clenched teeth.

"Anything for you" became pressure, unfamiliar and yet like coming home. Slow and gentle, but determined. Carson held him tight, and entered. A little.

Tim gasped. Strange and full and stretched and—good and weird all at the same time.

Carson pulled back. Out.

"Hey!" Tim twisted to catch Carson's eye.

"A little at a time. Turn around, relax." Carson rubbed his face against Tim's shoulder. "Trust me here, okay?"

Tim did, for sex and so much more. "Okay."

The blunt head of Carson's cock nudged again at his hole. "Breathe, boo. Bear down."

Little by little, with pushes and nudges and soft words, Carson worked in and out. "I want this to be good for you."

Good, mixed with strangeness, yeah. Carson was in

him! Had been, from that first penetration with only the tip, and now—oh fuck! He was all the way in, holding still. Too still.

"Try to let go of the tension." Carson brushed his lips against Tim's neck. "Can you melt into the mattress?"

Tim tried to loosen up, muscle by muscle, especially the one encircling his boyfriend's cock. "I feel so full."

"Like it?" wafted against his neck.

"I think so. Yeah." The more his ass relaxed, the stronger that yeah got.

At last. Everything he wanted. Nothing to stop them.

Carson moved slowly within him. Held him in strong arms, whispered encouragements and endearments in his ear from behind, and thrust gently into him. "I want this to be good for you."

It was. Oh it was. Carson could keep fucking him until the sun got cold.

Snaking a hand downward, he found Tim's cock, hard, leaking and utterly right in his grasp.

Everything Tim wanted, all at once, at the same time. Carson held him every way possible, rocking against an amazingly good spot inside. Every thrust lit him up from within, and the stretch of his opening was to let Carson be there.

He'd waited his whole life for this first time. Carson pushed into him tenderly and still hit every sensation, every dream of the sensation. Tim wasn't alone in a bed imagining, yearning, with no one to hold onto. Not any more. He gripped Carson's forearm with both hands, clinging to how real he was.

It all became too much—every nerve ending cried out for the beauty of their joining. His balls drew up tighter to his body with every stroke from in front and behind. Carson kissed his neck, soft whispers of caress with even softer words of encouragement. *Yeah, you feel so good, I wanna make it good for you.*

He was, oh, he was—Tim detonated in a fountain of bliss and come, his mouth saying something he wasn't even listening to. Carson quivered against him, and held on until the exquisite shudders passed.

Joy. Even if Carson wasn't inside him anymore. He'd be back.

"Oh man." Tim went limp. "That was... amazing."

"It was." Carson rolled away for cold moments that seemed longer than they were. The he was back, a warm hug from behind, his cock against Tim's butt, subsiding into satisfied flaccidness.

"Definitely milestone-worthy. Miles and miles of milestones." His V-card was folded, torn, shredded, burnt to ashes and blown away in a gale. *Bye!*

Tim pursed his lips and puffed hard. The speck of movement two inches away from his nose had too many legs. One good *whoosh* and it disappeared.

"Hmm?"

They'd been through much, much worse to arrive at this bliss—Tim chuckled. "The universe sent us a spider. I sent it back."

CHAPTER TWENTY-NINE

CARSON COULD GET USED to this "kiss to sweeten the day" thing.

Tim dropped him at the Monument Pharma admin building and headed back to the house for a busy day of looking for a job here in Colorado. They'd shared coffee and protein smoothies this morning, they'd share dinner and news tonight. Hopefully nothing more than, "I talked to Corden Pharma and MiraGen," and "Lorraine glared at me but didn't say anything."

Carson could really get used to driving together to work, but that was so out of the question. They'd be going opposite directions for work soon enough.

Lorraine's office door was closed. Good. Maybe she wouldn't come in today, with all the insurance stuff to deal with. He didn't want to see her face.

"What happened to you?" Angie stared openly.

Guess she would—his eye was open enough to see through, but the shiner was coming along nicely. Boxers who'd gone nine rounds with Deontay Wilder probably looked better.

"Lorraine happened to me." He didn't bother to keep his voice down.

The sudden breeze from all the flapping ears in the cubicle farm nearly knocked him over. "Long story, tell you at lunch."

"Aw, man!" one of the customer service reps whined. She didn't turn back to her monitor until he sat down.

Telling Angie meant telling Wes. And enduring the *I told you so*. Well, Wes had predicted they'd be good together, based off what, Carson didn't know, but since he was still smiling this morning, the little twerp could claim to be right. Of course, the state of his face meant that Carson was also right, but he'd heal.

While he reviewed the latest state legal updates, his phone rang. "Hey, Carson, it's Dave. You know Tim Ratliff, don't you?"

In every way possible wasn't the politic answer here, so Carson replied, "Yes," with what he hoped weren't overly-warm tones. "What about him?"

"The phone number on his application isn't active. I could email him, but if you have a good phone number for him, I'll call."

That hadn't taken long—was it the missing sim card or account-level deactivation? Good thing Tim had seen the wisdom of the pre-paid phone. Carson read off the new number.

He could save Dave the trouble of calling—all Tim's reasons for staying far away from Monument's laboratories quadrupled over the weekend. But that wasn't Carson's decision to make. It would hurt to turn the job down, but Tim deserved the triumph of the offer.

———

Tim had taken Carson to work still marinating in the sweat and musk from their good morning greetings. The memory of his scent and how he got it should make Carson happy about coming home.

But Tim needed to get down to business, and distracting himself with the odor of sex wasn't going to get him a new job.

Dang, he missed a couple of calls while he was in the shower. Tim dug jeans and a fresh T-shirt out of the pile destined for the burled dresser and grabbed his pen and pad.

A request for a phone interview at a polymer manufacturer in Boulder, awright! Tim wrote the contact information down. First step, definitely in the right direction. He didn't have any particular love of polymers, but he could develop a fondness for any kind of chemistry that paid the bills and kept him in Colorado.

And a message from a man whose voice he recognized. "This is Dave Pfeiffer at Monument Pharma. We'd like to extend a job offer, so please call at your earliest convenience."

Great. The job he wanted, on a plate.

The job he couldn't take.

He'd said he could maintain professionalism even if he worked at the same company with his mother. He'd said so because he never expected to test it, though he'd begun to hope that maybe, just maybe, he could spend his days in a building where his mother never went, and enjoy lunches with Carson and Wes and Angie.

While it might have been true last week, would it be true now?

Last week he could have figured out who to talk to in HR to keep Mom from scheduling his vacations without his input, but... Telling her not to contact him in any way and then turning up on the same campus every day was... Just mean.

Also, not too smart—sooner or later she'd get emphatic about talking to him. Much better to keep Mom from getting emphatic.

He'd call Dave Pfeiffer all right, and say thanks but no thanks.

But not yet. Tim wanted to bask in the glow of being wanted.

Carefully adding everything to his new job-search spreadsheet, Tim sent off résumés to a couple of places he hadn't already hit in the last month. He'd try again with the bigger companies he'd already lost into the void. It couldn't hurt to try again when he knew he could follow up.

His phone rang with guitars and voices, Thompson Square singing "Are You Gonna Kiss Me or Not." Carson. He could share the good news. Or the bad news, as the case might be.

Seemed odd that he wouldn't text, but hey, Tim was glad to hear the man's voice. "What's up, Carson?"

"Have you heard anything from Monument Pharma today?" Carson sounded so urgent.

"Yeah. They said they want to offer me a position." Tim couldn't get too excited about not accepting what he wanted most.

"Take it."

"Wait, what?" Had Tim really heard that come out of Carson's mouth? "I can't."

"You can. You should. It's what you want," Carson reminded him, as if he needed reminding.

"Carson, I know you know what's going on. You were there. Why exactly are you telling me to stick my hand in a whirring blender?" Tim jumped up to pace. Carson had protected him, encouraged him, and now he was advising Tim to walk back into the fire?

"About that." Carson slowed to a drawl. "I have good news, and I have bad news. Which would you like first?"

"Start with the bad news." Get it out of the way. Why was Carson being coy about this?

"The bad news is that the big Xerox printer workstation has to be replaced, the insides are busted."

"Does that somehow pertain to me?" Something didn't make sense here. "What's the good news?"

"I have only one black eye."

Carson had one black eye when he went to work this morning. Why was this news at all? Ohhh... No. Tim fell more than sat on the gray couch with the blue and aqua cushions. "Carson, what the hell happened?"

CHAPTER THIRTY

WHAT THE HELL HAD HAPPENED?

In a more perfect world, the all in one printer/scanner/fax would have taken a day off from eating the yellow sheets that never went through without a jam. But no, time to pull down Lever A, twist Knob B, and see if he could extract the shred of paper that had brought the workstation to a halt.

Carson leaned over to stick his hand into the depths of the misbegotten machine. Memories of where he'd put his fingers last night, and again this morning, made him smile. The fisheye camera on the ceiling had to be getting some good shots of his ass.

"I told you to stay away from my boy." Lorraine loomed over him, a dark shadow between him and the yellowish fluorescent fixtures. Fuck, she would have to show up today after all. "He shouldn't associate with the likes of you."

"Not your decision to make, Lorraine." Hadn't they had this discussion already? Wasn't her son not wanting contact a smack with the clue-by-four and not just a hint?

And damn, he could feel the paper scrap against his fingertip, just a little too far in to reach. He squatted down, trying to make his hand small enough to work a second finger against the scrap. Just a little farther…

"You're all smiles because you touched my son, didn't you? You put your degenerate hands all over my son, didn't you?" A drop of spittle flew—she had to have worked herself up on the way in. Or she could go from zero to eleven million in the space of a glance.

"Not the time, not the place to discuss this, Lorraine." There never would be a time or a place where he'd willingly discuss the weather, let alone his sex life, with her. If she'd just go away, he'd let the "degenerate" comment slide. Though Wes might get some mileage out of the degeneracy of the way Carson seemed to be fisting the printer.

But yes, yes, he had put his hands on Tim, and done a whole lot more than that. And Tim loved it. Wanted to do it again tonight, he'd said so, and try more besides. Carson was all over that idea.

"You're fucking my son, aren't you!" she hissed.

She just wouldn't let go, would she? She'd chase him down, she'd chase Tim down, she'd be fucking relentless… Carson had had enough, and more than enough. Honesty stomped right over discretion. Everything he hadn't said yesterday wanted to boil out of his mouth, but he wouldn't be the one to bring private matters to the office.

But he'd tell her the truth she didn't want to hear.

"Not at the moment."

"Don't you even dare!" Lorraine screamed and swung.

Right into his face.

His face, his poor, damaged face. He could anything but another blow to the face.

He could end this—be on his feet in a heartbeat.

Swing back. One blow would stop her. If he could stop at one. Every fiber of him yearned to fight back. But no.

He could take anything he needed to. For Tim, he needed to take this.

Her punch rocked his balance—he let momentum carry him down to the floor. His right hand twisted against the machinery, gouging his skin. He covered his face with his left arm, letting her hail blows against his forearm, but not touching his face. Something in the guts of the machine popped and yielded—he could pull his hand out and roll away from her.

"Quit fucking my son!" she screamed, smashing at him again. Doing a lot less damage than she was trying for. Doing a lot more damage than she knew.

Carson shielded his vulnerable head and didn't strike back. He let her wale away, shrieking foul things without answering. He yearned to stop her the way he wanted to stop his shitstain stepfather's abuse.

One blow would end it. Put her through the far wall. Stop the abuse, maybe permanently.

But he stayed down, he couldn't strike back. For Tim. Besides…

Never, ever, interrupt an enemy when they're making a mistake.

———

Reinforcements, at last. The shocked silence turned to a frenzied hubbub. "Stop it! Stop it!" and cursing rang out. Brave souls pulled Lorraine away from Carson.

He rose to his feet, on the far side of the circle of bodies that surrounded them. With one arm bent before him, ready to throw up a defensive elbow, he felt his nose. Angie pressed a tissue into his hand.

A mad light still glittered in Lorraine's eyes—she strained against her captors. Talk about having a tiger by the tail.

"What's going on here?" boomed through the office.

Dave Pfeiffer cut through the noise. For a moment, until everyone tried talking at once.

"Stop!" silenced them. "Carson! What happened to your face?" Dave demanded.

Dave hadn't seen yesterday's damages yet. Speaking wasn't possible—Carson choked on the blood trickling down the back of his throat. He had a firm grip on his nose —the blood had to go somewhere. But he didn't need words.

He pointed one finger at Lorraine, a wordless *She happened.* And then he pointed upward, at the fisheye camera.

———

Actions have consequences. Even hers.

Might be really awkward to run into Officers Anderson and Diaz a third day running, but Dave seemed willing to let Carson's refusal to call the cops stand. Didn't keep him from marching Lorraine back to his office for an extended stay in the Chair of Tears.

Nor did it keep the Vice President of Operations from marching down the hall to Dave's office, or from a call to one of the customer service reps to bring a large box to Lorraine's office.

Dave and the VP stood guard at the door while she

packed. With hunched shoulders and a bowed head, she carried her personal possessions out.

Dave closed the front door behind her. "Back to work, folks. Show's over."

Lorraine Ratliff was gone.

———

"I'm sorry, Tim. She came at me. I couldn't hit her back. Not hitting her back didn't work much better." Carson finished his story, not a trace of gloat to be heard.

"She shouldn't have been hitting you at all. What a fucking mess." Tim ran an angry hand through his hair. "I can't believe… Yes, I can. Damn it. I'm sorry." Two words Mom would never say, because she was always right, and look where that got her.

"My point is don't let your reaction to what happened to her keep you from accepting the job. If you still want it."

"If it still exists. They may decide Ratliffs in general are bad news." Hadn't his mother snatched away enough opportunities already?

"Only one way to find out, Tim. And I'm pretty sure Dave can tell the difference between you."

"I certainly hope so."

After Carson hung up, Tim leaned back, rubbing his forehead. What an entirely fucked up situation, and the irony of it all? Mom would get at least part of what she wanted.

Dave Pfeiffer had said to call at Tim's earliest convenience. Probably corporate speak for "five minutes before I thought to ask." Even if he'd like to wait long enough that Dave had come down off whatever rage high Mom provoked.

Welp, if his name was mud in the Monument Pharma world, it was time to find out. Tim touched his phone. "This is Tim Ratliff, returning your call."

Dave didn't mince words. "Tim, Monument Pharma would like to extend you a job offer, but there've been some developments that may affect how you feel about us. You should be aware before you say yes or no."

Oh boy, here it came.

"This is why we don't employ family members in the same department. You may have already heard about Lorraine being terminated."

"Yes. I did. Possibly not the whole story, but I heard enough to think you were justified." Much as it pained him to admit. Mom was no doubt devastated, but she'd have been quick to terminate anyone else who'd thrown a fist at work. Even if they'd been there for fifteen years like her. Even if they thought they were justified. Like her. "I'm really sorry she created a scene."

Dave had been upfront with him: Tim owed him the same. Even if it cost him the opportunity. "You should be aware that I have a pre-existing relationship with someone who works at Monument."

That got a wry chuckle. "That was, ah, made explicit this morning."

Oh shit. Of course it was.

But Dave had led with "job offer." So not a deal-breaker?

"You'd be in the lab, he's in regulatory affairs. Different departments. Different buildings. So, provided that you maintain professional decorum, it's not an issue." The sweet music of Dave's words barely penetrated the roaring in Tim's ears.

"We will absolutely maintain professional decorum."

He lived with the man—they could forgo dragging each other into the solvent room or the supply closet for hot humping. Tim refused to be the unprofessional Ratliff.

"In that case, Tim, let's talk about the job."

Once again, Carson called it. Dave knew one Ratliff from another.

Why, yes, a Chemist I position in the Product Development group was acceptable, and yes, that sounded like a good starting salary, and yes, first shift would work, and yes, he'd be happy to prove that he didn't partake in Colorado's green answer to pharmaceuticals: which lab should he leave a sample? Yes, yes, and more yes, and he'd be happy to start next Monday.

He ended the call not knowing whether to sing, dance, run ten miles, or turn cartwheels. At last! In spite of every obstacle, he was on his way.

CHAPTER THIRTY-ONE

TIM HAD the last of his clothing carried upstairs and piled neatly in the corner well before he expected Carson home. Did he have time to strip another surface of the dresser? Getting the solvent out wasn't his best idea today, much though he wanted to get the dresser finished. Eau d'turpentine wasn't the cologne he wanted for an evening of celebration.

The front door keypad beeped, announcing Carson's return. Tim came to greet him at the door.

Wes followed him in, a screaming green and yellow explosion of pineapples among the cool grays, blues, and aquas of the living room. "It's like an aquarium!"

Tim caught Carson's eye and laughed. "That's what I said."

Carson put one arm around Tim's waist, turning them as one to face Wes. Like they were both hosts, and Wes their guest, not just Carson's. "Welcome to the humble abode."

"Nice place." Wes nodded approvingly. "Can't believe I've never seen it."

Carson had said something about not having people over much. Tim cast a sideways glance at his boyfriend. Yeah. If every stitch of clothing he owned sat in the same bedroom with the bed they'd made love in, he'd call Carson his boyfriend. His first. His first for so many things.

"We'll have to throw a party sometime soon." Carson gave Tim a squeeze.

That sounded like a first for Carson—Wes's eyebrows rose. "The hermit awakes! I'd ask what's gotten into you, but I'm pretty sure I already know."

Tim's face heated. Why did everyone have to assume they knew what he and Carson did? Even if they were right? Or would be right soon?

"Wes." Carson made the name stand for an entire reprimand. "You had a reason for coming in and delaying me getting his clothes off?"

Tim burned hotter, not so much as to miss the squeeze.

"Oh. Yeah." Wes seemed surprised by the packet in his hand. He thrust it toward Tim. "Welcome to the Product Development group. Dress accordingly."

"I thought that meant sturdy shoes and lab jackets." Tim took the offering, a shirt bright as Wes's own, all blue surfers and green palm trees folded neatly inside the crinkly cellophane. "Thank you?"

"You're welcome." Wes smiled sunnily. "For the shirt and for that handsome hunk you're going to screw silly the moment I'm gone. Ta ta, boys, I'll see myself out."

He left just fast enough to not get a turbo assist from Carson.

"I can see he's going to make my new job interesting." Tim had no intention of wearing that shirt to work, or even to mow Mrs. Hedstrom's lawn. He set it down on the couch and returned to Carson's arms. Chest to chest, hip to hip, and rising fast.

"Once again, Wes is a pain in the ass, but not wrong." Carson dipped his head to meet Tim's mouth. A long moment of dancing tongues ended with a happy sigh. "It's nice to come home to you."

"This is home now." Tim stopped to savor the thought. "It's hard to believe how much has changed. I'm here, with you, the exact new job I wanted, and I never have to serve fried chicken again." Never have to hide who he was, or be forced into a life he didn't want.

"It's changed for me too. 'The hermit awakes' has some truth to it." Carson kissed Tim again, tenderly this time.

"I'm glad it's with me." Maybe Tim wasn't the only one to hesitate to reach for what he wanted.

"Me too." Carson rested his forehead against Tim's. "Welcome to the first day of the rest of your life."

"Hey." Tim tilted to brush his lips against his lover's. "First day of the rest of our life."

EPILOGUE

ONCE AGAIN, Denver had nearly skipped fall to go straight to winter. Fat flakes of snow swirled around in quick-melting eddies, landing in Tim and Carson's hair and eyebrows on their dash from the car. The sidewalks were wet, not snow-covered, but would freeze to a thin film of ice when the sun went down.

Woodsmoke teased their noses—this was a great day to light the fireplace and watch football games.

The neighborhood was clogged with cars—everyone's families came for Thanksgiving dinner. Even Tim's, though they weren't inside the house where he'd grown up.

No, Carson parked the replacement for the BMW, an equally tank-like Mercedes E350 (bought for a relative song because it needed a crankshaft position sensor and an hour of Carson's time) in Mrs. Hedstrom's driveway, next to Paul and Miyoko's Subaru wagon.

Tim carried the shallow glass pan of spinach soufflé casserole wrapped in a dishcloth for insulation. He'd googled recipes for the traditional Ratliff dish rather than asking Mom, and after Grams refused to respond to his request. Oh well—Tim wasn't going to use Cheez Whiz in his version anyway. Grams, of course, had taken Mom and Dad's version of events as gospel.

As if her disapproval was anything new. Tim activated his auxiliary grandparent into main mode.

He refused to spare a second glance toward his former home. His first showed a lit first floor and the porch light already burning, though dusk was still hours away. Grams's weary-looking Honda Accord sat in the driveway, next to the now-repaired Cruze. The upper window that had been his, partially hidden by the semi-stripped maple tree, was dark. Of course. Mom had probably turned the room into an office.

Tim wouldn't knock on their door. He'd reached out a month ago, just in case either of his parents had developed any insight into how they'd screwed up so badly. The screaming reception suggested not.

Carson wrapped his arm around Tim's shoulder for the quick journey to the front door. They were certain of their welcome and belonging here.

Inside, laughter and football mixed with the heady cinnamon and sage scent of hot spiced cider and turkey. Paul took the wrapped dish while Mrs. Hedstrom greeted them with hugs, passing Tim on to Miyoko so she could embrace Carson.

Miyoko had to turn slightly sideways to hug. "Say hi to Uncle Tim," she instructed her enormous belly, followed by "Say hi to Uncle Carson."

"Hello, sprat." Carson always played along with the conversations—he was a whole lot more taken with the idea of nieces and nephews than Tim was, but a guy who'd grown up without brothers or sisters probably never expected to have any. He was already planning to borrow the nibling for zoo visits and yet-to-be-released Disney movies.

The cacophony of greetings spread to the various Hedstroms who'd long ago begun to share their matriarch with the kids next door. Well, this kid was grown now, and bringing his boyfriend into the mix. Mrs. Hedstrom had absorbed both Miyoko and Carson into her loving circle and was affronted that others would not. She didn't have to name names.

Carson circulated easily with the rest of the family, sitting down to watch the Lions game in a flurry of "How've you been" and "Good to see you!"

"Getting excited?" Tim asked Paul to get him to stop fussing over whether Miyoko needed a footstool placed under the dinner table, now expanded out to seat a dozen.

"You bet. Also nervous. It could be any day now." Paul tried to drag his attention away from his wife, who cupped her hand over her stomach. "Um, how are you doing? Everything still good with you and Carson?"

"Getting better all the time." Tim sure had gone from zero to lightspeed on getting out on his own and into a relationship, but every minute was worth it. Even the occasional disagreements, because they learned to be better partners to each other. Tim had been genuinely shocked when Carson insisted he stand up for whatever he felt strongly about, and not just say, "Yes, dear." He didn't keep the peace—they made the peace.

And the make-up sex was mind-blowing. So was the not-make-up sex. Probably not a good idea to lick his lips right now. Even though he could see Carson's thin sweater ride up his middle when he flailed around cheering a Lions touchdown.

"How are things at the lab?" Paul about jumped out of his skin when Miyoko put her hand to her back and stretched. She went back to setting out napkins—Paul barely relaxed.

"You're going to have a heart attack every time the kid burps." Tim had to tease. "Work is fine. Been running hardness versus dissolution tests on varenicline. Should be a big seller."

"I understood the last sentence." Paul grinned. "Yeah, this first time stuff is nerve-wracking."

Yeah, it was. But in a good way. If they did it right, this would be the last time he and Carson would have to do first times on a lot of things. This was their first Thanksgiving together. They had so much to be thankful for.

"Heard anything from Mom or Dad?" Tim wanted to get the elephant in the room dealt with.

"Nothing I would share verbatim with Miyoko. Or you, if you're okay with that." Paul grimaced. "So we held an election for grandmother and Mrs. Hedstrom won."

"I'm sure she'll serve with distinction." Tim wouldn't ask what had been said—he didn't need the pain on a day meant for families and rejoicing. He was with his family, the ones who loved him unconditionally, and who loved Carson because Tim loved him.

This was their family. The family he and Carson had made for themselves.

The game ended, and Mrs. Hedstrom summoned the gathering to table. Everyone stood, their hands linked in a loving chain. Tim had Carson on one side and Paul on the other, and the Hedstrom grandson who'd been next best thing to a cousin right across the table.

"Carson, dear," Mrs. Hedstrom said. "Would you please say a few words?"

The quick squeeze of Carson's hand in his needed a squeeze back.

"We are blessed to be together on this day…"

ABOUT THE AUTHOR

P.D. Singer lives in Colorado with her slightly bemused husband, one proto-adult, and seventy-nine pounds of pets. She's a big believer in research, first-hand if possible, so the reader can be quite certain Pam has skied down a mountain face-first, been stepped on by rodeo horses, acquired a potato burn or two, and will never, ever, write a novel that includes sky-diving.

When not writing, playing her fiddle, or skiing, she can be found with a book in hand.

Keep current with Pam and the Rocky Ridge gang by joining the newsletter.

pdsinger.com
pd.singer@live.com

Concierge Service

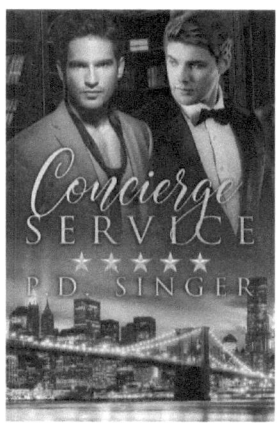

Joshua Hannes, the concierge of the Vivaldi Central Park Hotel prides himself on fulfilling every impossible request. Tickets to a sold-out show? A purple dye job for a purse dog? A last-minute table at a premier hotspot? No problem.

But the devastatingly handsome penthouse guest wants a friend?

Self-made billionaire Craig Ridley's in New York on business, but at the end of the day, he wants to relax with someone interesting. The concierge should be able to supply a friendly face. Just for a little conversation. Dinner and a card game. Not sex with a man he doesn't know or respect.

Craig didn't expect the concierge to personally volunteer. Nor to be the man Craig hadn't known he needed.

A billion reasons why they shouldn't be together. A billion and one reasons why they should.

A smoldering standalone romance with an HEA.

Spokes

Pro cyclist Luca Biondi lives for the race. For the star of Team
Antano-Clark, victory lies within his grasp—if he can
outdistance 200 other hopefuls, avoid suspicion from race
officials, and keep his lieutenant more friend than foe. Luca also
has secrets, and eyes for amateur cyclist and journalist
Christopher Nye.

Christopher understands Luca's need to keep their relationship
under wraps, but chafes at hiding in the shadows of his lover's
career. He's ready to cheer Luca's victories, but he knows too well
how triumph can turn to tears. While Christopher's heart sees
Luca the man, his inner journalist—and his editor—sees the
cycling world's biggest scoop.

From the jagged curves of the Colorado Rockies to the viciously
steep Belgian hills, Luca can ride out any bumps—except
rumors.

A few words in the wrong ear could crash everything. With miles
between them, hints of scandal, and Luca's fierce need to guard
his reputation, a journalist might have to let go of the biggest

story of his career or risk forcing his lover to abandon the race. Christopher and Luca face a path more treacherous than any road to the summit.

———

Returning Soon:

Fire on the Mountain

Snow on the Mountain

Fall Down the Mountain

Blood on the Mountain

Return to the Mountain

Make sure you know when it happens by joining the Rocky Ridge newsletter.